Marcos picked  **He made it st** **table, then he** **mug with a "grrraaawwrrr!"**

It was the most adorable thing she'd ever seen him do.

"Logan seems like a good kid," he said. "He looks like you."

"Oh, do you think so?"

"Yeah, in the shape of the eyes." He made a vague gesture to his own face. "His are brown, though."

Hazel, actually. Light brown flecked with green... like the ones staring across the table at her right now.

"Guess he gets that from his father," Marcos said.

Her heart was beating way too fast. She took a sip of her drink and burned her tongue. *Warning! Hull breach imminent! Change subject!*

But then again...

Logan didn't openly pine for a father like she had, but he needed a father whether he showed it or not. She owed him that much.

Dear Reader,

It's summertime at La Escarpa, the Ramirez family ranch—and Marcos, the oldest Ramirez child and only son, is home again after twelve years away. His mother and sisters don't know what brought him there, and Marcos isn't sure himself. He swore off the ranch when he joined the Marine Corps, but something is drawing him back.

Nina never had a settled home like La Escarpa. Now that she's moved to the Texas Hill Country, she's hoping she and her young son can finally put down some roots and belong somewhere. Her new friend Eliana Ramirez is ready to welcome Nina and Logan right into her own family…but one member of that family isn't a stranger to Nina. She and Marcos have met before, on a wild night eight years ago that changed the course of Nina's life.

Welcome back to Limestone Springs, that small rural town deep in the heart of the Texas Hill Country. I hope you enjoy your time here.

Kit

HEARTWARMING

The Texan's Secret Son

—

Kit Hawthorne

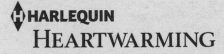

HARLEQUIN®
HEARTWARMING™

ISBN-13: 978-1-335-17991-3

The Texan's Secret Son

Recycling programs for this product may not exist in your area.

This edition published by arrangement with Harlequin Books S.A.

For questions and comments about the quality of this book, please contact us at CustomerService@Harlequin.com.

Harlequin Enterprises ULC
22 Adelaide St. West, 40th Floor
Toronto, Ontario M5H 4E3, Canada
www.Harlequin.com

Printed in U.S.A.

Kit Hawthorne makes her home in south-central Texas on her husband's ancestral farm, where seven generations of his family have lived, worked and loved. When not writing, she can be found reading, drawing, sewing, quilting, reupholstering furniture, playing Irish pennywhistle, refinishing old wood, cooking huge amounts of food for the pressure canner, or wrangling various dogs, cats, goats and people.

Books by Kit Hawthorne

Truly Texas

Hill Country Secret
Coming Home to Texas

Visit the Author Profile page
at Harlequin.com for more titles.

To my son Daniel, who started making up adventure stories almost as soon as he could talk and signed up to serve his country at the age of nineteen. He was the first of my children to stow plastic dinosaurs in my purse and is now my go-to guy for obscure questions about weapons and ammunition of various historical periods. Thank you for your service.

Acknowledgments

Thanks to all those who answered my questions about military life: Daniel Midkiff (Specialist, ARNG), Tony Perez (Corporal, USMC) and Sergeant First Class Stephen M. Zuniga, ARNG. Thanks also to all the other veterans in my life— my brother Stephen, my brother Kevin, my dad, my grandfather, my uncle Gary, my cousin Tony, my cousin Matt, my cousin Christian. It's a long list, and I'd need a lot more space to get to the end of it. Thanks, all of you.

Thanks to my critiquing partners for extra help and encouragement through a tighter-than-usual production schedule; to Johanna Raisanen, my editor at Heartwarming, for making my books so much better; to Greg for picking up the slack around the house while I worked to meet deadlines; to Isaac Dehoyos, Kathy Garner and Laura Woods for being quick and cheerful in sharing their expertise; and to my daughter Grace for her unfailing discernment and taste.

CHAPTER ONE

"ANY LUCK?" ELIANA called from the other side of the dressing-room curtain.

Marcos grunted in reply. He felt like he was fourteen again and any second now his mother would come barging in and start pointing out everything that was wrong with what he was trying on. Eliana even sounded like their mom, all cheerful and bossy.

"Come out so I can see," she said. "There's a three-way mirror out here."

"You don't need to see," said Marcos. "They're fine."

The curtain whooshed back, and his sister burst in.

"Hey!" Marcos said. "A little privacy here?"

"Oh, relax. I heard you zip the zipper."

Then her face got all focused. She looked him over and said, "No."

"What do you mean, no?"

"I mean those jeans are wrong for you."

"They fit fine."

"The cut is wrong. You need a roomier thigh."

"Are you saying these jeans make me look fat?"

"I'm saying you're too buff for them, Marcos. I'm saying that on your body type, straight-leg jeans look like skinny jeans."

He checked himself out in the mirror again. Hmm. Maybe she had a point. Marcos had been wearing mostly uniforms for the past twelve years, and there might be some things about men's fashion he'd missed.

But he wasn't about to learn from his six-years-younger baby sister. He'd been driving a tractor on the ranch while she was still rolling around on the floor with her stuffed bunny. He'd taught her to tie her shoes. She was supposed to look up to him, not order him around like some little kid.

Eliana frowned. "Although…you are thinner than when I saw you last. Like ten to fifteen pounds' worth, I'd say."

He shrugged. It had been more like twenty, but he was slowly gaining it back.

"Still," she went on, "your quads are too big for this cut. You need to try a regular and a relaxed in classic wash."

"These are good enough, Ana. I'm not

gonna go back out there and root around for regular this and relaxed that."

She handed him something folded and denim. "Well, lucky for you I already did. Now try them on. Both pairs."

They had a brief staring contest before Marcos took the jeans and said again, "Little privacy, here?"

Eliana went out and pulled the curtain shut, but not before Marcos saw that tiny triumphant smile.

He took off the straight-legs and pulled on one of the others, grumbling to himself. His last day off before the start of mandatory overtime at the factory, and how was he spending it? Shopping. For *clothes*. There was nothing wrong with the clothes he had. But Eliana always got her way. Part of it was bossiness, part of it was charm and part of it was bribing him with dinner.

Eliana stuck a green shirt past the curtain and waved it at him.

"Just *look* at this color, Marcos! It would be fabulous on you. Really bring out the green in your eyes."

"My eyes are brown."

"They're hazel. Brown on the outside, green on the inside."

Wow. She was correcting him on his eye color now?

"It's too bright," he said. "I'd look like a tree frog."

"It is not! It's a lovely rich shade and it would suit you perfectly. Just try it."

He snatched the shirt out of her hand and pitched it onto the floor.

Ever since Marcos had come back home, Eliana had felt like a stranger to him. She'd been so young when he enlisted, just fourteen. Still complaining about algebra and wearing sparkly stuff on her face and dotting the *I* in her name with a little flower. Now she was this elegant, confident woman with perfectly manicured nails and an unending stream of sophisticated boyfriends with names like Julian.

Of course, she'd always been pretty—the kind of pretty that attracted guys in droves. His other sister, Dalia, was pretty too, but she had a way about her that kept guys at a distance, and anyway she'd only ever had eyes for one guy, who was now her husband. So high school had been pretty straightforward for her, romancewise. Eliana was a whole 'nother story. But by the time she started high school, Marcos was gone, serving his country. From what he heard, he'd missed a lot of drama.

Huh, these jeans really did look better on him.

Yeah, and a lot of good that would do him in the days and weeks to come as he stood at his station in the factory, doing the same thing over and over, hour after hour, shift after shift, with nothing to make one minute any different from the next except the company of his asinine coworkers. They were such morons, with their lame private jokes and constant complaining about having to work for a living. At the end of the shift, they liked to go out for drinks together, as if eight hours in each other's company wasn't more than enough. They never asked Marcos to join them. Not that he wanted to, but it would've been nice to be asked so he could say no. They all looked at him like he was some kind of freak, like they were waiting for him to explode.

He hated that job—but it was the only one he'd been able to land since his discharge from the Marines.

He changed into his own jeans, picked up the pile of jeans and the green shirt and stalked out of the dressing room. He tossed all but one pair of jeans toward the discard rack.

Eliana gave a longing look at the green shirt, but perked up when she saw the jeans he was holding on to. "You're getting them? You're actually taking my advice?"

"Oh, are these one of the ones you brought me? Yeah, they're okay."

He couldn't let baby sister think she knew too much. It would set a bad precedent.

She rolled her eyes.

"You need to be more deliberate about this whole thing, Marcos. You need to learn to dress for both your body type and your fashion style."

"I don't have a fashion style."

"Of course you do. *You* are the rebel type. You've got that whole brooding bad-boy thing going on. It's a good look for you. But you have to be careful not to overdo it, or you'll just look like a criminal."

"I don't look like a criminal. I don't even have any ink."

"But you repel people with your glowering silence and overall demeanor. And then there's your hair."

"What about my hair?"

"What *about* it? You barely have any! You

need to let it grow. It's been ten weeks since you were discharged and still it's barely more than a quarter-inch long on top and nothing but scalp on the sides."

"High and tight. That's how I like it."

"It makes you look unapproachable."

"Good."

"And you have such nice hair too! So glossy and thick with that hint of curl. I'd like to see you try an undercut, or maybe a less extreme fade that's longer overall. What you have now looks like no guard at all, or maybe number-one guard. What if you tried a number eight on top, fading to a three or maybe a two? Wouldn't that be nice?"

"I don't know how you even know so much about men's haircuts and clipper-guard sizes, but an eight is way too long. I'd look like a hippie."

"Hippie? We're talking about one inch of hair!"

"Not doing it."

She sighed hard. "Oh, Steve. You're so stubborn."

The old nickname almost made Marcos smile. It had been a long time since anyone called him Steve.

In the end, he bought two pairs of regular-cut jeans and some new black T-shirts, a whole stack identical to each other and to the black T-shirts he already owned. Eliana didn't say anything, but he could feel her fuming all the way to the parking lot.

But she cheered up once they got in her car.

"I hope you're hungry," she said. "I'm *starving*."

Right on cue, his stomach let out a loud growl.

She laughed at that, and for a second she looked like the Eliana he used to know. He even smiled a little himself.

Then she took out her phone and started texting.

"Who're you talking to? Is it that guy Julian or whatever?"

Eliana didn't even look up. "His name is Nigel, and no, it's not him. That's over."

"Over? Since when? You were just telling me about him yesterday."

"I broke it off this morning."

She didn't look upset, but maybe there was more to the story. There had to be. This was just a brave front.

"What did he do? Do I need to pay him a visit?"

She smiled but didn't look up from her

phone. "Aw, Steve, that's so sweet. But unnecessary. Nigel didn't do anything terrible. He just wasn't very mature."

She put her phone away and started the car.

"Well, who'd you text, then?"

"Dalia. To tell her we're going to be late."

Marcos snorted. "She knows you're going to be late. You're always late."

"I am not! Anyway, I wanted her to be on the lookout for my friend who's joining us."

"A new boyfriend? That was fast, even for you."

"No! Just a friend."

Marcos smelled a rat. "Are you trying to set me up?"

She looked at him, horrified. "Of course not! I said this was a *friend*, didn't I?"

She was perfectly serious. He could see it in her eyes. He actually laughed. "All right. Good."

And then it hit him.

"Waaait a minute. It's your friend from that place, isn't it? That clinic you want me to go to, that quack shack."

"It isn't a clinic. It's a resource center for veterans."

"I don't need any help. I'm not broken."

"Nobody said you were broken. But there's

nothing wrong with accepting help when it's offered. It's not a sign of weakness."

"Is this why you wanted to drive me in your car and not take separate vehicles? Because you knew if I had my truck I'd bail."

She gave him that sweet look of hers, with her chin tucked low and her eyebrows raised.

"All you have to do is meet her," she said.

"Aha! So it *is* a she!"

"Oh my gosh, you are so paranoid. Relax. I told you, I'm not trying to set you up. She's married with a kid, okay? They're new in the area and want to meet people."

"Well, *I'm* not buddying up to her."

"I don't expect you to. That's what the rest of the family will be there for. You can sit there as silent as a tree stump for all I care. All you have to do is eat."

His stomach growled again. Something was gnawing away in there, right in that spot midway between his belly button and his breastbone.

He hoped that thing would settle down and cooperate.

CHAPTER TWO

BENDING OVER, Nina sprayed and sprayed the underside of her hair, then righted herself, tossed it back and checked the result in the mirror.

Her shoulder-length brown hair, usually straight, now hung in perfectly tousled loose waves.

She couldn't remember the last time she'd curled her hair. She'd forgotten she even owned a curling iron until she'd come across it while packing back in California. She hadn't forgotten how to use it, though.

It was kind of embarrassing how excited she was—and not because of the possibility of reeling in a new client for the Veterans' Resource Center of South Central Texas. That would either take care of itself, or not. If she'd learned anything in all her years of dealing with veterans, it was that you couldn't *make* them do what you wanted. If Eliana's brother decided to come to the center, he'd do it. If he didn't want to, no amount of coaxing or manipulating would change his mind. More likely, he'd dig in his heels.

So she wouldn't push him. She'd just do what Eliana said: be herself. Relax with Eliana's family. Let the brother see that she was a regular person and not some psychobabbler urging him to talk about his *feelings*.

That was fine with Nina. Eliana was the first friend she'd made in Texas, and Nina loved her already. They'd met a few days earlier at a coffee shop called Jittery Jim's, where they'd both ordered iced coffees. That had naturally led to some comments about Texas heat. When Eliana had learned that Nina worked at the veterans' center, she'd told her about her Marine brother, recently discharged, and after finding out that Nina and Logan were new in town, she'd said the two families ought to get together. It was the sort of polite but meaningless remark that usually led nowhere, but Eliana had immediately taken out her phone, started texting her mother and sister and set a date.

Eliana's family sounded nice too. And after two days of unpacking, assembling, cleaning, organizing, and setting up utilities, all while making sure Logan had three meals a day and didn't take apart any major appliances, on top of a week's worth of packing and driving before that, Nina needed a break in the worst way.

Aunt Cessy's text tone sounded on Nina's phone.

Sure you don't want me to keep L for you tonight?

Nina smiled as she typed her response. You're sweet to offer, but no thanks.

OK, Aunt Cessy replied. But you don't have to do it all alone anymore. I'm here for you, and I'm happy to help. Don't forget.

"Ha! Not much chance of that," Nina said aloud. It was downright luxurious, knowing there was a friendly, willing, responsible adult—a family member, no less—within easy driving distance. But Nina was no freeloader. She'd made it this far, and she wasn't going to take advantage of her aunt. Besides, Logan might like a nice evening out himself, especially at a kid-friendly indoor-outdoor riverside restaurant.

She opened her jewelry box—an old wooden tie box she'd picked up at a flea market in Alameda Point—and took out her favorite earrings, dangling columns of cubic zircs.

Last of all, she slid on her wedding band— white gold, tiny diamonds, very minimalist. Not much like the battered old pawn-shop ring hiding under the polish cloth in the box's back corner.

The alarm went off on her phone. Time to hit the road.

It had been a decade since her one and only trip to Gruene, so Nina wanted to allow plenty of time. Apparently you parked in a giant general-purpose parking lot and hiked the rest of the way to the restaurant, which was why she had on cute-but-practical thick-soled mules. They looked good with her simple summer dress in that perfect shade of teal.

All that was left to do was to grab Logan and go. He'd had his bath while Nina was putting on makeup and curling her hair. Only then had she taken his best jeans, shirt and sneakers from their zip-top bags in the top of her own closet. She'd have stored them in an armored safe if she'd had one.

Sometimes it seemed like all Logan had to do was *look* at a piece of clothing for it to get messed up. Whenever she took him out in public, she wondered if people were judging her for his unkempt appearance.

Logan had eyeballed her suspiciously while she'd stuffed him into his clothes. "Your hair looks different."

"I know. Isn't it nice?"

"It looks like wood shavings."

"That's because I haven't finger-combed it yet. All right, listen. I want you to stay here in your room while I finish getting ready. Play nicely and don't make a mess. Okay?"

"'Kay."

She would have told him to read a book, but Logan wasn't much of a reader. It worried her a little. Yes, he'd only just finished first grade, but when *she* was that age, she was already managing *Little Bear* and *Frog and Toad*, and stumbling through more advanced books by skipping the hard words and looking at the pictures. But Logan was completely uninterested in reading and disliked anything make-believe—unless you counted his games with his toy dinosaurs, which Nina didn't because it was nothing but roaring and stomping around.

What Logan liked was taking things apart.

It wasn't that he meant to destroy things. He just wanted to know how they worked.

Like the time he'd deconstructed Nina's ink-jet printer. Or the toaster oven. Or the electronic key fob to the RAV4.

Even when he wasn't actively disassembling anything, he managed to make colossal messes. Like when he'd slathered his body in petroleum jelly before plunging into an ice-cold bath. He'd seen that one on a kids' science program. It was supposed to show how blubber kept whales warm. The program had said to use one arm, but Logan scoffed at that. Whales didn't just put their *arms* in the water. Whales didn't even *have* arms. So Logan went full-body.

At the end of the day, he had a new respect for the physiology of marine mammals, and Nina had a new respect for the staying power of petroleum jelly. It took *days* to get her son degreased, and she kept finding slimy smears on bathroom surfaces for weeks. As for the bathtub drain pipe…ugh.

But there wasn't any petroleum jelly in Logan's room, or socket sets or tiny screwdrivers. Everything ought to be fine.

She turned the corner into his room and stopped dead.

Logan was covered with—

What *was* that?

Something white and frothy. Tiny balls, all over his chest and face and arms, in his curly red hair. He leaned forward, plunging his arms deep inside—

"*What are you doing*?" Nina shrieked.

Logan looked up soberly at her, then down at his gutted beanbag chair, then back at his mother, like this was a trick question.

"Sticking my arms inside my beanbag chair."

Truthful and terse—that was Logan. He was always precise with language; he said exactly what he meant, as pithily as possible. It was like living with a seven-year-old Calvin Coolidge.

"What did I tell you about taking things apart?"

"I didn't take it apart. I just opened it up. It had a zipper. That means you're *supposed* to open it."

Well, it could have been worse. It wasn't like anything was stained or mangled or torn. This was only polystyrene. It would come off.

Or would it?

Nina brushed and brushed at the tiny white balls, but they clung to Logan's black shirt. Sometimes they bounced around a little, only to settle elsewhere. Logan liked wearing black, and Nina always figured he might as well, because darker fabric would hide dirt better. Ha! Leave it to Logan to find the whitest thing in the house to make a mess with.

"Don't hit me," he said, sounding mildly offended.

"I'm not hitting you, I'm trying to brush this stuff off you." She held him by the arms and looked him in the eye. "Logan Walker! *Do not* tell our new friends that I was hitting you."

"'Kay."

She tried picking off the pieces one by one, but they stuck to her fingers, and there were so *many*. Maybe the vacuum cleaner...? But that would ruin Logan's nice new beanbag chair.

Anyway, the vacuum cleaner was still in pieces from when Logan had dismantled it.

"Why, why, *why* did you have to open up your beanbag chair? Why do you always have to take everything apart?"

"To see what's inside. I thought it'd be beans, but it's not, it's these little balls. They don't feel sticky, but they stick. Why do they?"

"I don't know. Static electricity, I guess."

"Look, now they're sticking to you."

Okay, it was time to cut her losses. Nina took out Logan's second-best jeans, with one small rip in the knee, and his second-best shirt, with faint ketchup traces down the front.

"Here. Put these on, fast. And don't take anything else apart."

So much for allowing plenty of time.

THEY SAID EVERYTHING was bigger in Texas, and so far they were right. The parking lot was *huge*, and stuffed full of trucks and SUVs. Nina drove and drove, praying for an empty space. Every time she thought she saw one, it turned out to have a dumpster behind it, which meant it couldn't be used. The pavement gave way to gravel, then dirt, then grass, before she finally parked the car and started trekking across the vast space, clutching Logan's hand, her purse clamped under her arm.

They crossed the street, turned and kept going, booking it past low wrought iron fences and gracious old houses converted into shops. The little town swarmed with humanity, all dressed up in flounces and fringe, boots and spangles, with big hair and big smiles. A dozen whiskey-barrel planters stood near the white clapboard dance hall

Nina had visited once as a teenager, along with a sign for the restaurant she was headed to—a good idea, because at this point people probably needed the encouragement to keep going.

And there it was at last, the Gristmill. And they were only…she checked her phone… seven minutes late.

She slowed to a sedate, unhurried pace. Just as she reached the hostess station, a tall, slim woman stepped up from the crowd.

"Nina?"

The woman looked familiar, but Nina couldn't quite place her. "Yes?"

"I'm Dalia, Eliana's sister. She texted and told me to look out for you. She's going to be a little late."

Nina followed Dalia down a mulched walkway, past flower beds and more whiskey-barrel planters, to a huge outdoor waiting area.

"I'm sorry Eliana's not here yet," Dalia said. "I don't know why it is, but that girl can't seem to get anywhere on time."

"Cut her some slack," said a pretty, fifty-ish woman with a lapful of knitting. "She's been clothes shopping with your brother all afternoon."

"I'm just glad someone's later than I am,"

said Nina. "Logan had a last-minute wardrobe mishap."

The knitting woman smiled. "It doesn't matter. We have to wait for a table anyway, and waiting is part of the experience."

A live band played on a little roofed stage, next to a humongous chalkboard filled with names of parties waiting to be seated. People sat on stone ledges or picnic tables, or milled about or sidled up to the bar.

Dalia made the introductions, but Nina had heard so much about Eliana's family that she'd already put names to faces. The big, affable guy with the megawatt smile was Dalia's husband, Tony; the long-haired, slightly less massive version of Tony, with a baby girl in his arms, was his brother Alex. Alex's wife, Lauren, had a diamond chip in her nose and an artistically messy hairstyle.

The knitter was Renée, Eliana's mom. She scooted over to make room for Nina, and Nina sat down beside her.

"What are you making?" Nina asked.

Renée held up her knitting. "Woolen socks."

"Nothing better under your work boots on a cold winter's morning," said Dalia.

"You and Tony are the ones who live on the old family ranch, right?" Nina asked.

"That's right," Dalia said. "Been in the family since the early nineteenth century. Ignacio is the eighth generation to live there."

Ignacio was Tony and Dalia's little boy, a sturdy toddler with a shock of black hair standing straight up. He was busy scooping mulch into ridges and hills, and Logan had gone right to work alongside him.

"We're ranchers too," said Lauren, who looked way too boho to be a rancher.

"Yeah, but we're Johnny-come-latelies compared to you Ramirezes," said Alex. "Peri is just the seventh generation of Reyeses to live on our place."

He kissed the top of the baby's head in a gesture so tender and natural that it made Nina's throat ache a little. She knew, because Eliana had told her, that Peri was not Alex's biological child, but it didn't seem to make any difference to him.

"And I live in town," said Renée, "in the little house my husband and I bought when we were first married."

"That sounds idyllic," Nina said. "All that extended family living so close together. It's really special."

"Do you come from a big family yourself?" Renée asked.

"No. Only child. It was just me and my mom when I was growing up, and we moved around a lot—California, Colorado, Oregon. But my father was from Texas. I visited his parents a few times and loved it here. It was actually my aunt, my dad's sister, that got me my job at the center. She's almost the only family Logan and I have left."

"Well, I hope you'll consider us your family now," said Renée. She looked as if she meant it too.

"Thanks," said Nina. "I might just take you up on that."

She liked these people, and this place, with its stonework and blossoms and big old oak trees. Moving here was the right choice. It was just what she and Logan needed.

Nina kept stealing glances at Dalia. There was something very familiar about her—the way she moved, the serious hazel eyes, even her voice.

Finally Nina asked, "Have we met before?"

"I don't think so," Dalia said.

It didn't seem likely that they could have crossed paths in the short time that Nina and Logan had lived in Texas. But this felt more like a long-ago type of thing. Was it possible they'd met on one of Nina's childhood trips here?

One thing was certain: it wasn't Eliana that Dalia reminded her of. The sisters looked nothing alike. Dalia was tall and queenly; Eliana was small, vivacious and daintily pretty.

"Where in California did you live?" Lauren asked.

Nina told her. Lauren had spent a lot of time in California during her years traveling around in a customized live-in van, and in Colorado and Oregon too. Turned out they'd been to some of the same places.

Then Alex said, "The real question is, why'd your father ever leave Texas to begin with?"

"He joined the Marine Corps," Nina said. "Went to Iraq for the first Gulf War and never processed out. He went to Afghanistan too, and Iraq the second time."

"That must have been hard," said Renée.

"Yeah, it wasn't easy, for any of us. He and my mom split up after he got back from his first tour, and I didn't see him at all for a long time. We managed to reconnect a little before he died. Better late than never, I guess."

"Speaking of which," said Dalia, nodding toward the entrance.

And here came Eliana, sparkly, chic and gorgeous. No sensible shoes for her! She had on a pair of high heels that Nina couldn't have managed even on smooth ground.

Trailing behind her was a man.

A big man, dressed in jeans and a black T-shirt, with a distinctive Marine haircut. There was something defiant in his posture with his long slouching steps and lowered head.

Eliana hurried over and gave Nina a quick, light hug.

Then she said, "Nina, I'd like you to meet my brother."

The man raised his head and met her eyes. His sullen expression gave way to shock, then horror.

And suddenly Nina knew exactly who Dalia reminded her of.

CHAPTER THREE

MOST OF MARCOS'S dreams were like amped-up, over-the-top action-adventure movies. He didn't mind those. They were kind of entertaining. But the other dreams, the ones where he found himself in some awkward social situation with no idea how it had come about—those were the ones that woke him with a jolt, leaving him staring at the ceiling, breathing hard and telling himself, *It's okay. It's not real*.

That was what this would turn out to be, just a horrifying dream. What other explanation was there? It wasn't possible for Nina to be standing here, in the flesh, not two feet away from him, with his family all around. Any second now, he'd wake up and it would all go away.

Aaaaany second now.

No one spoke. Dalia shifted impatiently, clearly annoyed at Marcos for just standing there stock-still with his mouth hanging open.

And then Nina smiled.

"It's Marcos, isn't it?" she said.

She said it in a what-a-pleasant-surprise voice, not a what-fresh-hell-is-this voice.

Marcos nodded. He couldn't deny it.

"We've met," said Nina. "Years ago, in San Diego. Maybe you don't remember. It's been a long time."

She sounded friendly and confident, like it was true, like there was any chance he'd ever forget her.

Marcos dredged up a smile. "Oh, yeah, right. I thought you looked familiar."

Like they hadn't spent the night together on an air mattress in the bed of his truck, with the Pacific Ocean pounding in the background.

Eliana looked from Nina to Marcos and back again. "You two already know each other? This is fantastic!"

Yeah, fantastic.

"A little," Nina said. "We're just friendly acquaintances."

Just former husband and wife.

"We only ever saw each other a time or two," Nina went on.

Once when they met and married, and again in court to finalize the annulment.

Marcos wasn't a good talker at any time. He wasn't one of those slick guys who could lie and get away with it. He never really had to be. He just left stuff out.

But Nina—wow. Look at her go. Everything she said was exactly right. She didn't make it sound like they were buddy-buddy, but she didn't let on that there was any tension between them, either. Just friendly casual acquaintances with no disastrous romantic history whatsoever.

It was impressive. And it saved Marcos from what would otherwise have been a nasty situation.

That was one of the things he'd liked about her, eight years ago in that San Diego bar, The Bad Oyster. Her quick confidence, her total self-assurance. He'd looked at her and thought, *Now, that is one squared-away woman.*

Also, she'd been really hot.

And still was. She looked dressier than when he'd seen her last, and with fancier hair. But the fearless blue eyes and strong chin were the same, and her waist still had those same slender curves.

And how did Marcos look? Like a criminal. For a second he almost wished he'd worn his new jeans out of the store and bought that stupid green shirt.

Then he saw the wedding band on her left hand, and it wasn't the one they'd picked out together at the 24-Hour Pawn.

A wall dropped down inside him. Well, then. She'd moved on—as she should. As he'd told her they both would.

But wait a minute. What was he thinking? *Of course* there was a husband. A husband and a kid. Eliana had told him so.

"Don't ask about the husband," she'd said as she parked the car. "He had to stay behind while the house sells, and it's a sensitive topic for the little boy."

That was all Marcos needed to hear. It wasn't like he was big on small talk anyway, and he sure didn't want some stranger's kid whining its way through dinner. He wouldn't have asked about the husband regardless. And if Eliana had told *him*, that meant she'd told everyone else too. She was thorough that way. Which meant that *no one* would ask about the husband. Marcos wouldn't have to hear about him, so yay for that.

Nina turned to Eliana. "Hold on a minute. You told me your brother's name was Steve."

Eliana and their mom chuckled. Dalia just shook her head.

"My husband's name was Martin," his mom told Nina. "Which sounds a lot like Marcos, especially from a distance. So to avoid confusion, whenever I'd call out from a ways off, I'd call Marcos by his middle name, Esteban. And later that got shortened to Steve, and turned into a nickname."

"Not for me," said Dalia. "I always called him Marcos." She sounded proud of this.

"Well, that explains that," said Nina.

Then she turned those clear blue eyes on Marcos. "But *you*."

Marcos swallowed. "Me what?"

"You mentioned having sisters, but you said their names were Ana and Dee."

Tony spoke up. "Wow! You have a really good memory."

Marcos shrugged. "That's what I call them."

"See, that's just lazy," said Dalia. "That's just dropping syllables. And instead of *avoiding* confusion, like was supposed to be the case with the Esteban thing, it *caused* confusion. So going forward, let's all call people by their actual names."

Typical Dalia, trying to set policy for the entire family.

"Guys, our table's ready," said Alex.

Marcos silently followed his family toward the smiling server standing ready with a stack of menus.

Well, that was one crisis averted. But, hey, the night was young.

CHAPTER FOUR

NINA HAD NEVER forgotten Marcos's face, though close to eight years had gone by since she'd seen him last. She had a small square photo of him in her jewelry box, underneath the secondhand wedding band, but it was a memorable enough face without the tangible reminder. Broad through the cheekbones, with straight, heavy brows. Strong, but with something oddly vulnerable in the shape of the lips, the ever-so-slightly dimpled chin.

And the eyes…oh, the eyes. Heavy-lidded, almost sleepy, but changeable, quick to flash into intensity or humor, or turn sad. She'd seen them go through a whole gamut of emotions over the twenty-plus hours of their first meeting.

Now they were hard and cold as stone.

Eliana had contrived to get him and Nina seated across from each other. Marcos looked like he'd rather be anywhere else in the world.

"So, Nina," said Renée, "where are you living?"

"I'm renting a house in New Braunfels, not far from work. It's small, but it's on a big lot. Plenty of backyard for Logan to play in."

"Good! Are you all unpacked and settled in?"

"Not even close."

They went on that way for a while, about the move, the town, even the weather. Renée kept up an easy flow of small talk, and Nina was grateful. It helped ground her, and right now she needed all the help she could get. She was still reeling from the impact of the discovery that Eliana's brother "Steve" was actually Marcos Ramirez.

At least she didn't have to talk about the fake husband, and no one would ask any awkward questions about him. She had Eliana to thank for that. Clever, coming up with that thing about avoiding the subject because Logan missed his dad so much that he might get weepy if he heard him mentioned. Pretending to have a husband made Nina's life a lot simpler; it cut back on unwanted come-ons by about 60 percent. But it only worked if she didn't have to lie in front of her child.

The irony of Eliana's ruse was that Lo-

gan's father had been missing all his life, and
Logan didn't seem to care one bit. It worried
Nina a little, how unemotional he was about
the whole thing.

Really, though, that was only the first layer
of a whole onion of irony in this particular
situation.

Marcos was the only one not contributing
to the conversation. He sat right across from
her, grim and silent, not even meeting her
eyes.

The Marcos Nina remembered was worlds
away from this guy. Singing along with the
Lyle Lovett track at that San Diego bar. Flash-
ing her that daredevil grin. Pulling her to her
feet for a dance. Looking down at her with
those gorgeous green-flecked brown eyes,
saying, *I, Marcos, take you, Nina, to be my
wife*...

And she wasn't the only one who'd noticed
the change.

We all thought he'd go career military, Eliana had told her. *He always said he would,
and he was past the halfway point to retirement. Then all of a sudden he got discharged
and showed up at home with no explanation.
Now all he does is sleep and work. He was
always quiet, but this is different. Scary. I*

look at him and there's this wall, and I don't know what's behind it.

"This is a weird-looking restaurant," Logan said.

They'd followed the hostess through a huge open-air building and out again to a multi-level deck. Past the deck, the land sloped down to the river. A tabby cat kept ambling by, making a circuit of the whole place. Ignacio meowed every time he saw it, and his parents told him how smart he was.

"That's 'cause it used to be a mill," Alex said from beside Marcos. "A hundred years ago, farmers used to bring their cotton here and run it through a machine that took out all the seeds. There was this big wheel set up in the river, and the water would turn the wheel, and the wheel powered the machine."

Logan was silent a moment, taking that in. Then, "Where is that wheel? And the machine? I want to see."

Alex shook his head. "Sorry, bro. That stuff all got destroyed in a fire a long time ago. But the building is still here, and someone thought it'd make a good place for a restaurant."

"And cats," said Logan.

"Yep. And cats."

Renée smiled at him. "Do you like machines, Logan?"

Logan nodded, lips pressed together in the way that meant he'd already reached his talking quota for the night.

"Does he ever," said Nina. "He loves taking things apart. We got a late start tonight because he decided to open up his beanbag chair."

"Oh, no! Did he get those little balls stuck to him?"

"All over. He looked like he was covered in soap suds."

"How did you ever get them off?"

"I didn't! I had to change his outfit. I don't know how I'm ever going to get those darned balls off his clothes and floor and furniture and back in the beanbag chair where they belong."

"Maybe a dry sponge? Or a clothes brush?"

Marcos spoke up. "Nah, that won't work. If anything, it'll build up more of a charge. Get you some antistatic spray. That's basically deionized water and alcohol in a conducting polymer. Or if you've got some liquid fabric softener, you could make your own. Say one part rubbing alcohol to one part fabric softener to fifteen parts water. Mix it up and spray it on. It'll make everything mildly conductive and prevent the charge from building up."

It was the longest speech he'd made all evening. He rattled it off in a bored, slightly impatient way, without even looking up from his glass of tea.

"Thanks," Nina said. "I'm no physicist, but that sounds like it would work."

Renée put a hand on her son's shoulder. "Marcos has always been the mechanical genius in our family. Saved me a fortune in appliance repair over the years."

"What was your MOS, Marcos?" Nina asked.

She already knew his military occupational specialty, of course. It was one of the first things she'd found out about him the night they met. But they had to keep up appearances as casual acquaintances. It wouldn't do for her to remember too much about him. She'd already slipped up once that way, and Tony had been quick to notice. And it would be weird if she didn't at least try to engage him in conversation.

Marcos actually made eye contact for a second. "Oh-eight-eleven, Field Artillery."

"Ah, the Cannon Cockers."

Marcos almost smiled.

"Unfortunately, it's a skill set that doesn't transfer to the civilian world," said Dalia.

The smile vanished. "Yeah, thanks for the reminder," Marcos said.

Alex looked at Marcos. "You know that Texas living history group I belong to? We use artillery pieces in our battle reenactments— Béxar, Goliad, the Alamo. We shoot 'em off at our regular gatherings, too, just for fun. You should join us. We have a good time."

"That's a great idea!" said Eliana, a little too eagerly. "You'd love it, Marcos. Alex has all these cool costumes and old weapons and things. The San Antonio paper did a nice interview with him last year where he told all about the group and the things they do. It'd be a great way for you to meet people."

Marcos made a scoffing sound. "Yeah, I don't think so. After being shot at for real by ISIS, I'm not about to dress up in costume and play at it."

An awkward silence fell. There was nothing sleepy about Marcos's eyes now. They looked mad—at Eliana's bossing, mostly, but maybe a little at himself for being rude to Alex.

But what did Nina know? She wasn't exactly an expert on this new Marcos, or his facial expressions.

She caught Eliana's eye and tried to remind her telepathically of what they'd agreed. *No pressure, remember?*

But Eliana didn't catch the message, or refused to acknowledge it. "Well, you've got to do *something*," she said. "You can't go on like this, sleeping and working with no social life, and only putting in appearances with the family long enough to scowl at everyone. It's not right. It's not healthy. We're worried about you, Marcos."

Marcos flicked a tortured glance at Nina. "Do we have to do this now, in front of—a guest?"

"Yes, I think we do. I'm tired of dancing around the issue, and I'm just saying what everyone is thinking. You need to go to Nina's center. Tell him, Nina."

Wow. The soft-sell approach hadn't even lasted long enough for them to order entrees.

Marcos was staring into his tea again, swirling it around in an overflow of nervous energy, the spoon rattling against the tumbler. His mouth had flattened into an angry line, and Nina could see the muscles in his jaw flexing.

One of the best things Nina had learned from her Texas grandmother was how to smooth over awkward moments. In this case, the best thing to do was to pretend Eliana's outburst hadn't happened, and move on.

"So, Marcos," Nina said, "did you visit San Diego a lot when you were at Camp Pendleton?"

The tea sloshed over the edge of the glass. Marcos took out his teaspoon and set it on the table. Cautiously, without looking up, he said, "As much as anyone, I guess."

"What neighborhoods did you like? Gaslamp Quarter? Ocean Beach? Little Italy? You don't strike me as a North Park or La Jolla kind of guy."

She could almost see the gears turning in his head.

"Yeah, La Jolla's too upscale, and North Park's a bit hipster for me," he said at last. "Ocean Beach is okay, but it has too many yoga studios. My go-to neighborhood was Pacific Beach."

"Oh, yeah, Pacific Beach is nice," Nina said. "The boardwalk. Kate Sessions Park. Oscar's Mexican Seafood."

"Those fish tacos," said Marcos.

"Mmm, yes."

His lips twitched in another almost smile. "Sounds like we frequented a lot of the same places."

Eliana looked back and forth between the two of them, clearly not following.

Then Lauren said innocently, "I like the beach at San Elijo."

Marcos choked out a sound between a laugh and a cough. Nina felt a flush rising into her face, along with a bubbling wave of hilarity. If he looked at her now, she would lose it for sure.

Marcos cleared his throat. "Yeah, San Elijo's nice," he said. "I used to go there a lot. Kept an air mattress in my truck under my camper shell so I could camp out whenever I felt like it."

He darted a quick glance at Nina.

Seriously? Was he *trying* to get her to crack up?

Now it was her turn to fake a coughing fit.

"Are you okay?" Eliana asked. Tony thumped Nina on the back.

By the time she'd regained control, the appetizers had arrived, and the subject of San Diego neighborhoods and beaches was forgotten. Marcos looked at her again and flashed that old daredevil grin, the first real smile she'd seen from him all evening.

The whole situation was beyond bizarre. Sitting here, talking and eating, almost flirting with her one-time husband in front of his oblivious family, who just happened to be exactly the sort of family she'd longed for all her life. If things had been a little different—if Marcos had been willing to hold on and had a little more faith—they *would* have been her family. Her mother-in-law, nephew, brothers-and sisters-in-law, and whatever Alex, Lauren and Peri would have been to her. Her almost family.

And Logan's actual family, with no might-have-beens about it. His grandmother, his aunts and uncles, his cousin…

His father.

And she was the only one who knew it.

CHAPTER FIVE

"THANKS FOR NOT putting any pressure on me tonight in front of your new friend, Ana," Marcos said. "I reeeaally appreciate it."

He couldn't bring himself to say Nina's name, but he could feel it there in his mouth, wanting to be said.

Eliana shot him a guilty glance from the driver's seat. "I deserved that. I'm sorry, Marcos. I did exactly what I said I wouldn't do. It's only because I love you, and I'm worried about you, but that's no excuse. I was wrong, and I'm sorry."

That was the aggravating thing about Eliana —she was so quick to own up when she did wrong that you hardly got a chance to chew her out. Marcos had a lot more sarcastic things to say and no reason to say them now.

"It's all right," he said grudgingly. "At least your friend had the decency to change the subject."

Of course, the change of subject had nearly

been the undoing of them both, but it sure had been fun—a lot more fun than being grilled by Eliana. As far as Marcos was concerned, it had been the high point of the evening. He'd stayed quiet after that, and kept his eyes off Nina except for a few quick glances.

Eliana smiled. "Yes. She's such a sensible person. I didn't used to think that was much of a compliment, but it *is*. The world needs people with sense, to balance out the people like me."

Marcos shut his eyes and leaned his forehead against the glass. A deep aching knot was forming in his stomach. *Go away, pain.*

"So?" Eliana prodded.

"So, what?"

"Will you go to the center?"

He opened his eyes. "What? What happened to *I'm sorry* and *It was wrong of me* and all that?"

"I meant it was wrong of me to pressure you in front of Nina, after I'd said I wouldn't. But it's just the two of us now. You liked Nina. You said it yourself. So—"

"I didn't say I liked her. I said she had the decency to let me off the hook."

"Well then, what do you think of her?"

Marcos grunted.

Eliana let out an exaggerated sigh. "Why do you have to be so difficult, Marcos? Would it kill you to communicate honestly and openly, with actual words?"

Why was everyone so hung up on communication, anyway? What was so great about it? Once you said things, they were out there, forever, where other people could hear them and remember them. It was dangerous.

During that all-night gabfest with Nina, Marcos had told her things he'd never told anyone else before or since. He'd been a regular chatterbox. And now she knew all that stuff about him. Maybe she'd forgotten—it was eight years ago and they'd both had a lot to drink—but somehow he didn't think so. They'd both been sober enough in the morning at the county clerk's office, making their vows.

Marcos shrugged.

"Stop it! Talk to me, Marcos. Tell me what you thought of Nina. Human speech only! No grunts."

She says exactly what she means with no messing around. She doesn't talk noise or try to make herself look smart by making other people look dumb. She stares reality in the

*face and doesn't blink. All that, and she ac-
tually cares about people too.*

"She's all right, I guess."

"Wow! That's high praise, coming from
you. So you'll go? To the center?"

"Nope."

"Marcos! Why not?"

The pain was getting worse. "I just don't
want to, okay? And I don't owe you an explanation. You're not my commanding officer."

"I don't know why you have to be so *hostile* all the time. I'm just trying to help you,
Marcos. I—"

"Pull over."

"What?"

He undid his seat belt and grabbed the door
handle. "Pull over. Now!"

The car hadn't come to a complete stop
when he opened the door, lurched out and
emptied his stomach onto the grass.

It took a while, and it hurt. When it was
over, he felt only slightly better, and he tasted
blood.

He belted himself back in and reclined the
seat. His shift started in a matter of hours.

"Are you okay?" Eliana sounded chastened.

"What do you think?"

"I'm sorry. I didn't know you were sick. Do

you think it's a stomach virus? Or something you ate at the restaurant?"

"Ana, you said you wanted to help me. Did you mean that?"

"Of course."

"Then I need you to do something for me right now."

"Sure. What is it?"

"Stop talking. Drive me home without saying another word."

Silence. Then she shifted gears and pulled back onto the highway.

Marcos shut his eyes again.

Nina had moved on, just like he'd told her they both would. But not Marcos. He was stuck.

And he didn't see any way out.

CHAPTER SIX

"COME IN, COME IN!" Aunt Cessy waved Nina and Logan through the front door into her light-filled, minimally furnished house. "Logan, go look in the sunroom. I got you an old hard drive and a whole set of tiny screwdrivers to take it apart with."

Logan took off, eyes gleaming. He was, Nina thought grimly, his father's son.

Minutes after they'd gotten home from Gruene the night before, she'd found him in the laundry room with a spray bottle of window cleaner in his hand, ready to empty into the sink so he could repurpose it to hold his homemade antistatic spray. A bottle of rubbing alcohol and a jug of fabric softener sat on the counter. How did he even know which bottle was the alcohol when he couldn't even read the labels? The kid had an encyclopedic memory, at least for the things that interested him.

"Don't worry," Cessy said to Nina. "There's

no residual power in the hard drive—he won't be electrocuted."

"Oh, okay. Good," Nina said, as if she'd already known that was a thing you had to be aware of.

Cessy took her arm. "Come out to the patio and have some wine. You can tell me all about it while Logan's occupied with his electronics."

"All about what? What makes you think there's anything to tell?"

"I'm a professional, Nina. I know."

It was so comforting to be bossed and coddled, to not have to be the adult. It was a luxury Nina had rarely experienced growing up.

Nina settled into an Adirondack lounge chair on the flag-paved patio while her aunt filled two wineglasses.

"So?" Cessy said.

"So. That dinner I had, with my friend and her family? The brother she wanted me to meet, Marcos? *I knew him.*"

Cessy handed her a glass. "In a good way, or a bad way?"

"Both. We met eight years ago in San Diego—met in a bar. How cliché is that? He was a Marine, stationed at Camp Pendleton and out celebrating his reenlistment. And I…"

She sighed. "You have to understand, this was right after I'd tracked Dad down the first time. I'd been waiting and trying and hoping so long, I was so excited to connect with him at last and have a *father* for a change, and… well, you know how that went."

"I do indeed."

"So I was in a bad place emotionally, and ready to do something crazy. But it was Texas that actually got us together—Marcos and me. We were playing trivia, and the quizmaster asked what was the state mammal of Texas, and we both shouted *armadillo*! And so he asked me what part of Texas I was from, and I said I wasn't actually *from* there, I just visited my grandparents' place a few times as a kid. And he asked where was that, and I told him, and he said that wasn't twenty miles from where he grew up. We started comparing notes, figuring out what people and places we had in common. Remember that time I went to Gruene Hall to hear Lyle Lovett? Marcos was there, that very night. We might have brushed past each other, smiled at each other, who knows? So next thing I knew, we'd left the trivia game and gotten a table together. We talked for hours, and when the bar closed, we went to a park and went right on talking. I have never connected that deeply with anyone, Aunt Cessy. He said the same thing about me. So the long and short of it is, we found a pawn shop and bought two wedding rings, and when the county clerk's office opened that morning, we went in and got married."

"Wow! That escalated quickly."

Nina sipped her wine.

"It was unbelievably stupid of me. I know that. I'd never done anything like it before, ever. I knew better. I'd seen the devastation a failed marriage could wreak. I was usually so cautious with men. I don't know what made me take leave of my senses that day."

"Don't you? I think it makes a lot of sense. You'd just been rejected by your father, after longing all your life for the strong, abiding male presence you never had. Then suddenly here was an attractive, vital man—a Marine, no less—with whom you had instant chemistry and common experience. It was a perfect storm."

"I guess."

"So what happened next?"

Nina was silent a moment, remembering. The drive to the beach at San Elijo. The sea tang coming in through the cracked-open windows of the camper shell over the bed of Marcos's truck. The pounding of the surf intertwined with the plaintive melodies in Nina's alt-country playlist. Most of all, Marcos himself. This man, this strong, gorgeous, tenderhearted man who'd given himself to her. Falling asleep in his arms, perfectly happy. Waking at the exact same instant hours later, facing each other and smiling, perfectly in sync. There was no shock in Marcos's eyes, no what-have-I-done horror. He recognized her. He was *glad* to wake up with her. It was something she held on to later, a shred of comfort—proof that the whole thing hadn't entirely been a drunken mistake as he'd claimed.

"We drove to the beach and spent the night there—well, morning, really," she told Cessy. "And in the morning—afternoon, I mean—he got a phone call."

He'd made a joke of rejecting the call, saying things like *Sorry, Mom, I'm on my honeymoon,* and *Seriously, Mom? I'm a newly married man here. I want to pay attention to my beautiful wife.* But it kept ringing, and finally Nina told him, *Go ahead and answer. But keep it quick.*

So he did.

He was lying on his back beside her, his phone to his ear, and she was staring at him thinking, *Wow, he's ripped. My husband is seriously ripped.* She ran her fingers lightly along his pectoral muscle. His hand closed over hers, caressing it.

Then he froze. He pulled her hand away from him and sat up.

What? he said. *When? How?*

"It was his mother calling," she told her aunt now. "His father had died, not even an hour earlier. Heatstroke. He was making hay. I told Marcos I was sorry, tried to comfort him, but he flinched away from me. And he said, *This was a mistake.*"

Nina blinked back tears. "What could I do? He was in shock—he was grieving. I wanted to help him, but he wouldn't let me. So I didn't push. I gave him his space. I thought he'd come around. He drove me back to town and dropped me off at my car, said he'd be in touch. And the next time I heard from him was when I got served with annulment papers."

"Oh, Nina," Cessy said. "That's rough."

"Yeah. It's not like I had any right to be surprised. I'd married the guy after knowing him less than a day. But I was crushed.

I actually thought our hours together meant something. I wanted us to stay together. I'd made a vow—a foolish and impulsive vow, maybe, but still a vow. And I wanted to honor it. But how could I fight for a marriage built on such a flimsy foundation?"

The tears spilled over. Nina wiped savagely at them. Cessy didn't say anything, but Nina could feel her sympathy.

Once she had her voice back under control, she said, "When I was nine years old, my mom had this boyfriend named Ray. He was a great guy. They were together about a year, which was a long time for her. When it ended, I begged him not to go, not to leave us. And when I say begged, I mean *begged*. He looked really torn up, but he still left. I'd made a fool of myself for nothing. I told myself I'd never do that again. I never did—and Mom had a lot more boyfriends after Ray. Every time she took up with a new guy, I'd tell myself not to get attached. I'd remind myself that it wouldn't last and I'd just get hurt. I did my best—I hardened my heart and held out as long as I could, but eventually I always gave in. I couldn't help it. It would have been easy if they were jerks, but in spite of being such a flake, Mom had appallingly good taste in men. They were all really sweet to me—they wanted me to like them. And after I finally opened up and allowed myself to get close to them and feel secure and believe that maybe this time would be different, Mom dumped them—and I mean, like, *right* after. We're talking a matter of days—sometimes hours. Every single time. It felt like I was *making* them go, just by wanting them to stay."

Cessy said gently, "You realize you weren't, right?"

Nina started to say yes, of course, but the words wouldn't come. Finally she said, "It was a ridiculously short time in between, Aunt Cessy. It was hard not to think the two events were related."

"Related, sure, but not causally. It was all about the passage of time. The more time went by, the more likely you were to get attached—and the more likely your mother's romances were to crater. That's all."

"I guess. I remember I had this picture of Dad, taken when he was in Iraq the first time—the only picture of him I had back then. And every time Mom told me she'd ended it with another guy, and I felt that sick sense of loss all over again, I'd go to my room and take out that picture and stare at it. I'd tell myself, *This is your father*. I'd promise myself never to fall for another substitute. I fell for them anyway—but you know what? I never begged again. And I didn't beg Marcos. I just signed the papers and closed that particular box. Annulled is like it never happened, right? It was a glitch, an anomaly. And now it was over and it was time to move on. No reason it should ever trouble me again. Except..."

"Except that you were already pregnant," Aunt Cessy finished.

Nina took another swallow. "Yes. Except for that."

Nina had never told her family anything about Logan's father. She'd just said that she'd had a lapse in judgment and didn't want to talk about it. And she never had, until now.

"So what happened when you saw each other yesterday? Did he recognize you?"

"Oh, yeah. Things looked pretty dicey for a minute there with the two of us gawking at each other and his whole family watching, but I pretended we'd met in passing in San Diego, and he played along. It was surreal, sitting right across the table from him, with his son right beside me, and him not realizing it."

"Surely he suspected."

"Honestly? I don't think he cares enough to do the math. He barely noticed me, barely looked at me all evening. It was humiliating."

"Oh, I don't know about that. He may have noticed more than he let on."

Nina downed the last of her wine and reached for the bottle.

"You know what's funny about it, aside from…well, everything? I went to that dinner for two reasons—to meet some new people in my new home, and to give Eliana's brother a chance to get to know me in a casual, no-pressure setting so he'd go to the center. Well, I met people, all right! And if the circumstances were different, I'd *love* to spend more time with them. They were all so friendly and hospitable. The mom is a knitter. Isn't that rich? Logan has a knitting grandmother. She was so sweet. Said I should think of them as family. And the middle sister, Dalia, invited Logan and me to spend a day at the ranch. It's a real working ranch with cattle and goats and I don't know what all. Logan would love to see that! But I can't actually *go*. And as for Marcos going to the center, we can forget about that. And that's a shame, because he needs help. His family is worried about him, and I can see why. But he'll never come now."

Aunt Cessy took a sip from her own wine-glass. "Never is a long time, my dear."

CHAPTER SEVEN

MARCOS WOKE FROM a dead sleep to see his mother standing over him with an anxious face. The anxiety was nothing new—everyone is his family looked at him with anxiety these days—but it was more intense than usual.

"Mmmyeah, I'm awake," he said. "What is it?"

She glanced over her shoulder toward the living room. "There's a police officer here, and he wants to speak with you."

"A police officer?" Weird. Ever since dinner at the Gristmill, Marcos hadn't been anywhere but work, and he hadn't broken any major laws that he knew of. Maybe he'd taken the highway a little fast coming home, but that was hardly a reason to send a cop to his *house*.

"'Kay," he said. "I'll be right out."

His mom left the room, shutting the door behind her.

Marcos threw on some clothes, checked the

time on his G-Shock wristwatch and groaned. He'd been woken in the middle of prime sleep time. His shift at the factory wouldn't start for four hours yet. It wasn't very interesting work—making plastic handles on an assembly line—but it did require him to be alert.

He'd lived in this house in little old Limestone Springs until he was five years old. The living room seemed to have shrunk since he'd gone away, just like everything else in his hometown. Marcos didn't fit anywhere anymore.

The cop was a tall, bearded guy dressed in a dark blue uniform with a gold star on the sleeve that said Constable, Seguin County and a name tag that said Kowalski. He had an air of quiet self-assurance, of strength under control. Marcos used to have that too.

"Marcos Ramirez?" Kowalski said.

"Yeah, that's me."

"Our office received a call about a threatened shooting at your place of work. Can you tell me about that?"

"About a what, now? Who made the threat?"

"The caller said you did, Mr. Ramirez."

"Me?" Marcos was baffled, then—oh, good grief. Surely this wasn't about—

"Okay," he said, "here's what happened.

We'd been working on the line for seven hours, and there was this one machine that had an alarm that would go off whenever something needed to be reset—only the alarm was malfunctioning. It kept going off over and over and no one could stop it. It was one of these obnoxious blaring alarms. We'd complained about it early in the shift but no one from Maintenance ever showed up to fix it. Everyone was worn out and on edge—I was, anyway. And so I said, *If there's ever a shooting in this place, that alarm's going to be the first thing to go.* That's it. That's all that happened."

His mother almost wailed, "Oh, Marcos! You can't say things like that!"

"It was a joke! A tension-breaker!"

"You don't break tension by joking about shooting things! That's like joking about bombs in airports!"

"I didn't threaten to shoot anything or anybody. I just said *if.*"

"But they can't ignore something like that," his mom said. "What if they didn't do anything, and then you really did shoot up the place? They'd be liable. Don't you see?"

He did see, now. But the whole thing was so *dumb*. The things guys joked about in the military—now, *that* was dark humor. This was *nothing* compared to that.

Well, this was just great. Here he'd finally loosened up enough to make a friendly joke at work, and now his coworkers thought he was homicidal.

This is exactly why I don't talk to people.

"Mr. Ramirez," the constable said, "I'd advise you not to attempt any more firearm-related humor at work, or anywhere in public, really. I understand that this is Texas, and we Texans like our firearms. But joking about them is not a good idea for you."

"Yeah? Why me in particular?"

He shouldn't push. He should just say, *Yes, I understand, I'm sorry, thank you, officer.* But he wanted to hear him say it.

"Because your coworkers are afraid of you, Mr. Ramirez. They describe you as unsociable, even hostile. They know you're a veteran, and that's fuel to the fire."

"Why? Because all veterans are scary? Loopy? A heartbeat away from shooting up their workplaces?"

Marcos's mom spoke up again. "In fairness, Marcos, you're a scary-looking man. You're big, you have strong features and your expression doesn't do anything to soften the effect."

Wow. Thanks for the support, Mom.

The officer hesitated, then said, "Look, I get it. I'm ex-military too. But this is the reality of our society and how veterans are perceived in it."

"It's crazy, is what it is," Marcos said. "I can think of three coworkers right now who I'm positive have criminal records. One of them has prison tats. And *I'm* the scary one?"

"Evidently, yes. It's not fair, but it's how things are. And you're simply going to have to adjust."

Marcos sighed, looked at the ceiling. "So what happens now? Do I still have a job?"

Kowalski smiled a little. "That's outside my purview. I've done what I came here to do. Good luck to you, Mr. Ramirez." He nodded at Marcos's mom. "Ma'am."

"Thank you, officer," she said.

After Officer Kowalski left, all the energy seemed to drain from the room. Marcos's chances of getting any more sleep were shot, which was a shame, because he was bone tired. He felt bad for his mother, who looked more anxious than ever. That wasn't right. At thirty-two, he was her oldest child. He ought to be making her life easier, not causing her stress.

He took out the trash, just to do something useful.

"Are you hungry?" his mom asked.

He thought about it before answering. He did a lot of thinking about his stomach these days. About whether that empty, gnawing sensation right between his navel and his breastbone was hunger, or something else. About what would happen if he ate, or didn't eat. Eating wasn't much fun anymore.

"No, I'm good," he said. But he wasn't good. He was lousy.

For the next two hours, he felt like he was waiting for the other shoe to drop, and drop it did. When his phone rang, he knew who it was and what it was about before he answered. He stepped outside on the porch to take the call so his mother wouldn't hear.

The guy was super nice and polite about it. He said it was a simple response to a reduced demand for the product—clearly a lie, considering all the mandatory overtime, but Marcos supposed some excuse had to be given.

"Is there a problem with my work?" Marcos asked. He could hear the desperation in his voice, and the unspoken question, *Is this about what I said*?

"Oh, no, not at all," the guy said in his soothing way. "I can assure you, sir, you were not personally targeted in any way. This was a last-in, first-out kind of thing. And there's every reason to expect it'll be only temporary. If demand picks up again, we'll be sure to give you a call."

Man, this guy was *good*. They must've gotten the smoothest-voiced HR rep to make this call. Probably he handled all the nutcase terminations.

He had to admit it was smart. If you were going to fire a guy because you thought he might shoot up the factory, clearly you couldn't tell him that was the reason. You had to make it sound like it was just one of those things and he'd most likely get his job back. It was like his mom said: the company had to protect itself, and its employees, from the crazy veteran.

He stared at his darkened phone screen. How had it come to this? Just months earlier he'd been a decorated gunnery sergeant with twelve years' service, past the halfway mark to retirement and well on his way to Officer Candidates School—all set to make a successful, satisfying career out of the Marine Corps. Now here he was, getting fired from a job he hated, staying in his mother's house and sleeping on a twin bed under the quilt he'd had as a boy.

He went inside and headed straight to his room, moving fast to avoid more conversation with his mom. He pulled on his boots, did some basic grooming, went out to his truck and found the address on his phone for the Veterans' Resource Center of South Central Texas.

CHAPTER EIGHT

NINA'S BODY RECOGNIZED the backlit form of the man walking through the glass door before her mind did. Before she thought his name or even made out his face, her heart gave a great swell as if to go to him. The set of the shoulders, the devil-may-care stride—who could it be but Marcos?

He walked through the waiting area and straight on to her desk. Then he stopped, frozen, like he'd been powering through on sheer bravado and it had just run out. His posture was defiant, but his expression was scared.

"Can I help you?" she asked. The words came to her automatically, in her usual friendly professional work voice—as if Marcos had been just *anyone*.

His mouth started working, but it took a while before any sounds came out. "I, uh—I need to see someone, I guess."

"Do you have an appointment?"

The work voice again. It felt wrong, talking this way to the father of her child, instead of asking him straight out what terrible thing had happened to him. He'd been dead set against coming here, and he wouldn't have done it unless he thought he had no choice.

Marcos's face fell. "No. I came straight over without calling first. That was dumb. This isn't Supercuts—you don't take walk-ins. I don't know what I was thinking. I don't know what I'm even doing here."

No, he didn't know what he was thinking. For him, to decide was to act. It was one of the things she'd liked about him, his boldness.

But boldness had its limits. It got him through the door, but it wouldn't keep him here. If she didn't stop him, he'd walk right back out.

She stood. "That's all right. Let's get you started on some paperwork."

She took him to a small room and gave him a clipboard with intake forms. He folded himself into a chair, looking out of place and forlorn.

"So what changed your mind?" she asked as she took a seat across the narrow table from him.

"I lost my job."

A deep flush rose from his neck, and he

couldn't meet her eyes. "Worst job I ever had. Unskilled, low pay. And I couldn't keep it."

He dropped the clipboard and stood. "I shouldn't have come. Sorry I wasted your time."

"Sit down," she said sharply.

He sat.

"What do you mean, wasting my time? How is this wasting my time?"

"People lose jobs every day. They don't have to get counseling for it."

"Sometimes they do, or they should. Sometimes these things have underlying causes."

"I don't need fixing! I'm not messed up. Not like some guys."

"There's no minimum threshold here, and you don't have to wait until things get bad. This is a veterans' resource center. Resources for veterans—that's what we have. We're here to help."

"Veterans in the past didn't have centers and resources and things. They didn't wallow around in their trauma. They came home and went back to work. They took care of business."

Nina felt her face get hot. "Oh, that's not even *close* to the whole story. The Greatest Generation might not have talked about it much, but they were traumatized *plenty*. Lots of World War II veterans were functioning alcoholics, and veterans' hospitals back then were full of men with serious mental health issues. And they weren't the first by any means. The term *shell shock* goes back to World War I, but even veterans of the Napoleonic Wars showed signs of post-traumatic stress—all that drinking and gambling and risk-taking behavior."

"But that's not me. I wasn't injured or gassed or taken prisoner."

"You did see combat, Marcos."

"Yeah, but I don't have PTSD. Lots of other guys sacrificed more. Putting me on a level with them is wrong."

Survivors' guilt, Nina thought but did not say. She had to tread carefully here. If she tried to put a label on him, he'd rebel.

"This place isn't just about injuries or PTSD. Lots of things are hard for discharged veterans across the board. They tend to have a terse communication style—just the facts, no niceties. That's fine in a military setting— it's essential there—but in the civilian world it comes off cold or combative. And that's just one example. Things you were valued for while serving, habits that were drilled into you, can turn into liabilities out here. That's a sacrifice you made, Marcos. Not like dying or losing a limb, but still a real sacrifice because it exacts a cost, just like you're experiencing right now. And that's a real shame, to us as a society. We owe it to men and women who've served their country to help make their transition to the civilian world easier. No, most previous generations didn't get that kind of help. But they should have. And now we know better."

She pushed the clipboard back to him. "So fill out those forms and stop arguing with me."

While she'd been talking, he'd stared straight into her eyes with that wooden expression. Now his chest swelled with a deep breath. He grabbed the pen, gave it an aggressive click and bent over the clipboard.

Nina left him to it, walking out quietly before shutting the door behind her as noiselessly as possible, then went straight to Cessy's office.

Her aunt looked up from her laptop. Before she could speak, Nina whispered, "He's here."

"Who's here?"

"Marcos Ramirez. Walked in off the street with no appointment. I have him filling out forms now, but he's nearly bolted twice already. I know he doesn't have an appointment and you don't usually see clients this time of day, but we've got to strike while the iron's hot. You'll see him now, won't you?"

Cessy slowly shook her head. "Nina, I can't see Marcos at all in a professional capacity, ever. He's my niece's ex-husband and my great-nephew's father. It would be unethical for me to treat him."

Nina dropped into a chair. "Oh, no. You're right. I didn't even think of that. Oh, Aunt Cessy, what am I going to do? I can't just let him walk out of here. I convinced him to stay. I told him it was okay to ask for help."

A knock sounded at the door. "Come in," Cessy said.

A man entered. Nina had met him before; his name was Kevin or Keith or something. He was Black, tall and lean with impeccable posture, ruggedly dressed in plaid shirt, cargo pants and work boots. Retired Army, so he had to be in his forties at least, but he looked younger than that. Had some lingering medical issues from an old injury sustained while he was serving.

He held up a file folder. "I came by to drop off that paperwork we talked about, but there wasn't anyone in reception. Oh, hi, Nina. There you are."

Cessy studied him for a bit, her head to one side. Then she said, "Keith, how would you like to kick off our brand-new mentoring program?"

Keith put a hand to his chin, considering. "When?"

"Right now."

"YOU SHOULD KNOW that I don't like doctors," Marcos said.

He was sitting in a cushy armchair across from a fit-looking man in practical, outdoorsy clothes. Not what he'd have expected for a shrink, but maybe the casual clothing was supposed to put Marcos off his guard.

The man replied, "Well then, we're both in luck, because I'm not one."

"Oh. Who are you?"

"Lieutenant Colonel Keith Randall, Army. Retired."

"What was your MOS?"

"Twenty-one-S. Topographic Survey."

"Combat gardener?"

Keith smiled. "Not exactly. My job was to provide data for mapmaking, as well as artillery and aviation support."

"Okay. So…how does that apply here? You going to survey my brain?"

"Nothing that invasive, no. You've been assigned a mentor, and I'm it."

"So you're not a shrink. You're just a guy."

"Yeah. A guy who's been through some of the same things as you and has had a lot more experience coping with them."

Marcos could almost taste the relief. For some reason he'd been expecting a woman, all softness and sympathy. That probably wasn't fair, but it had been the picture in his mind. Just one more woman in his life worrying over him, mothering and sistering him. Keith was a different story. He looked like a tough, no-nonsense guy, the kind Marcos was used to dealing with. Army, but oh well.

"Why don't you like doctors?" Keith asked.

"Because they think they're so godlike with their fancy education, so much better than everyone else. And they don't listen. When you talk they just sit there with that superior look on their face. Waiting for you to quit saying words so they can tell you what's *really* wrong with you, or that there's nothing wrong with you, or whatever it is they've already decided."

"Boy, I hear that," said Keith. "I got the

same sort of runaround when I hurt my back. Got three different diagnoses from three different doctors who reviewed my files."

"Exactly! You're constantly going to a new one because one of you gets deployed, or changes duty stations or their availability doesn't work with yours. You're always starting over."

"It's a hassle, all right. So what's the source of your trouble? Were you injured?"

"No. It's my stomach. And when I say stomach I mean my actual stomach organ. Here." Marcos clutched a fist to the spot below his sternum.

"When did it start?"

"About a year ago."

"And what's happening to it?"

"Pain."

Keith waited. "Can you be a little more specific?"

"Deep, burning pain. Like my body's eating itself up from the inside out."

"That sounds bad. What'd your slew of doctors have to say?"

"What *didn't* they say, is more like it. Every one of them had some pet thing. The first guy was all about diet. Took me off dairy, even though the symptoms of lactose intolerance are completely different—I looked it up. Surprise, surprise, didn't help. Next he took me off gluten. That didn't help either. Then he acted like I was lying to him, like I'd only pretended to change my diet, like I *wanted* my stomach to hurt. That made me mad, so I didn't go to him anymore. The second doctor thought maybe I had a stomach ulcer. She said most ulcers are caused by this one type of bacterial infection that's easy to treat. So I thought, *Great*! *A solution to the problem.* But I tested negative for the bacteria, and after that she didn't have much to say to me. The next one said I had stress-induced gastritis and needed to change how I reacted to things on an emotional level. Gave me all this info on stress management, said I should do yoga. Basically he thought the pain was my own fault and I just needed to chill. And it was bull! The pain had nothing to do with how stressed I was feeling. I told him that, and you know what he said to me? He said, *Well, you certainly appear agitated now.* Well, yeah, I was agitated! I was agitated because my stomach hurt and my doctor wasn't listening to me!"

Keith just nodded while smiling grimly— the "been there, done that" look.

"Worst of all was the one who thought I was faking, trying to get a medical discharge," Marcos said. "He didn't say it right out but I could tell. A discharge of any kind was the last thing I wanted. But that's what I got."

"Oh? How'd that happen?"

"I got worse. Ended up in the hospital. Turned out I had an ulcer, all right, but no one could figure out what was causing it. I got tested for all kinds of things—pancreatic stuff, parasites, fungus, Crohn's. All negative. But I couldn't do my job with a bleeding hole in my stomach. So suddenly I'm up before a Medical Evaluation Board, and next thing I know I'm out on my ear."

"That's rough. How's your stomach now?"

Marcos shrugged. "The hospital doctor prescribed some meds. They help."

"But you're not a hundred percent."

"No."

Keith wrote something on a sticky note, tore it off, and handed it to Marcos. "As I said, I'm not a doctor, so this isn't a referral, just a recommendation. This is the name of a gastroenterologist I know. She's good. And her billing department will work with Tricare."

Marcos silently took the paper. He was past the point of feeling hopeful about new doctors.

"So how's your transition to civilian life going?" Keith asked. "Not so hot, I gather. According to your intake form, the immediate cause of your being here today is—" he read from the form "—'Got fired from a crappy job and told I look scary and suck at communication.' That sounds like a fun story. You want to fill in the details?"

No, Marcos thought. But he did it anyway. Then he sat back and waited for Keith to lecture him on how you couldn't crack jokes about firearms in the workplace and blah blah blah.

But Keith didn't say any of that.

"What I don't get," Keith said, "is how you ended up working in a place like that to begin with. It sounds awful."

"It wasn't my first choice. It was the only place that would hire me. Guess I don't interview well."

He shook his head. "It wasn't supposed to be like this. I ran artillery crews in Syria. I fought against ISIS and helped take them down. But now I'm out and that doesn't mean squat. And I'm sick of being told that it's all my fault. Yes, I chose an MOS that doesn't transfer to the civilian world. No, there's not much demand in the private sector for cannon cockers. But that wasn't why I joined, to get my job training and then leave. I joined because I believed in the Marine Corps mission. 'To win our nation's battles swiftly and aggressively in times of crisis'—that's what I wanted to do. And I did it, and I was good at it, and I wanted to keep on doing it. Now that's over. And I've got to start all over on the whole stupid process with online job applications, hour after hour of type and click and scroll. It makes me want to—"

He stopped himself, but Keith just chuckled.

"What? Shoot your computer screen? It's okay—you can say it. I'm not your boss at the factory—I'm not going to fire you. And I get it. I hate desk work. I just about lose my mind if I don't get in plenty of outdoor time every day, doing something tangible."

"Exactly! If my ulcer really was stress induced, this would be just the sort of stress that induced it."

Keith leaned back in his chair. "Okay. So would it be fair to say you feel let down? Betrayed, even? I know, you didn't join for what you could get out of it, but I think all of us expect our military service to make us *more* hirable, not less. To bring us honor and respect. Not make people afraid of us."

"Yeah. It would be fair to say that."

"All right. Now let me ask you this. Do you think all veterans are in the exact same boat, stuck in dead-end jobs with people afraid of them?"

"No."

"What do you think might be different about the ones who are succeeding?"

Marcos shrugged. "Probably they're better at working the system. Better with people. But that's not me."

"Okay, then. Who are you?" He glanced again at Marcos's paperwork. "It says here that you were a field artillery cannoneer. What does that mean?"

"It means I operated an M777 howitzer."

"That's it? That's the complete job description?"

"No."

"Then elaborate. What specifically did you do?"

"Lay the guns for elevation and deflection. Construct field fortifications. Handle ammunition. Perform preventive maintenance. Load and fire."

"You worked with a crew?"

"Yeah."

"And you achieved the rank of gunnery sergeant, which means you had to direct some of them."

Marcos shifted in his chair.

"So after all that, are you telling me that 'working the system' in the civilian world, and dealing with people, is too hard for you?"

"It's not the same."

"Why not?"

"Because I'm not good with people—not outside the military, anyway. I hate small talk. How are you, what do you do for a living, where do you live—I don't care about any of that."

"Yeah, well, I'm going to let you in on a little secret, Marcos. *It doesn't matter.* You can make small talk without caring a hill of beans about the answers. It's just a social ritual. It makes people comfortable, takes the pressure off. So try it. You might end up hearing something interesting in spite of yourself. And even if you don't, you'll make someone else happy."

"I don't have anyone to try it on. I don't have any friends around here."

"Then go out and make some. You're not

a bad-looking guy. Go to a coffee shop or something. Take your laptop and knock out some of those soul-crushing job applications. Make an event of it. Get spiffed up, go to a nice venue, treat yourself to some good food and drink, ulcer permitting."

Marcos didn't answer.

Keith shrugged. "I can't make you do it, of course. But I'd consider it a personal favor if you gave it a try. If it doesn't work, you can come back and tell me what a lousy idea it was."

Marcos gave a brief nod.

"So how about your family?" Keith asked. "How are things with them?"

"Okay."

"Just okay?"

"Not great. They're on my case and driving me crazy. Treating me like I'm about to break."

"Because of the ulcer?"

"No, just my 'mental state.'" He made air quotes. "They don't know about the ulcer."

"Oh? Why's that?"

"Because I'm sick of talking about it and being fussed over."

Keith leaned forward. "So you're telling me

your family doesn't actually know you were medically retired?"

"No. It happened right at the twelve-year mark, so they think I just processed out."

"And you didn't think it was important to tell them the truth?"

"Like I said, I didn't want them to worry."

"Yeah? And how's that working out?"

Marcos didn't answer.

"Look," Keith said, "they know you're holding out on them, they just don't know why. At this point, whatever they're imagining is probably a lot worse than the truth. Tell them."

Marcos nodded again.

It was refreshing to be told what to do, and to be outside his own head for a change. He felt like he'd been pacing in a narrow cage for a long time, wearing ruts in the floor. And now he was outside, with a different view and new places to go.

You've got this, he told himself, and tried to believe it.

CHAPTER NINE

MARCOS TOOK A SEAT at the bar and opened up his laptop, ready to fill out job applications and interact with some fellow human beings.

He could do this. He was a likable enough guy, or had been once. Sure, he'd always been an introvert, but he didn't used to be so closed off. He'd had friends enough in high school. His pasture parties had been the stuff of legend.

Tito Mendoza was standing behind the bar in his crisp white shirt and black vest, polishing a glass. He and Marcos had gone to high school together, but they weren't friends. Tito wasn't a pasture-party kind of guy. He was the kind of guy who said, *Actually...* before telling you a bunch of obscure facts that you never wanted to know, didn't care about now, and wouldn't remember afterward.

"I like your place," Marcos told him. "It's very...clean."

It was the best compliment he could come

up with. Marcos was more of a dive-bar guy himself, but Tito's place, with its combination bar and taproom on one side and casual restaurant on the other, was the closest thing to a coffee shop within easy driving distance.

Tito looked taken aback. Maybe Marcos should have led with *Hello.*

"Uh, thanks!" Tito said. "My uncle always prided himself on keeping a clean bar, and so do I."

Oh, yeah, the uncle. Original Tito. Young Tito had taken over for him some years back. Should Marcos ask how Original Tito was doing? That would be small-talkish and pleasant…unless the uncle was dead and not retired. Yeah, probably best not to risk it.

"So what can I get you?" Tito asked.

Now, that was a good question. In the absence of helpful medical advice, Marcos had observed some things about his ulcer. Alcohol didn't seem to directly cause a flare-up, but he had fewer flare-ups overall if he didn't drink.

"Something nonalcoholic," he said.

It was pretty lame, coming into a bar and asking for something without alcohol. It would have been okay if he'd sat on the restaurant side, but he'd chosen this seat because it was a strong defensible position, with a good view of the front door, and close to the corridor leading to the restrooms and back exit.

"Sure thing. We've got craft sodas at the soda fountain next door, and iced tea, sweet and unsweet."

"I can't have soda either. And I'm not sure about black tea."

"Stomach ulcer?"

Wow, that was a really good guess.

"Yeah."

Tito rubbed his chin. "Would you care to try some turmeric-ginger tea? I could brew you a cup."

Marcos drew back, repulsed. "Turmeric? That's what mustard's made of."

"Actually, it's a spice that's commonly used in mustard preparations, but it isn't mustard per se. It has a lot of health benefits—it's an antioxidant and an anti-inflammatory. And ginger has been used to treat stomach ailments for centuries."

Yeah, well, ibuprofen was an anti-inflammatory too, but no one sat around drinking it.

"Tell you what," Tito said. "I've got some chilled in the employee fridge. How about

I pour you some in a shot glass so you can give it a try?"

"'Kay," Marcos said. He knew he was being difficult, making trouble over a low-price beverage. But turmeric and ginger? No way could that be anything but awful.

Only it wasn't. Tito was right—the tea was good. Marcos finished his shot glass and said, "Go ahead and brew me some."

"Sure thing. If you want, I can brew it double strength, add some ice and give it to you in a stein glass. The ice will melt right away and it'll look like you're drinking a nice blond ale."

Huh! Apparently there were all sorts of tricks, besides the old club-soda decoy, for people who wanted to drink something non-alcoholic at a bar without anyone noticing. Maybe Marcos's whole life had been a lie.

Or maybe Tito was just really thoughtful.

"S'aright," Marcos said. "I'll just sit here at the bar with my little teacup. Might as well get used to it."

"How about I give it to you in a manly stoneware mug?"

"Perfect."

Marcos pulled up a job application form on his laptop and started filling it out. When

Tito set the steaming mug on the bar, Marcos set the laptop aside.

Time to make some small talk.

"What have you been doing since high school?" he asked. "You went away and came back, right?"

"That's right. Went to school in North Texas."

"What'd you study?"

"Philosophy."

"*Philosophy?* That's as impractical as my Field Artillery MOS."

Tito laughed. "Yeah, not a lot of market demand for philosophers as such, but I loved it. And it turned out to be a pretty handy field of knowledge for a bar owner."

That made sense. "Did they have a good philosophy department where you went to school?"

"Good, but not world-renowned or anything. Mainly I just wanted to get away from home. It was nice, being someplace where I could be myself, and not just the runt of the Mendoza brothers."

"Yeah, you got that right," Marcos agreed, a little too vehemently. "I mean—not about being a runt, but—I know how it can be, all the stuff family can put on you. My family's great and all, but it was a lot to live up to, being a Ramirez of La Escarpa. Especially for someone who didn't want to be a rancher."

Tito nodded. "There are a lot of expectations that come along with a strong family identity."

That was a nice way of putting it.

"So why'd you come back?" Marcos asked.

"Well, my uncle died and left me the bar."

Aha! Dead, not retired. Good call on not asking about the uncle earlier.

"My initial plan was to get set up with a good manager and be a hands-off owner," Tito said. "But my standards were so high, I had a hard time filling the position. So in the meantime I did it myself. And before long I realized I loved the work, and I moved back for good."

"Was it weird moving back home?"

"At first. But I'm not the only one from our class who's living here now. There are plenty of people we went to school with who never left, or came back like I did. I was afraid it might be confining, being around people that remember me the way I was. But it hasn't worked out that way. In general I find that high school is over, and everyone's grown up and moved on. People are just as ready as I am to let go of the past and live in the present."

A shadow darkened the front door, and a big man with a shaved head and a handlebar mustache walked in.

"Rigoberto!" he called.

"Hi, Dad," Tito said. His smile had gone stiff, and he gave Marcos a quick glance that said clear as words, *Well, most people, anyway*.

Mr. Mendoza clomped over and took the seat right next to Marcos, though there was plenty of room along the bar.

"How's it going, *huerco*?" he asked his son. "Working hard, or hardly working?"

He laughed at his own joke. Somehow Marcos got the idea that Mr. Mendoza said those words a lot.

"Hanging in there," Tito said. "What can I get you, Dad?"

"Gimme a pint of Thirsty Goat."

"Coming right up."

Mr. Mendoza looked at Marcos and did a double take. "Marcos? Marcos Ramirez? That you?"

"Yes, sir, it sure is."

Mr. Mendoza gave a great roar of a greeting and shook Marcos's hand. He had a heck of a grip.

"How you been? I haven't seen you since you joined the service. Are you on leave?"

"No, sir, I'm home for good. How are you?"

"Can't complain. Business is booming."

"What business is that?"

"Dirt work and land clearing. I did a lot of mesquite grubbing out at your family's place a few years back, right around the time your sister and brother-in-law took it over. Got the fence lines all cleaned up too."

"Right, I remember now. So where are you working these days?"

"Oh, I got me a big job. The old Masterson place is being parceled out and sold, and me and my boys are clearing out some brush so the surveyor can get back there and do his thing. Then there'll be pad sites to make and fencing to put up when the new owners are ready to build."

Tito handed him his beer. He took a draw from it and shot Marcos a sidewise glance. "But hey, I'm forgetting who I'm talking to here. You're old ranching stock. Probably think it's a disgrace for an old property like that to get carved up and sold off."

Marcos shrugged. "Nope. Doesn't bother

me a bit. Just because a ranch has been in the family for umpteen generations doesn't mean it has to stay in it forever. If other people want to pay good money for their own piece, I say more power to them."

Mr. Mendoza clapped him hard on the shoulder. "Haha! That's the spirit! You ought to come work for me."

"Are you hiring?"

Mr. Mendoza blinked. "Whoa, seriously? You in the job market?"

"Yes, sir."

"Well, yeah, I could use the extra help. Javi, my next-to-youngest, just went off to West Texas to work in the oil fields." He rolled his eyes. "Thinks he can make more money out there."

He gave Marcos an appraising look. "Do you have experience with earth-moving equipment?"

"I drove a tractor a lot growing up, and moved a lot of earth in Syria with M777 howitzer shells."

"Close enough. You're hired!"

The tight knot of worry that had been constricting Marcos's chest all day suddenly dissolved in peace. "Thanks, Mr. Mendoza. I appreciate it."

"You bet. We veterans have to stick together, right?"

"Are you a veteran? I didn't know."

"Oh yeah. I enlisted at the same time as your uncle Marcos, for Desert Storm. So when can you start?"

"How 'bout tomorrow?"

"Great! Oh, hey, one thing. I can't guarantee forty hours a week. It'll probably be closer to twenty. That all right?"

Twenty hours a week? No wonder Javi lit out for the oil fields. Still, part-time was better than nothing.

"Sure," he said.

The door opened again, and Mr. Mendoza's voice boomed out. "Tony! How you doing? Get yourself over here and have a beer. Look who I'm with! Your brother-in-law! He's gonna come work for me!"

Tony sat around the corner of the bar from Marcos. "No kidding? When did that happen? I thought you were at that factory making those handle things."

Only a few hours had passed since Marcos had lost his job, but it felt like days. After his session with Keith, he'd gone home, cleaned himself up and come to Tito's. Mom had already left for work. No one in his family knew about his phone call from HR.

"Nah, I'm not there anymore," Marcos said. "I was sick of being shut in a windowless room doing repetitive work for hours on end." Which was true as far as it went.

"Well, good for you, brother. You'll get plenty of fresh air and exercise working for Mr. M."

Mr. Mendoza set down his empty beer stein and motioned to Tito for another. "So Tony, when're you gonna come out to my place for some time on the Brush Hog?"

Tony shook his head regretfully. "I want to, Mr. M, but I just can't get an afternoon free."

Was Tony clearing brush at Mr. Mendoza's property? That didn't make any sense.

"Brush Hog is Mr. M's mechanical bull," Tony explained. "I've started competing in rodeos again, but I haven't had much time lately to train."

"I didn't know you were riding again," Marcos said. "I remember you rode in high school. Didn't realize you'd made a comeback."

"Well, I haven't made much of one so far. I'm crazy busy with work and helping my brother. This is the first time in months that

I've set foot in this place, and I'm only here today because I had a few minutes free after going to the bank. I've competed in a total of six rodeos over the last four years. Haven't taken home a prize yet, but I came close once. I don't think I'm likely to get rich off riding a bull, but man, is it fun."

"I'll bet. Wouldn't mind trying it myself."

"Seriously?" said Mr. Mendoza. "You want to take a spin on Brush Hog, you come out any time."

"I might do that. Got a lot of time on my hands all of a sudden."

"What do you mean?" Tony asked. "I thought you said you hired on with Mr. M."

"Part-time. Going to have to find something else to supplement."

Tony stroked his beard. "Listen, Marcos, you might not want to hear this, but Dalia and I could really use some help on La Escarpa."

Tony was right. Marcos didn't want to hear it. He'd been ignoring the hints ever since he'd first come home.

He looked at the job application on his laptop screen, with all its asterisk-marked required fields. The cursor blinked at him.

"What kind of help?" he asked.

"Everything. I've been working with Alex

out at my grandparents' place, trying to get their house ready for him and Lauren to move into. I've been stretched pretty thin, and I'll be playing catch-up for weeks to come."

Marcos sat up straighter. "Alex and Lauren are moving out of the bunkhouse? When?"

"End of the week, we hope."

"Do you have another tenant lined up?"

"Noooo," Tony said, in a what-an-interesting-thought kind of voice. "Are you interested in some sort of work-for-room type situation?"

Marcos thought. He'd walked away from La Escarpa once and said he'd never be back. Ranching was work he knew, though, and he was good at it. Plus, he really needed his own place. Much as he loved his mom, living in the bedroom he'd had as a baby was not helping his state of mind. Not that a bunkhouse on his family's ancestral ranch, within a short walk of his sister's house, would be much of an improvement, but at least he'd have the four walls to himself.

"Yes," he said. "I am."

"Awesome! We'll have to talk to Dalia to get the details straight—you know how she is about accounting. But I'm sure we can work it out. She's been holding out on looking for a hired man because it's so hard to find a good, steady guy you can trust. I know she'll be relieved to have her own brother."

Marcos closed the job application window and shut his laptop. Then he drained his turmeric-ginger tea and held up his empty mug to Tito. "Bartender! Another."

His heart suddenly felt lighter than it had in a long time.

CHAPTER TEN

NINA STARED AT the wall of nail-polish bottles. They ran the gamut of colors and textures, including metallic, neon and glittery. The variety boggled the mind.

"Do you know what you want?" Eliana asked.

She stood there, perfectly poised, with her already immaculate nails shining dark red against her Kate Spade handbag.

"Honestly?" Nina said. "I don't even know what any of it means!" She looked down at the price sheet the salon attendant had handed her. "A reverse French manicure? What is that? Hot stones and seaweed? How do they figure in? And what on earth is a powder dip? It sounds like a coating for the bed of a pickup truck."

Eliana's exquisitely sculpted eyebrows rose. "Exactly how long has it been since you visited a nail salon, Nina?"

"Um…senior prom, I guess."

The eyebrows rose higher. "You're kidding me, right?"

"No. I've been busy raising a child! I mean, I like how a nice manicure looks, but for the past seven years I've had way too much going on to ever go to a salon and pay for one. I paint them myself sometimes, but I'm always cleaning something at home or opening packages at work, and the polish usually starts to chip on the very first day. And once that starts, I end up peeling it all off."

Eliana made an indignant sound. She whisked the price sheet out of Nina's hands and said, "You're getting a gel manicure in a nice neutral shade—number 229, I think. Gels are extremely durable. But you do need to protect them from hot water, so get yourself some good latex gloves and wear them. And if you should somehow manage to chip the finish anyway, *do not* try to peel it off! You'll damage your nail. Gels should be removed only with professional-grade tools. We'll meet back here in two to three weeks. I'll make our appointments before we leave today. Got that?"

Nina opened her mouth to protest. She couldn't possibly keep imposing on her aunt for something as frivolous as a manicure.

Then she remembered what Aunt Cessy had said when she'd half-apologetically asked her to watch Logan today. "Oh, my goodness, yes. Meet your friend. Have your manicure, and have lunch afterward. Do it! Go!"

"Got it," Nina told Eliana.

Behind her, she heard the door to the salon open and a voice say, "Eliana? Is that you?"

Eliana's face lit up. "Annalisa!"

She hurried over to the newcomer, gave her a featherlight hug and turned back to Nina.

"Nina, this is my friend Annalisa Cavazos. She graduated with Marcos, and she used to live in the same neighborhood as my Casillas grandparents in town, so we'd all play together as kids."

Annalisa had a sweet smile, and the biggest, most soulful eyes Nina had ever seen. "Eliana was such a cute little girl," she said. "I used to dress her up in my old ballet costumes. She was like my very own life-size doll."

"I remember that! And we rode together on the float in the Persimmon Fest—once when Annalisa was queen and I was part of the junior court, and later when I was queen and she came back as a past queen."

"I still have my dress," said Annalisa. "And my tiara."

"So do I!" Eliana looked at Nina again. "Oh, and she wrote a book! *Ghost Stories of the Texas Hill Country*. One of the ghosts was an ancestor of mine! That book was part of what got Alex and Lauren together."

"Yes, I'm very proud of that," Annalisa said.

"You should be! Alex and Lauren are perfect together." She turned back to Nina. "Tony and Alex are Annalisa's cousins."

"Second cousins. We share a set of great-grandparents on the Cavazos side."

Nina enjoyed the whole disjointed back-and-forth introduction. It was lovely how intertwined people's lives were in a small town. She wished *she* had a complex network of connection to a whole community.

Of course, her life was already intertwined with Eliana's family, far more than they realized.

"And this is my friend Nina," Eliana went on. "She just moved here from California, but she's not one of *those* Californians. Her grandparents used to have a place in Comal County, and she used to visit them as a kid, so she's an honorary Texan. And now she's moved here for real. She works at that new veterans' center."

"It's good to meet you, Nina," Annalisa said. "You showed a lot of sense in moving to Texas."

"Thank you! I think so too."

The salon attendant led them to their seats. Nina and Annalisa were side by side, with Eliana a row ahead of them.

The attendant sat across the counter from Nina, pushed a small bowl of some fragrant solution toward her, and motioned for her to soak her nails in it. Nina saw Annalisa taking off her rings before dipping the nails of one hand in her own bowl, so Nina took off her wedding band and set it on the counter.

She placed the fingers of her left hand in the bowl, and the attendant took her right hand and started clipping and filing. She was glad she had Annalisa's example so she wouldn't make a mistake.

"I like your ring," Annalisa said.

"Thanks. It's fake. I mean—the ring is real enough, but I'm not married. I bought myself a ring off Amazon, so the men I work with won't ask me out."

Eliana turned around. "Isn't that smart? I wish I'd thought to do that when I started at my current job. It's unbelievable how many creepy stalkers are out there. My Instagram is private, and I'm not on Facebook, but they find a way. I once had a client stalk me on *Pinterest*. Can you imagine?"

"How is that possible?" Nina asked.

"He followed my boards and sent me a private message." Eliana didn't say what the message was, but she did shudder at the memory. "And he was *married*! I'd met his wife! Can you believe the nerve?"

"I believe it," said Annalisa. "What did you do?"

"Blocked him, and told my boss. She made sure I never had to deal with him again."

"Good for her," Nina said.

"I know, right? Not every boss would take an employee's side against a client that way."

"So who are you dating these days, Eliana?" asked Annalisa.

"An Italian filmmaker. His name is Rinaldo. He has lovely eyes."

"What?" said Nina. "What happened to Nigel?"

"Oh, Nigel's long gone. I broke it off with him the day you and Logan went to the Gristmill with my family."

Wow. Clearly Eliana's definition of *long gone* was not the same as Nina's.

The woman doing Eliana's nails took out what looked like a tiny sander and started working away with it, putting a halt on conversation with Eliana, and leaving Nina and Annalisa to themselves. Annalisa smiled shyly at Nina. She'd made the last overture; now it was Nina's turn. But she was sadly out of practice. These days, most of her nonwork conversations were about Logan, or with Logan.

"So you went to school with Eliana's brother?" Nina asked.

She felt shy about saying Marcos's name. She wondered if maybe Annalisa was an old flame. She was certainly pretty.

"Sure did! Kindergarten through high school. I used to go to his pasture parties, until he joined the Marine Corps. Hey, maybe you know Marcos through the center?"

"I can't really comment on whether someone is a client," Nina said apologetically.

"Oh, of course. That makes sense."

So much for that topic of conversation.

"Eliana said you wrote a book?" Nina said. "That's impressive."

"Oh, not really. It's more of a compilation.

I grew up hearing all these stories from older relatives and finally decided to get them written down. Their voices were so rich and distinctive. I didn't add much beyond a bit of polish."

"Actually, I would imagine that would take a lot of skill. Preserving those voices and not imposing your own personality."

"Well, yes, I guess that's true. Especially considering I don't even believe in ghosts."

"Really! What made you write the book, then?"

"Mostly I'm interested in the psychological and cultural aspects of the stories. The kind of things people find frightening, or horrifying or sad, and why. How they use storytelling to deal with that, to find a sort of closure. There are a lot of recurring themes in ghost stories—the suicide ghost, the woman in white, the haunted house, the ghost with unfinished business. Some themes are almost universal in ghost folklore throughout the world, but of course Texas ghost stories have their own flavor."

"What about the one Eliana mentioned, with her ancestor?"

"Oh, yes, Alejandro Ramirez. The theme of that one is return of the dead lover."

She told Nina how Alejandro, a well-off *ranchero*, left his *rancho* and his pregnant wife, Romelia, to fight in the Texas Revolution, promising to return in time to lay a cluster of yellow *esperanza* blossoms in the cradle of their newborn child. But he was killed in battle, and his body was never brought home. Years later, when a wildfire threatened La Escarpa, Romelia saw a shadowy figure through the smoke, fighting the fire along with the hired *vaqueros* and her young son, and saving the *rancho*.

"So you see how an event like that could be subject to interpretation," Annalisa said. "A ghostly figure in a smoky haze? That could be almost anything. But Romelia believed Alejandro had come home, trying to fulfill his promise, and protecting what was his. My great-uncle Miguel used to swear up and down that it was true, that Alejandro's ghost had walked the earth. He was the great-grandson of Alejandro and Romelia's son, Gabriel. Gabriel remembered the fire and the ghostly figure in the smoke. He believed it was his father, and he told the story to Miguel. Miguel passed it on to his grandsons—Tony and Alex."

Nina sorted that out in her head. "Wait,

are Tony and Alex cousins to Eliana and her brother and sister?"

"That's right! Fourth half cousins. So Eliana is Tony and Alex's cousin but not my cousin—at least, not that I know of. There's a lot of extended family in and around Limestone Springs. I'm sure plenty of people are related and don't realize it."

I'll bet.

"Alejandro sounds like a typical veteran," Nina said. "If they come back at all, they come back changed."

"Yes, I suppose you're right. Have you worked with veterans long?"

"All my adult life. Some of their issues are age-old, and some things change with time. These days, with advances in medical care and the use of Kevlar body armor, most of the wounded survive their injuries—about ninety percent. That's a lot of scarred men and women walking around in society. And then of course there are all the invisible injuries, like PTSD and traumatic brain injury—not to mention depression, anxiety and all the everyday problems of making a transition to civilian life. Our culture is supportive of veterans in theory, but most people don't really understand what they've been through or the challenges they face. Someone needs to bridge that gap."

"Sounds like you're passionate about your work."

"I am. My father was a veteran, and I didn't have much of a relationship with him. If he'd gotten better help at a critical time, a lot of things might have been different."

She hadn't been able to help her own father, but she'd been given an opportunity to help the father of her child. She'd managed to get him connected to Keith, and she wished she knew how their meeting had gone. It had been hard to tell much from his face when he'd left the center.

"So what made you come to Texas?" Annalisa asked.

"Work and family—which in my case are pretty much the same thing. My aunt is a licensed therapist at the Veterans' Resource Center of South Central Texas. She got me to move here so I could work as office manager at the center, and also so she could help me with my son."

"And how old is he?"

"Seven. He's great, but he's a lot to take care of on my own. He's with my aunt right now. It feels so luxurious, having another adult I can depend on. I'm not used to it yet. I keep thinking I have to keep an eye out for Logan and make sure he doesn't take those nail-polish bottles off the shelves and start pouring them out on the floor."

Annalisa chuckled. "I can imagine. It must be hard to get time to yourself with friends when you're a single mother."

"Well, most of my pre-Logan friends dropped away a long time ago anyway."

Part of that had been Nina's own fault. She could admit that now. She hadn't told anyone who the father was, hadn't confided anything about the whole impromptu marriage and annulment. That had put up a barrier between her and her friends. None of them had had kids of their own, which was another barrier. And when they started getting married, Nina had felt sore about being around all the happy couples. She soon found she would rather be with Logan. There was a you-and-me-against-the-world vibe to it that got her through the worst of the loneliness.

"Well, we're your friends now," Eliana said over her shoulder. "We're meeting up here again in three weeks and having lunch together afterward. I'm not letting either of you leave until we set a date and time."

She had her chin high in the air and a fixed look in her eyes. Nina hadn't even realized she'd been listening, or that the nail sander tool wasn't whirring anymore.

"I don't see why we can't have lunch today too," said Annalisa.

"Oh, we will," said Eliana. "That's a given."

MARCOS LEANED AGAINST Mr. Mendoza's truck and took a bite of his taco—potato and egg, no salsa. The idea of avoiding spicy foods for the rest of his life was a depressing one, but so was the thought of another ulcer flare-up.

The truck was parked under the shade of a post oak tree. It was shaping up to be a hot day, but not as hot as it would be a month from now. This was early June, so the mornings were still fresh, and the heat didn't have time to build up like it would later. And after Syria, he couldn't find much to complain about in Texas, weatherwise. Plus no one was shooting at him, so there was that.

He'd been working at the Masterson place all morning, clearing hackberries and other brush from an old fence line. He finished his taco, crumpled the foil wrapper and tossed it into the trash bag in the truck bed.

"Surveyor's here," called Johnny, the oldest Mendoza brother. Seconds later, a Chevy 4x4 with an extended cab turned onto the dirt driveway. A decal on the door said Randall Surveying. Something about that rang a bell.

Then the truck parked and the guy got out—a tall Black man dressed in Fire Hose pants and a nice button-down with cowboy boots.

"Keith?" Marcos said.

"Marcos!" Keith strode over with his hand extended. "What are you doing here?"

"This is my new job," Marcos said as he shook Keith's hand.

Mr. Mendoza joined them. "You two know each other?"

"We've met," said Keith. "I didn't know he was part of your outfit."

"He just started," said Mr. Mendoza. "Funny thing. He was at my youngest son's bar just the other day, filling out job applications online. We got to talking, and the long and short of it is, he works for me now."

"That's great," Keith said. There was no I-told-you-so in his voice or face. He just looked pleased.

"Sure is," said Mr. Mendoza. "Hey, you hungry? One of my boys just made a run to that taco-*kolache*-espresso place in town."

"Quite a combination," said Marcos.

"Yeah, kind of a Mexican-Czech-Italian fusion," said Mr. Mendoza. "I like the chorizo *kolache* myself. You want one? We've got plenty."

"That does sound good, but I already ate," Keith said. "Thanks just the same."

"All right, then. Let me know if you need anything."

Mr. Mendoza headed back to his bulldozer, leaving Marcos and Keith alone.

"So how's the new job going?" Keith asked.

"So far so good. Beats working in that windowless factory."

"Did you tell your family about your ulcer?"

"I told my mom."

"And?"

"And she was worried, but mostly relieved that I didn't have anything worse going on. She's probably told my sisters by now. I guess I'll find out, when I start my other job tomorrow."

"You got a second job?"

"Yeah, on the ranch."

"Which ranch?"

"La Escarpa. My family owns it."

"I didn't know your family had a ranch."

"Yeah, it's where I grew up. My sister and her husband run it now."

Keith thought a moment. "If your family has a ranch in the area, why not work there in the first place?"

Something clenched tight in Marcos's stomach. "It's not a good fit long-term."

Keith waited, but when Marcos didn't go on, he asked, "Do you get along with your sister and brother-in-law?"

"Yeah."

"Do you think they're doing a good job running the ranch?"

"Yeah."

"Then why—"

"It's not happening," Marcos said sharply.

"Okay," Keith said.

There was a silence. Then Marcos said, "What about you? You seem to be doing all right, judging by your truck."

Keith laughed. "Yeah. I enjoy what I do, and I keep busy. It's interesting, active work. You never know what you're going to see, walking around on these old ranches. Architectural ruins. Old wells and cisterns. Cemeteries with sandstone markers, the names worn away. And wildlife! Cougars, feral hogs, peccaries."

"Chupacabras."

"Very likely."

After another pause, Marcos said, "Thanks."

"For what?"

"All the stuff you said yesterday. You were right."

"You're very welcome. I remember what it was like when I got out and—well, I'm happy to help. We still on for our next appointment?"

"Yeah."

"You know, we don't have to keep meeting at the center. We could meet someplace closer to home for you. Your boss mentioned his son's bar—Tito's, right? I've heard a lot of good things about it, and it's got that restaurant right next door."

Marcos thought of Nina, the way her blue eyes flashed when she talked about veterans of the past, how they needed help but mostly didn't get it. He'd have walked right out again if she hadn't stopped him.

"I'd just as soon keep meeting at the center, if it's all the same to you," he said.

"Fine by me. Neutral territory, huh?"

Sure, that's the reason. It had nothing to do with Marcos wanting to see Nina again.

CHAPTER ELEVEN

Nina placed her order at the counter of Jittery Jim's and handed the barista her own mug from home—a pretty, dainty, pearlescent pink thing that Logan had somehow never managed to break. Reaching for her wallet, she felt something hard and spiky and palmed it. These days, her purse always seemed to have small plastic toys knocking around in it.

As she was signing the card reader, someone behind her said her name, and her heart leaped into her throat. She knew that voice.

Marcos was seated at a small round table, hands around a steaming mug, wearing a gray T-shirt and a chambray overshirt with the sleeves rolled up, snug against the biceps. His hair was longer than when she'd seen him last. A close layer of black velvet covered his scalp on the sides and back, and the top was just starting to curl.

But it was his face that really caught her

attention. The expression was open and relaxed, not tight as a clenched fist like before.

"Marcos! Hey! What are you doing here?"

"Being around people without looking like I'll bite the head off anyone who tries to talk to me."

"Let me guess. Keith?"

"Yep."

He was almost smiling. He looked more comfortable in his own skin than she'd seen him in—well, ever. Not that the two of them had a lot of history to draw on.

He made an awkward gesture for her to sit down, and she did. Maybe it wasn't the smartest thing to do, considering the big secret she was keeping from him, but he was making such an effort, and she wanted to encourage that.

They both started to talk at once, then both abruptly stopped.

"Go ahead," she said.

"Do you come here a lot?" he asked. Then he winced. "Sorry, that's the worst."

"I do, actually. Come here a lot. It's a treat. As a—" she started to say single mother, but caught herself just in time "—mother of a young child, I'm on call most of the time, so I like to build in little minivacations for myself, to rest and recharge. How about you? Are you on your way to the center?"

"Yeah. Meeting Keith, then going straight to work."

He had a new job, then. "Good! What sort of work?"

The almost-smile broke through at last. "Ranch work."

"Seriously? Not at La Escarpa, surely?"

He nodded. "I'm Tony and Dalia's hired man."

"Wow! I didn't expect that."

"Neither did I."

"So? How are you liking it?"

"S'aright. Been riding the fence line, mending as I go, clearing cactus and brush. Nice to be left alone, not micromanaged. Nice to be outdoors."

"That's wonderful, Marcos. I'm so glad to hear it."

"There's more. I'm moving into the bunkhouse."

"The one Alex and Lauren fixed up?"

"Yep. They're moving to the Reyes place. Alex and Tony both own it, but Alex works it. They've been getting the house fixed up."

"Wow, all you people with your ancestral ranches and extra houses. I guess Tony and

Dalia must be doing well, if there's enough work to support a hired man."

"It's not full-time. I'm also working for an outfit that does dirt work."

"Dirt work! What's that?"

"Earth moving, excavation, grading, brush cutting. We're clearing some land that's going on the market. And who do you think the surveyor is? Keith."

"No way!"

"Yep. He was a surveyor in the Army."

"Huh! I didn't know that. Now, *there's* an MOS that transfers."

"That's just what I thought. Funny how connected people are, if only they thought to ask."

"Yeah. Six Degrees of Kevin Bacon."

He gave her a blank look.

"It's a game," she said. "You take some random actor and see how many links it takes to connect him to Kevin Bacon. It's based on the idea that any two people in the world are only six removes apart from each other at most."

"In the *world*? I don't know about that."

"Well, it's what they say."

The muscles in his forearms twitched as he tapped his fingers against his mug. Nina peered into the amber liquid. "What is this you're drinking?"

He looked embarrassed. "Turmeric-ginger tea."

"Whoa! That sounds pretty hippy-dippy for you, Marcos."

"It's for my ulcer. But it's not bad."

"Oh, no! How long have you had an ulcer?"

"Don't know when it started, but it perforated earlier this year during Iron Fist. I passed out from blood loss, got peritonitis—that's an infection from your stomach contents sloshing around all over your insides. I was a mess."

Iron Fist was an artillery exercise held at San Clemente Island every February. Marcos had been discharged two months later, in April.

"You didn't process out," she guessed. "You were medically retired."

He held his hands up in a "you got me" gesture.

"Yeah. Sucks, doesn't it? To make it through Raqqa and Deir ez-Zor with hardly a scratch, only to get laid low by my own stomach eating a hole in itself."

"Well, what about now? Are you seeing a doctor?"

He shook his head. "I take my meds, watch what I eat. I do okay. It's been ten days since my last flare-up."

"You had a flare-up that day at the Grist-mill?"

Great, now he knew she'd kept track of the days. Okay, so he had too, but he had the excuse of an ulcer attack to make the day memorable.

"Yeah, but it wasn't bad. And I haven't had one since."

Nina wondered why he wasn't seeing a doctor, but she wasn't about to push. He'd just dig in his heels, and it wasn't like she had any claim on him.

Instead she said, "Well, you look good, Marcos."

"Thanks. You do too. You look—you look real good."

"Thank you."

Marcos took a sip of tea. "Has your husband joined you in Texas yet?"

Her heart gave a sickening lurch. "No. Not yet."

"Eliana said he was staying in San Diego while the house sells?"

His tone was flat and wooden, like he was forcing himself to ask.

"Yes. Yes, that's right." *Liar!*

"What does he do? Is he military?"

Nina blanked out. Naturally she had a fake backstory for her fake husband, but suddenly she couldn't remember a word of it.

At that exact moment, the barista called her name. She went to the counter and picked up her drink.

This was her chance. All she had to do was pretend to get a message from work and take off. A lie to cover up another lie. But then she turned and saw Marcos waiting for her—alert, interested and so very attractive—and suddenly found herself sitting back down.

"Is that a *Pachycephalosaurus* in your hand?" he asked.

"Is it?" She set the little dinosaur on the table. "It was in my purse. I forgot I was holding it. How'd you know the name?"

"I loved dinos when I was a kid."

"So does Logan. These days I always seem to have a dinosaur or two on my person, and I've learned more about them than I ever wanted to know."

Marcos picked it up. He made it stomp around on the table a bit, then headbutted it into his tea mug with a "grrraaawwrrr!"

It was the most adorable thing she'd ever seen him do.

He set the dinosaur down. "Logan seems like a good kid," he said. "Doesn't run off at the mouth."

"True. He's a boy of few words."

"He looks like you."

"Oh, do you think so?"

"Yeah, in the shape of the eyes." He made a vague gesture to his own face. "His are brown, though."

Hazel, actually. Light brown flecked with green…like the ones staring across the table at her right now.

"Guess he gets that from his father," Marcos said.

Her heart was beating way too fast. She took a sip of her drink and burned her tongue. *Warning! Hull breach imminent! Change subject!*

But then again…

Did she really have to protect the secret?

By the time she'd realized she was pregnant almost eight years ago, her marriage to Marcos had been annulled, and she hadn't seen him since they'd both appeared in court. She could have tracked him down, but she didn't. She'd told herself that she and the baby were better off without him, but the plain truth was that she couldn't handle another rejection. And so she'd inflicted a repeat of her own childhood on her son.

Logan didn't openly pine for a father like she had, but he needed a father whether he showed it or not. She owed him that much.

And now here was Marcos, open and available all of a sudden.

Did she dare?

"Speaking of fathers," she said, and then she lost her nerve and took a step back from the precipice. "I found my dad. Again."

"Yeah? How'd that happen?"

"My aunt acted as a go-between. She kept after both of us and basically wouldn't let it go until we finally agreed to meet up. When I tracked him down the first time—right before you and I met—he was so cold and brusque, I thought he didn't care about me at all. But he just didn't know how to be a father. I was born while he was away for Desert Storm, and when he came back, he was—well, different, you know. At least my mom says he was, and I don't doubt it. And she said he couldn't be around me. But looking back, at her relationship history after they split up… I think she was more in love with the idea of a deployed husband, the romance of it all, than she was with him. You've heard how it was back then, all the patriotism. And when he came home, and she had the reality of a man in her life, a man with issues, she didn't have the patience to deal with it. Of course I was too young to remember any of it, so this is all guesswork on my part. From an adult perspective, though, I think they could have made it work. I think they gave up too soon."

He listened without comment, his hazel eyes fixed on her, his mouth sober. Then he said, "Honestly, I think that's true more often than not."

Heat spread through her face. Did he mean that the way it sounded?

"So how'd the reunion go?" Marcos asked.

She took a sip of her drink to steady her voice. "It was good. Not everything I wanted, but good."

"Do you still see him?"

She shook her head. "He died not long after we reconnected. He was already sick by the time he agreed to meet with me. I think that's a big part of why he was willing to talk to me again. I'm grateful for the time I had with him, and that he got to meet Logan, but I wish we'd had more."

"Yeah."

Nina's heart pounded. Now the stage was set for her to tell Marcos about his son, right here in Jittery Jim's Coffee Shop.

"I'm happy for you, Nina," Marcos said. "It's great that you got to connect with your father, even a little. And now here you are helping veterans. Turning your own experience into something positive for other people. It's admirable. I know it's made a difference for me."

"Thank you," she said. That couldn't have been easy for him to say.

He looked so tranquil and happy and…free. Like the guy she fell in love with eight years ago. Fell impulsively infatuated with, she corrected herself.

Then he looked down into his tea mug. "Can't imagine what it was like for your dad. A brand-new kid that he'd never even met— of course he was freaked out. I've got my issues for sure, but at least I don't have anyone depending on me."

The words felt like a hit to the solar plexus. "Yeah," she heard herself say. "At least you don't have that."

An alarm went off on Marcos's watch. It was a G-Shock, a watch favored by members of the military, and it looked like Marcos had "stealthed" it by going over the reflective paint with a black Sharpie. She could see the painstaking rows the marker had made over the watch's surface.

"Got to go meet Keith," he said as he switched it off. "It was good seeing you, Nina."

"You too," she said.

He downed the last of his tea and was gone.

The little *Pachycephalosaurus* was lying on its side where Marcos had left it after stomping it around on the table with his strong, capable-looking hand—the same hand that had slid the pawn-shop ring onto her finger eight years ago. She picked it up and held it tight.

CHAPTER TWELVE

IN THE DAYS since he'd run into Nina at the café, Marcos had set up a procedure. Leave twenty minutes earlier than necessary to meet Keith on time. First stop, Jittery Jim's. If he happened to catch Nina there on one of her minivacations, great. If not, get his turmeric-ginger tea to go, and move on to the Veterans' Resource Center. That wasn't as satisfying, because he couldn't really talk with her there, but at least he could keep an eye on her.

Which was what he was doing now, in the center's waiting room.

It was nice, as waiting rooms went. Peaceful enough, usually, but a hive of activity today. Something big was going down—several somethings. Computers getting upgraded. Air conditioner being serviced. New clients coming in, like that guy with the Navy tats and the woman with the prosthetic leg, both filling out paperwork. The room where Nina had taken Marcos to do his paperwork was out of commission for some reason today, so the waiting room was more crowded than usual. Cardboard filing boxes were stacked in the hallway.

And Nina was handling it. Keeping track of all the threads, switching gears as needed, from client to computer guy to air conditioner repairman. Always cheerful, always competent.

Marcos still hadn't told Keith why he wanted to keep meeting here at the center, or about his history with Nina. There was plenty else for the two of them to talk about, and if Keith knew Marcos was staging "accidental" meetings with his former wife, who was now married to another guy...well, that might come across as something that was not okay.

Marcos didn't have a high opinion of the guy Nina was married to. She clearly wasn't happy with him. Never spoke of him voluntarily. Always looked uncomfortable when Marcos asked about him, and gave quick answers before changing the subject. Marcos didn't even know the guy's name. He just thought of him as *the guy*.

Why wasn't the guy here in Texas yet? Something about the waiting-in-California-while-the-house-sold story smelled fishy.

Was it possible that they were separated? Or was the guy really that clueless and insensitive?

He'd *have* to be clueless, to have a wife like Nina and not do whatever it took to be near her. Marcos looked at her— that sleek brown hair that swung around her shoulders when she moved. Those clear, fearless blue eyes. That strong-set chin. He'd been wild about that chin, the night they met, though he'd never thought of himself as a "chin man" or particularly noticed any other woman's chin ever in his life. But Nina's chin was in a class by itself. He remembered kissing it, on the air mattress in the bed of his truck, as the sun climbed into the sky over San Elijo Beach.

Stop it! She's not for you. You had your chance and you blew it.

Looking at her was all he could do now, and he had only himself to blame. He could have chosen differently that day after he got that terrible phone call. He could have held on—like he'd talked about at Jittery Jim's, when she'd told him about her dad. That was the closest he'd come to apologizing for what he'd done.

She hadn't wanted the annulment. She'd pushed back as much as she decently could under the circumstances. But Marcos had been too hardheaded to budge—though looking back, he wasn't sure why. His feelings had been so jumbled. A lot of guilt about his father, for sure. Now that he was talking to Keith so much, he'd started identifying and labeling emotions. It was an eye-opener.

So he'd left—like that would fix anything between Marcos and his father, like Nina was in any way to blame for the man's death. The truth was, if Marcos's father had lived long enough to know about the marriage, he'd have chewed him out good for doing something so reckless and impulsive, but then he'd have told Marcos to get his butt in gear and honor the commitment he'd made. *Time to cowboy up*, he'd have said.

Marcos wished he could tell Nina everything. That he was wrong, and he was sorry. That he should have held on.

But it wasn't the sort of thing a man could say to another man's wife—especially considering all the feelings that he had yet to put a label to that were stirred up every time he saw her.

So he just looked.

The AC crew was finished. The head guy was going over the invoice with Nina now, and she was reading along and nodding, her pen poised and ready to sign. She flipped her hair back, saw Marcos and flashed a quick smile. He smiled back.

Then her gaze shifted to somewhere past his shoulder, and her expression froze.

He turned and saw a young woman coming through the glass door. That was what you were supposed to call them now, apparently— young women. Not girls, and not females, as they were referred to in the military. This particular young woman was around college age. One hand clutched the strap of a large expensive-looking purse. The other held on to a little redheaded boy—Nina's son. Logan.

She was walking faster than seemed possible in those heels. *Click! Clack! Click! Clack!* Logan was almost stumbling as he tried to keep up. He had a backpack on that was shaped like a T-Rex.

She marched Logan to Nina's desk and turned loose of his hand with a dramatic sweeping gesture.

"That's it!" she said. "I'm done. I can't take it anymore."

Nina set down the pen. "Hi, Chloe," she said weakly. "Is something wrong?"

"Uh, yeah! What's wrong is that I had a

live demo scheduled on my YouTube channel today, which I've been promoting for *weeks* across all my platforms. But now I can't do it, because this child of yours *demolished* my set."

The color drained from Nina's face. "Oh, no. What—what did he do?"

"He completely emptied my Caboodles Rock Star Grande and filled all the trays with his stupid *lizards*! This in spite of the fact that I had it locked up and the key on me—because of *course* I knew better than to keep it unlocked around him. But that didn't stop him! Oh, no. He picked the lock with a *hairpin*, which I thought was only a thing that happened in movies, but apparently not. You seem to be raising a criminal, so congratulations on that."

Nina's shoulders sagged in relief. "Is that all? I mean—I understand that would be very aggravating, but when you said demolished, I was thinking *demolished* demolished, as in permanent damage."

Chloe took a step back and let her jaw drop open. "How dare you make light of this situation? What about the permanent damage to my reputation? Until today I was a respected vlogger, with *hundreds* of followers regularly tuning in to see my demos of new products.

What am I supposed to tell them now? How is this going to look to whoever assesses my channel for Partner Program access? How can I *ever* hope to monetize my site with a black mark like this against me?"

"Can you reschedule?"

"Well, I don't have much choice now, do I? But that means starting all over with my promotions."

"I understand. I'm sorry, Chloe. But—"

Chloe held up a hand palm out to stop her. "Look, Nina. When you first approached me with this babysitting gig, I thought it was a way I could bring in a little cash while getting my business off the ground, building my brand—and also doing you a major favor, because let's face it, you aren't paying me that much. But now? I've had it. I'm *done*."

"I'm so, so sorry, Chloe. Please will you keep Logan just for the rest of the day? I'll pay you double."

"No money is worth this! And I'm going to be busy all afternoon trying to salvage my image and appease the viewers who were cheated out of my demo."

All this time, Logan was standing beside his mother's desk with his little backpack. Nina had a protective hand on his shoulder. Marcos couldn't see his face, but he saw Chloe's sneer as she looked down at him.

"This kid is *not normal*," she said. "He's into things *all the time*. You can't sit him down to watch TV. You can't give him an iPad to play with, because he'll take the iPad apart. It's like he doesn't understand what electronic devices are *for*. All he cares about is how they work. Honestly, I think you should have him tested."

Marcos's heart sped up, and he heard the blood rushing in his ears. Chloe had crossed one line too many. Now it was time for Nina to let her have it—and he for one was looking forward to seeing that happen.

Until that moment, Nina had kept her gaze firm and her chin high. But now...

Her face flushed. Her eyes filled with sudden tears. And that perfect chin trembled.

Marcos snapped. He let out a sharp "Hey!" that made Chloe jump and turn around.

"Who do you think you are, telling this woman to get her kid tested? Talk about *normal*. You think it's normal for a kid to go around with his eyeballs glued to a screen all day? I got news for you, *Chloe*. Kids play. They like to handle things and take them apart. *That's* normal. And where were you when Logan was emptying that canoodle thing? Why was he unsupervised that long? She's paying you to look after him, and you left him alone?"

Chloe's mouth fell open. "Wh— How dare you speak to me that way, jerk? You have no idea what I've been through today. Who do you think you are?"

"I know who I am. Marcos Ramirez, gunnery sergeant, United States Marine Corps."

The guy with the anchor tattoo spoke up. "And I'm Terence Wilson, boatswain's mate, United States Navy. And I didn't come here today to listen to you gripe, missy."

"Yeah," said the woman with the prosthesis. "Lose a leg to a roadside IED and then tell me how hard your life is."

Chloe made some more huffing sounds, then said, "I don't have to stand here and listen to this!"

"Go, then," Marcos said. "No one's stopping you."

"Whatever," said Chloe, and walked out.

The waiting room suddenly seemed weirdly quiet. The atmosphere wasn't exactly relaxed, but at least Nina didn't look like she was about to cry anymore.

The AC guy held the invoice clipboard out again and said gently, "Ma'am?"

Nina picked up the pen and signed.

Marcos's heart rate started to go back to normal. It felt good to take Chloe down. But she was just a silly young narcissist, not a real enemy. And with her gone, Nina's problems were only beginning. The office was still in chaos, and now she had a young kid to look after.

Could Marcos help with *that*?

Little children tended to be frightened of him. Ignacio had screamed at the top of his lungs the first and only time Marcos had held him, and Peri always stared at him like he was a *chupacabra*. He'd never be one of those guys like Tony who were naturally good with kids. But he could try.

"Hey, Logan," he called. "C'mere, bud."

He said the words without thinking. They were the same words his dad always used when calling him over. It felt a little funny hearing them come out of his own mouth.

Logan turned and looked coolly at Marcos, then at his mother. She smiled, sort of, and nodded.

She didn't have to look *that* uneasy. Marcos was capable of overseeing a kid for a little while. Okay, maybe he had gone off like a mortar shell just now, but he'd been justified. He wouldn't go off that way on a little kid.

He could do this. He'd show her.

Logan walked on over. He didn't look traumatized by what had just happened.

Marcos said, "Your mom's real busy right now, so how 'bout you play over here for a while."

"'Kay," said Logan. "Hey, I know you."

"That's right. You and your mom went to dinner with my family. My name's Marcos."

"Huh," said Logan. "That's like my name. Mark Logan."

"Oh yeah?" Marcos didn't care much for the practice of giving a kid a first name that was just for show and then calling him by his middle name. He'd known some guys like that and they all said it was a major pain. But who was he to judge? For all he knew, Logan was the kid's *last* name, and Nina and "the guy" were preparing him for future military service. Whatever the case, it was no business of Marcos's.

Should he ask Logan about school, or what he wanted to be when he grew up? Seemed like those were the standard topics of conversation with this age of child. But Marcos always used to think it was tedious when adults talked to him that way. Maybe he should just talk to Logan like a regular person.

"So, that was pretty wack back there with Chloe, huh?" Marcos asked.

Logan let out a long, weary sigh. "Yeah. Chloe doesn't like me very much. She didn't want to babysit me anyway. She's a vlogger."

"A what, now?"

"A video blogger. She has a YouTube channel where she shows how to do makeup."

"That's a thing?"

"Yeah. She's trying to reach a thousand followers. She's always checking to see if she got any new ones."

"What was it that you took apart?"

"A makeup case. You open it up and it's got these trays and things that come out on the sides. I didn't really take it apart. I just took out all the makeup stuff. I wanted it for a dino fort."

"Yeah, I get that. But you know what works well for dino forts? Cardboard boxes. You get lots of different sizes and plenty of duct tape and you can make a real nice fort with entryways and ledges and towers and such."

"Yeah, cardboard's best, but Chloe won't let me have any." He gave Marcos an aggrieved look. "She says I make a mess when I cut it up. She always has lots of Amazon boxes, too. Her makeup comes in it. Today she had some really good ones, and I asked nice if I could have them, but she said they were for recycling and she took her utility knife and broke them down."

"Broke them down right in front of you? Dang, that's cold."

What was wrong with this heartless excuse for a babysitter? Had she never even *been* a kid?

"Where are your dinos now?" Marcos asked. "You didn't leave them at Chloe's place, did you?"

"No, they're all in my backpack."

"Can I see?"

Logan unzipped his bag. One by one, he took out his model dinosaurs and lined them up in order from smallest to largest. He never hesitated and got it exactly right the first time. Marcos recognized the *Pachycephalosaurus* from that one day at Jittery Jim's.

"Nice," Marcos said. "Do you know their names?"

Logan rattled them off with perfect, precise pronunciation. *Deinonychus*, *Struthiomimus*, *Velociraptor*, on and on.

"That's good," Marcos said. "You know your dinosaurs, all right."

"Chloe says it's not normal that I know so much about them. She says I should get tested. People are always saying that."

Marcos made a scoffing sound. "Don't listen to those fools. The way you are is a good way to be."

He meant it too. Usually he felt awkward with kids but not this one. This was the most sensible kid he'd ever met.

Logan picked up the *Pachycephalosaurus*. He stomped it around on the table, head-butted it into a magazine basket and said, "Grrraaawwrrr!"

Marcos went cold all over. He felt disconnected, like he was outside his own body watching himself, like some guys said happened to them when they got hurt bad and almost died. It was a little bit like before, when he'd heard his voice speaking his dad's words. Only now he was seeing himself as a kid, playing with his own dinosaurs.

"How old are you, Logan?" he asked, dimly surprised by how calm his voice was.

Logan didn't even look up. "Seven."

"Do you know your birthday?"

"May seventeenth."

He went on playing, like everything was fine, like the world hadn't just been turned upside down.

Marcos couldn't move, couldn't think, couldn't breathe. He looked at Logan, really looked at him. The shape of his hands. The cowlick on the right side of his forehead that made his hair stick up in a big wave.

Marcos raised his head and looked at Nina. She hadn't heard; she was dealing with the computer guys now. He watched, waited, until she finally met his eyes.

There must have been something telling in his expression, because she actually rocked back a bit. Her face flushed, and she bit her lip. Confirmation, if he'd needed any.

Marcos spoke again in the same weirdly calm voice. "I have to go do something, Logan. Can you stay right here and play with your dinos?"

"'Kay," Logan said without looking up.

Marcos stood, looked back at Nina, and jerked his thumb toward the front door. Then he stalked out.

CHAPTER THIRTEEN

WELL, SHE'D WANTED him to know. Now he knew. That much was clear from his face—and that commanding jerk of his thumb.

You. Me. Outside. Now.

Marcos was pacing like a caged tiger near the corner of the building, away from the windows. Nina's legs shook as she closed the distance between them.

Then he turned to face her, and she took a step back again. That set jaw, those blazing eyes—he was in full warrior mode. His posture was what Nina's Texas grandparents would have described as *all bowed up*—chest out, shoulders back, arms held out from his sides like parentheses. Making a display. She could almost feel the heat coming off him.

But when he spoke, his voice was lower than usual.

"He's mine? Logan is mine?"

"Yes."

He drew in a deep, raw breath and let it out again. His gaze bored into her.

"You passed my son off as another man's child?"

Oh, boy.

She took a quick look around to make sure they were alone and said quietly, "Marcos, I'm not married."

She wouldn't have thought it possible for him to look more shocked than he already did, but he managed it. He looked at her left hand, like maybe he'd imagined the ring, but no, it was still there. "What is *this*, then?"

"A wedding band I bought off Amazon. I wear it as a safeguard."

"Safeguard? Against what?"

"Against men coming on to me."

He looked as mystified as if she'd said the ring warded off evil spirits. "Why would you need a safeguard against that? If a guy comes on to you and you're not into him, what's wrong with just telling him no?"

"It's not that easy! I work around a lot of vulnerable, emotionally damaged men. The position I'm in, helping them, taking an interest—it's easy for them to get attached. Sometimes that attachment takes the form of an attraction—and that causes problems.

If they think I'm married, they might not act on it."

He shook his head in disgust. "That's a pretty fancy explanation, but I think it's bull. I think lying is just your go-to response."

Her voice shook. "You have no right to say that, Marcos. You have no idea what it's like for a woman to raise a child alone."

"Yeah? And why are you raising him alone, Nina, huh? Why didn't you tell me I had a kid?"

She threw her arms out. "Because you were gone! You took off without leaving so much as a phone number. You made it perfectly clear I was nothing to you but a drunken mistake."

His eyes clouded with something that might have been shame, but he didn't back down. "That was nearly eight years ago! What about now? How many times have we seen each other in the past three weeks? You have my contact information—you know where I live. Why didn't you tell me *recently*?"

"How could I, after what you said?"

"What I said when?"

"That day at Jittery Jim's, when you said how glad you were that you didn't have anyone depending on you. I couldn't jeopardize your recovery by dropping an emotional bombshell on you."

"My *recovery*?" He spat out the word. "What are you saying? You—you thought I was too *fragile*?"

He laced his hands behind his head like a runner cooling down, turned his back to her, took a couple of paces away, and spun to face her again.

"I have to get out of here," he said. "I can't be around you right now."

"Yeah, I know," she said. "That's *your* go-to response."

The bitterness in her voice was a surprise even to her. Marcos stood a moment, looking like she'd slapped him, and walked away.

CHAPTER FOURTEEN

MARCOS RODE PAINTED PETE along the fence line in the northwest pasture. He had his fence-mending kit in his saddlebags, his Colt .45 in a low-ride shoulder holster and his Ka-Bar sheathed horizontally at the back of his belt.

After his blowup with Nina, he'd driven home and saddled up. He didn't want to talk to anyone. Couldn't. Had to be alone someplace quiet to process things. Out here in the pasture, the only sounds were Pete's steady hoofbeats and some distant highway noise.

He had a son. That redheaded kid who liked taking vacuum cleaners apart—that was *his* kid. His DNA and Nina's were forever linked in that little person.

Raw emotions knocked around inside him, bouncing off each other. Shock. Anger. Pride. An overwhelming desire to see Logan again. An overwhelming fear of the same thing.

Then a cloud of dust rose from beyond a ridge, and Marcos forgot everything else.

Ever since Deir ez-Zor, any kind of powder or vapor in the air always took him straight back to Syria. Sandstorms were among the worst of his wartime memories. They used to come down from Iraq year round, driven by roaring sixty-mph winds. Goggles and protective clothing could only do so much. The fine dust worked its way into tents, covering every surface. For his entire tour, Marcos had gone around with ever-present grit on his skin, in his hair, ears, eyes, mouth, lungs. The coughing around the camp sounded worse than a TB ward, or cedar allergy season back home.

Worst of all was how ISIS used the cover of the sandstorms to launch surprise attacks. You couldn't see them coming through the thick haze, couldn't see your own hand in front of your face, couldn't hear the firing of enemy artillery miles away. Your first clue that an attack was taking place was the impact and concussion of detonating shells—unless the shell got you, in which case you never knew at all.

So in Marcos's mind, clouds of dust meant

either maddening irritation or sudden death—
or both.

But this wasn't Syria. This was home,
where dust meant nothing worse than cali-
che driveways and dry summers. He concentrated on his breathing—slow and deep—and
kept riding.

And when he crested the ridge, he looked
down into a bare, rocky hollow and saw some
cow-calf pairs kicking up dust with their
hooves.

He let out a dry chuckle, proud of himself
for keeping his cool. *That's right. That's how
it's done. No trauma here.*

The cows and calves stared at Marcos,
tracking him with their eyes as he rode past,
heads slowly turning.

A stretch of fence up ahead needed fixing.
Pete stopped almost before Marcos was con-
scious of telling him to with the change in his
seat. He dismounted and gave the horse a pat
on the neck.

Then a series of loud pops rang out, and
next thing he knew, Marcos was facedown
on the ground.

He spat out a brown stream of dust. *Just a
backfiring truck on the highway, idiot.*

He got back up, brushed off his jeans and

picked some thorns out of his shirt. Pete hadn't moved a muscle. Old roping horses like him were pretty steady characters—not much like old artillerymen.

Marcos got his fence-mending tools and walked over to the sprung wire. He hadn't been much bigger than Logan when he first started riding fence with his dad—Martin on Buck, still a young horse in those days, and Marcos on Jaycee, a gentle sorrel mare who stood just under fifteen hands, easy for Marcos to mount from the ground. Whenever Marcos would see a stretch of fence that needed repair, he'd dismount and hurry over before his father had even come to a halt, and his father would say how smart and quick he was. Marcos was a grown man before it even occurred to him that his father was *letting* him get there first.

Back then, seemed like everything he did made his father proud. He was a quick study, clever with his hands, physically tough and a good problem solver. Tack repair, rough carpentry, cattle work—they all came easy to him. Whenever Martin took him to the feed store, someone was sure to say what a fine ranch hand Martin had there, or how much the two of them looked alike. It didn't bother Marcos back then.

The bottom strand of fence wire was hanging in a coil. Marcos started to reach for it, then slowly pulled his hand back. A rattlesnake lay curled up by the post, perfectly camouflaged in the dappled shade.

Marcos drew the Colt, aimed and fired.

The bullet caught the snake right through the neck. It writhed and rattled a while before lying mostly still.

If he were fifteen, Marcos would've cut off the rattle, cured the skin and added them both to his collection. Now he didn't even bother stretching the snake out to see how long it was. He found a fallen branch with a fork in the end, hooked the snake, tossed it into some prickly pear cactus and went back to his fence repair.

What would Logan think of riding fence? Did he even know how to ride a horse? If he was anything like Marcos, he'd be a fast learner—and it was pretty clear that Logan was a *lot* like Marcos.

And Marcos was a lot like Martin.

That Ramirez kid is his old man all over again. Marcos had overheard one of the hired cowboys saying that, the first year Marcos had ridden in the roundup. He'd been ten. No doubt the cowboys had expected him to be in the way—but he'd proven them wrong.

He understood his father's pride in him now, in a way he never had before. He could actually feel his chest swelling when he thought of Logan breaking in to Chloe's high-security makeup case. Seven years old, and he'd figured out how to pick a lock, all by himself.

He gets that from me, Marcos thought. He felt it again, that thrill of connection. It was exhilarating.

But it wasn't enough. Not for Marcos and his father, or for Marcos and his son. Sooner or later a boy wanted to be more than his father's shadow.

The middle strand of the fence had been mended previously. The half-hearted repair looked like something Marcos might have done thirteen years ago while hungover, which it might well have been. He'd been hungover a lot in the two years after high school graduation. His dad wanted him to live at home, work on La Escarpa and take ag courses at the university. Marcos had complied, sort of, but by then his work ethic had fallen off pretty sharply from what it had been when he was a boy. He'd stay out all night partying and come home minutes before his father got up to start his day—like he was *daring* his old man to kick him out.

And in the end, after Marcos went to the recruiting office on his own, enlisted and didn't tell anyone until it was too late to do anything about it, his dad was glad to see the back of him. His fine ranch hand had turned into more trouble than he was worth.

The boy needs to get his head on straight, Martin had said to Renée when he thought Marcos wasn't listening. *Learn some discipline. Then he'll come home and settle down.*

But Marcos had reenlisted.

Twice.

Another four years? his father had said over the phone after the second time. *What is wrong with you? You've gone away, had your big adventure. Now it's time to come home and get to work.*

It was the last conversation they'd ever had. By the time he ended the call, Marcos was pretty wound up—so wound up that he went out to The Bad Oyster, got drunk, met Nina, married her and fathered a child. Whereas Martin went out and—

Marcos shook his head hard. No sense in thinking about that.

Martin was a good father. Marcos could see that now. And still things had gone sour between them. What hope did Marcos have with a son he'd basically abandoned for the first seven years of his life? He'd looked so innocent and small in the center today, with his T-Rex backpack, kneeling at the coffee table and playing with his plastic dinos. He'd seemed to enjoy talking with Marcos. What would he think of Marcos when he knew the truth?

He gave a last twist to the fence wire, stood and said aloud, "I'm a father. I have a seven-year-old son."

The words rushed through him like a shot of liquor. So many things to sort through in his head. Ignacio wasn't the only grandchild anymore, or the first. Peri was not Ignacio's only cousin. He had to keep thinking of it all until the strangeness wore off.

He took out his phone. Keith had texted to ask where he was—because Marcos had taken off from the center without telling him. Typical Marcos. Selfish and shortsighted, never thinking beyond what was right in front of him, or what he wanted in the moment.

He texted back an apology, then texted Eliana and asked for Nina's number.

He was back at the horse paddock before sundown. While he was tying Pete to the fence, Dalia came out of the feed barn.

"Been riding fence?" she asked.

"Yep. You?"

"Just tidying up the barn. Baling wire and feed sacks."

That was one thing about Dalia. She never bogged down in small talk.

"Killed a rattlesnake," Marcos said.

"How big?"

"Pretty big."

Marcos unbuckled Pete's breast strap. As he was passing it over the saddle seat, Dalia said, "Your shirt's torn."

He looked down at himself. "Yeah, I got snagged by some thorns."

Dalia patted Pete on the neck. "Settling in all right at the bunkhouse?"

"Yep. Place looks real nice. Alex and Lauren did a good job."

Back in the days before the Texas Revolution, the bunkhouse had been just the cabin, and the Ramirez family of that time had lived there until the big house got built. Then the cabin got added on to and turned into quarters for hired men—which was exactly what Marcos was now. A hired man on his own family ranch. Wasn't that the prodigal son's original plan, to come back home and work on his father's place as a hired man? Things ended up working out a whole lot better for him.

But there wasn't any father to welcome Marcos home. And it wasn't like he wanted to stick around anyway. He'd stay long enough to get his feet under him again, and then he'd move on.

Marcos lifted off the saddle and laid it on the top rail of the fence.

"Remember when Dad used to give us the history spiel, about Alejandro Ramirez and La Escarpa and the whole seven-generations thing?" he said. "You would always listen so hard, all solemn and respectful. I just liked the part about Alejandro going away to fight in the revolution, and dying for his country."

"Yeah, so?"

"So it's right for you to be running the place now. You're good at it. Dad should have been grooming you to take over all along."

Dalia shook her head. "I wouldn't have listened. I wanted to get away, just like you did."

"Yeah, but you came back."

She gave him a half smile. "Look who's talking."

"Who, me? I'm just marking time until I figure out what to do next."

"I wouldn't be so sure. This place has a hold on people. Even Alejandro came back, or so they say."

CHAPTER FIFTEEN

I need to see you.

THE TEXT CAME out of nowhere, from an unknown number, but Nina was pretty sure who the sender was. Her hunch was confirmed by a second message a moment later: This is Marcos.

Eliana had texted Nina a few minutes earlier. My brother asked me for your number. OK to give it to him? Nina had said simply, Yes. She was glad Eliana didn't press for details.

She replied to Marcos. I can be at Jittery Jim's in 20 min.

Then she waited, staring at the screen, as if by looking hard enough she could see through it into Marcos's mind.

His reply came quickly.

K.

Nina sighed, uncurled herself from the corner of the sofa and set down the half gallon of Dulce de Leche with the spoon still stuck in the top. She'd driven straight to H-E-B after work today and picked it up. Cessy had taken Logan for the evening; she'd volunteered, after hearing about the afternoon's waiting-room drama. So Nina had come home with her ice cream and left it on the counter while changing into her favorite sweats and soft T-shirt. She'd been all set to do some serious stress eating when Marcos's text had appeared.

She put the ice cream away and pulled on some dark-wash jeans and a linen peasant blouse. She was glad she hadn't taken off her makeup yet. Looking good was a kind of armor. She brushed her hair smooth and took a last anxious look in the mirror before heading to the door.

Her purse hung from a hook in the entry closet. She started to reach for it, then glanced at the box on the top shelf. Should she…? Might as well. She took down the box, put it in a big tote bag, grabbed her purse and left.

She arrived early, but Marcos was already there, sitting at a secluded corner table by a window. He looked more formal than usual in a white button-down with a woven stripe. A mug of his usual turmeric-ginger tea steamed beside him, next to what looked like Nina's usual order.

The thoughtful gesture unnerved her. Placing an order would have given her time to gather her wits. And after seeing Marcos, so strong and self-contained but with that restless energy just beneath the surface that had drawn her to him from the start, her wits needed gathering.

Now there was nothing to do but sit down. She did it, setting her tote bag on the floor by the window.

"Where's Logan?"

Interesting that it was the first thing out of his mouth. No hello, no *thanks for coming*. The words sounded stiff and strange. It must feel weird for him, saying Logan's name, now that he knew it was his son's name. Everything was different now.

"Aunt Cessy's watching him."

Marcos nodded. He looked calmer than he had this afternoon, or at least not angry.

"He doesn't know, does he?" Marcos asked.

"No."

"Yeah, I didn't think so." He took a deep breath. "I'm sorry I lost my temper today. I was out of line."

"Not entirely. You had a right to be angry. It was wrong of me not to tell you I was pregnant."

"Yes, it was. But the way I was acting at the time—I understand why you did it. You're right. I left you alone."

"You were in shock. You were grieving."

"Stop making excuses for me. Yes, my father's death threw me for a loop, but that doesn't make my behavior okay. I took a vow, for better and worse and all that. And at the first sign of trouble I bailed. It was selfish and stupid and cowardly and wrong."

It seemed impolite to agree with him out loud, so Nina just said, "Thank you for saying that. Oh, and for what it's worth… I really did almost tell you that day we ran into each other here for the first time. But even before that—before I left California—I was starting to at least consider the possibility of finding you and telling you. After I connected with my father, I realized that a lot of my resentment toward you was really anger at him. Once he and I were square with each other… I don't know. I just didn't feel the same about it anymore. I know that doesn't count for much when I didn't actually do anything about it, but it's true."

"Sounds like we both got tangled up in issues with our fathers. That's what kept us apart—but it's kind of what brought us together too."

"Hmm. That's really astute."

"Yeah, I'm Mister Emotional Intelligence now. Anyway, I'm sorry. I wish things had been different——that I'd been different. Did you have any help at all? Your mom? Your aunt?"

"I wasn't really in touch with Aunt Cessy until later. And my mom was horribly smug about the whole thing. I'd made no secret of what I thought about *her* lifestyle over the years, so she was thrilled to see me knocked up with the father nowhere in sight. She didn't know the whole story. I didn't tell anyone."

"Anyone? Seriously?"

She shook her head. "It was kind of a sore subject."

"I'm sorry you went through all that alone. But I'm here now, and ready to take responsibility. I don't even know what child support for seven years would add up to. Probably more than I've got. But I'll do what I can now, and do more as I'm able."

He had his jaw set and his head held high.

Nina would have to proceed with care. Male pride was such a delicate thing.

"We can sort that out later," she said. "Right now, there's something you can provide that Logan needs a whole lot more."

"What's that?"

"You."

He drew in a quick breath.

"Raising a child is about more than food and shelter," Nina went on. "Right now I'm all he's got, and I have been for seven years. I do my best, but he needs a father—not just as a provider, but someone to spend time with him, and show him how to be a man. I can't do that. I'm strained to the limit being his mother."

"Y-you want to tell him? That I'm his—"

Marcos looked almost panicked.

"We don't have to," Nina said quickly. "Not right away. But you can still spend time with him. Start laying a foundation you can build on later."

"I don't have experience with kids. Just Ignacio, and he's little. Logan's big enough to ask questions."

"You did fine today, before you knew he was yours."

"Well, I know now, and it's not the same.

Plus that was for, like, five minutes. I wouldn't know what to do with him all day."

"Relax, Marcos. I'm not going to drop him off with you and expect you to take sole responsibility for hours or days on end. I wouldn't do that to either one of you. I'll help you."

He nodded, then lowered his head and started running his fingernail along a groove in the table. "Has, uh, has he ever asked about his father?"

"Oh, yes. When he was five. That's pretty typical for kids in a one-parent household, from what I've read. Before then, they don't give it much thought, but at four or five they start noticing other families with two parents. One day he straight-up asked me, *Do I have a father*?"

"What'd you tell him?"

"I said yes, he had a father. And he asked why you didn't live with us like other kids' fathers. And I told him that when he was born, you weren't ready to be a father yet."

"You didn't tell him I was dead?"

"What? No! That would be a terrible thing to do."

"Did you tell him I walked out on him? On both of you?"

By now he was pressing so hard into the groove that his hand was going white. Nina took his hand in hers and held it tightly.

"Marcos, he was five years old. There was no need to burden him with any of that. All he needed to know was that it wasn't his fault that you weren't around."

"What'd you tell him about me, then?"

"Good things. That you were a Marine like his grandfather. That you were strong and brave and good at your job, and smart, and handsome…"

She was still holding his hand. It wasn't weird yet, but it might be soon. She let go.

"I also told him that one day, if he wanted to find you, like I found my father, I'd help him."

He looked up. Were those tears in his eyes?

"Thank you for that," he said. "It was better than I deserved."

"Well, I wasn't exactly shooting from the hip. I'd had time to think about what to tell him when he asked. Years. I read a lot of articles, asked my aunt. And I remembered what it was like for me, when I was a kid."

"What, uh, what did you put on his birth certificate, for who his father is?"

"I left it blank. I couldn't name you without your cooperation."

"We should change that. I want him to be able to get death benefits if I die."

"We can. It's doable. You just have to sign an affidavit."

"I'll get on it, then."

He look a gulp of tea. "So, back to this whole spending time together thing. How do we handle that? Will he be suspicious? Will he wonder why he's spending time with this strange man all of a sudden?"

"I don't think so. He knows I want us to make friends in our new home. I told him that the night we met your family at the Gristmill. I'll tell him that's what we're doing with you, and he'll take it at face value. He's not one to look beyond the surface and ponder motives."

"How do you know all these things? Like when a kid is old enough to be suspicious, or whether he's a suspicious type of person at all?"

"Well, they're usually newborns when you start out. Newborns are demanding, but not very nuanced. You get to know them as they grow and learn things, and you have time to adjust."

"I guess I'm basically screwed, then. I'm getting a late start, and I've missed all that."

"Well…maybe this will help."

She moved their drinks to the windowsill, reached into her tote bag and took out the box. It was a decorative storage box, covered in images of vintage cars and airplanes. The nameplate on the front said Mark Logan Walker.

"I started this when he was a baby," Nina said. "I've been putting things in it—pictures, keepsakes, things he made. I thought it would be good to have in case there ever came a time when you were in his life. Logan knows about it—he knows it's for his father. Sometimes he gives me things and says to put them in the box."

Marcos ran his finger along the nameplate. "The Mark part, did you, uh… Was that for me, or did you just like the name?"

"What do you think?"

"I don't know. That's why I asked."

She smiled. "Yes, Marcos. I named him for you."

"I guess he doesn't know that, huh? Because when I told him my name today, he didn't seem to think it was any big deal."

"No, I never told him your name. Didn't

want him looking you up online before he was actually ready to make contact."

He smiled a little. "You really thought of everything."

They stared at each other a moment. Then Nina said, "Are you going to open the box?"

"Can I? Is that okay?"

"Of course! That's why I brought it. It's for you."

The magnetic front flap parted from the end of the box with a soft pop. Marcos raised the lid, then drew in a deep breath and covered his mouth with his hand.

He picked up a Lego creation. "He made this?"

"Yes, it's a—I don't remember what it's supposed to be, but it says on the label."

Marcos turned the thing over until he found the label. "'*Ankylosaurus*,'" he read. He turned the hunk of plastic around in his hand. "Yeah, it looks like an *Ankylosaurus*."

"There should be a date, also," Nina said.

He checked the label again. "Yeah, there is. Wow, this was right at the end of my tour in Deir ez-Zor."

"I know."

He gave her a quizzical look.

"I've always more or less known where you

were," she said. "Not in a stalkerish way—I just kept up. I worked at the VA, so it was easy enough to follow the movements of Echo Battery."

"That makes sense."

He set down the Lego *Ankylosaurus*, picked up a tiny lock of red-gold baby hair and ran his finger along it.

He went through the entire box, item by item. The crayoned pictures, the toy car with the broken axle that Logan had replaced entirely on his own with a section of paper clip. The toddler-size T-shirt with a T-Rex mouth made of a cloth flap that opened and closed.

The coffee and tea were both long gone by the time Marcos put the last picture back in the box and shut the lid.

"Thank you, Nina. For all of it. Keeping the box. Not running me down in front of Logan. I know you said it was better for him that way, not to be told bad things about me, but a lot of people in your situation would have done it anyway, and never mind what was healthy for the kid. And thank you for doing such a good job with him."

Nina's throat swelled, and she had to swallow before saying, "You're welcome. Thank you for standing up for Logan and me to Chloe today."

He chuckled. "Oh, no thanks needed. It was a pleasure, believe me."

He stared out the window into the darkening sky. "You know something funny? All this time I've been thinking what a deadbeat that fake husband of yours must be. Here you were, taking care of the move to Texas on your own, taking care of Logan, while he sat tight back in California. Turns out I'm the deadbeat. And I'm worse than I ever thought he was, because I was *never* there for you. All these years, you've had everything to do by yourself. It isn't right."

He turned back to her. "I can't change that, but I can do things differently going forward, and I will. From now on I'm going to do right by Logan—by both of you."

He looked so strong and big and deadly serious, sitting across the table from her with his hand still resting on the lid of Logan's box. She swallowed again and said simply, "Okay."

Her heart was too full to say more.

CHAPTER SIXTEEN

MARCOS'S MOTHER AND sisters sat side by side on the living room sofa at La Escarpa. He faced them across the coffee table, sitting on the edge of his recliner.

"Thank you all for coming so quickly when I asked," he said. "I know you're wondering what this is all about. So I'm just—I'm just going to say it."

They waited, wide-eyed.

"You remember Ana's friend Nina?"

Nods all around.

"Remember how we said we knew each other from San Diego?"

More nods.

"Well…" He took a deep breath. "We knew each other a little better than we led you to believe. Her son, Logan? Well—he's—"

Eliana let out a snort-laugh and quickly covered her mouth. Renée elbowed her, and she snort-laughed again. She shook her head and said, "Y'all. I can't do it. I can't keep a straight face."

By now Dalia was trying to suppress a smile and not succeeding very well. "It's okay, Marcos. We know."

"You—you know?" said Marcos. "How?"

"How?" Eliana repeated. "Have you *seen* him? He looks just like you!"

"He does not look just like me!" said Marcos. "He has red hair!"

"I think he favors Nina, mostly," said Renée, in the same sweet, grandmotherly tone she used when talking about Ignacio. "But his mannerisms, Marcos! His voice! The way he stands and moves! *That's* what reminds me of you."

"His eyes are like Marcos's, though," Dalia said. "Not the shape so much, but the color."

"Mmm-hmm," said Eliana. "Hazel."

Marcos couldn't believe it. "You mean to tell me you all figured out he was my son after seeing him one time?"

"Oh, no," said Eliana. "We had a lot more to go on than that. When Nina and I first met, and she was telling me about the whole fake husband thing—"

"You knew about the fake husband?"

"Of course! She told me that right away. And I told Mom and Dalia, naturally."

"But—but it's supposed to be a secret!"

"Only from men! That's the whole point, to fend off unwanted advances."

"Totally understandable," said Dalia. "I never did it myself, but I knew lots of women in Philadelphia who did. It can be a real time-saver."

"So then I asked her about Logan's father," Eliana went on.

"Seriously?" said Marcos. "You asked her about that when you'd only just met her?"

"Well, of course! I was curious."

"Eliana can get away with stuff like that," said Dalia. "People always feel safe confiding in her."

"So…what'd she say?" asked Marcos. "About…the father." He felt a little shy all of a sudden.

"That he was a good-looking Marine with a chip on his shoulder, and that she'd gotten involved with him at a vulnerable time in her life while caught up in her own daddy issues."

"Oh." Marcos wasn't sure how he felt about that description.

"And then when the two of you saw each other at the Gristmill—your faces, that shock of recognition, that spark that passed between you—well, clearly you were more than acquaintances, no matter what Nina said. And Logan really does look and act a lot like you as a kid, Marcos. And you would have been in San Diego around the time he would have been conceived. I know, because it was…"

"When Dad died," Marcos finished. "Yeah. It was actually the day before he died that Nina and I met and got married."

If Marcos had felt let down by his family's reception of his first piece of news, they more than made up for it now.

"Married!"

"You and Nina got *married*?"

"Did you say *met and got married*? As in, all in one day?"

"Yep, all in one day. We, uh, we met in a bar, and—well—"

"Did you have an instant connection?" Eliana asked dreamily.

"Yeah, actually."

"Love at first sight?"

"Oh, don't grill him about stuff like that, Eliana," said Dalia. Then, to Marcos, "So… I take it you're not married anymore?"

"No. No, we're not. We got it annulled—

or I did, and she went along with it. Nina actually wanted to stay together, but I was…"

"Grieving," said his mom.

"Overwhelmed," Dalia said at the same moment.

Stupid, thought Marcos.

"Well," he said. "Got to say, this is not the reaction I was expecting. Here I thought I had this shocking piece of news, but the three of you already knew all about it and thought the whole thing was funny."

"It wasn't the news itself that was funny," said Eliana. "Just your delivery. That solemn face and that whole *I suppose you're all wondering why I've called you here today* vibe, when we had it figured out weeks ago."

"More like suspected," said Dalia.

"We were pretty sure," said their mom. "We've had a group text about it for a while."

"Wow. Well, now I feel like a moron for not figuring it out right from the get-go. But I never even suspected. I thought she really was married, like Ana said, and the kid was her husband's."

"Didn't you at least do the math, out of simple curiosity?" Eliana asked.

"I wasn't curious. I didn't know how old he was and had no reason to ask. If I'd thought about it at all, I would've figured that if he *was* mine, Nina would've told me."

They all shook their heads at this.

"Well! I'm glad we know for sure now and everything's out in the open," said Renée. "Did Nina finally just break down and tell you?"

"No. As a matter of fact, I figured it out for myself. I may not be as quick on the uptake as you all, but I do notice things."

"What was it that clued you in?" Dalia asked.

"It was a whole lot of things in a row. But the kicker was the way he played with dinosaurs."

Renée grew teary. "Now that's something I would dearly love to see."

"Well, as a matter of fact, you should have a chance to do that soon. Nina and I have decided it would be good for me and Logan to spend some time together."

Renée let out a trilling little "Yay!" and Eliana clapped her hands.

"Have them come out to La Escarpa," Dalia said. "We'll make a day of it, the whole family."

This was exactly what Marcos had been hoping for. With all his relatives around, his own shortcomings wouldn't matter as much. And with so many acres to run around on, so many things to do and animals to see, there wouldn't be a lot of downtime for sitting around staring at each other.

His mother and sisters started planning right away.

"Is this Saturday good for everyone?" Dalia asked. "Weather's supposed to be nice, not too hot. Tony can grill."

Eliana opened her rhinestone-studded phone case and started swiping. "Works for me," she said.

"I'm going to get Marcos's old dinosaurs out of storage for Logan to play with," said Renée.

"Good idea," said Dalia. "But don't let them be where Peri and Ignacio can get to them. Some of them are small enough to be a choking hazard. Wait 'til they go down for their naps."

"Peri?" said Marcos. "Why would she be around for it?"

"We've got to invite Alex and Lauren," said Eliana.

"They're not even related to me," Marcos grumbled, but he was just grumbling for the sake of form. He was fine with it. The more the merrier.

"Hold on," he said. "There is one more thing. We haven't told Logan yet that I'm his father." The words still felt new and strange in his mouth. "And I don't know when we will. So for now, we don't talk about that in front of him. You got that? Can you keep it secret?"

They all just stared at him.

"Never mind," he said. "Dumb question."

CHAPTER SEVENTEEN

NINA SCOURED THE kitchen sink as if her life depended on it. Anticipation had strained her nerves almost to the point of pain. They were actually going to La Escarpa, she and Logan, this very day. In less than an hour they would see the ranch where Marcos had grown up, and be with his nice family again.

They'd all been so sweet to her before, but that was when she was just Eliana's friend, a stranger to be welcomed into town. She couldn't have gone up in their estimation now that they knew her history with Marcos. What if they thought she made a habit of picking up men in bars and marrying them? What if Renée resented her for keeping her grandson away from her all these years? And how about Dalia? She couldn't possibly understand. She looked as if she'd never done anything reckless or impulsive in her life.

Nina had to make a good second impression. Logan too.

She'd bought Logan some cowboy boots for the occasion, in case he went anyplace brushy with potential for snakes. Marcos had told her to do that. But what if it looked presumptuous, like she was trying too hard to make Logan fit in at La Escarpa, to insinuate the two of them with Marcos's family?

She herself was dressed sensibly for a day at a ranch, in boot-cut jeans, a plain V-neck T-shirt and her own new pair of cowboy boots. She'd thought about a new pair of jeans for Logan, but that seemed silly and extravagant when he had so many old pairs. Problem was, none of his old pairs looked right on him. She wished she could find jeans that fit his dimensions.

She put away the scouring pad, took out the eraser sponge and wiped every inch of the enamel sink. She'd prepped like crazy the night before, scrubbing Logan within an inch of his life in the bathtub, and making German potato salad from her Texas grandmother's recipe. She'd fed Logan his breakfast early this morning, then sent him to brush his teeth while she cleaned the kitchen. Her nervous energy needed an outlet.

Nina had told Logan only that they were going to spend the day at their friends' ranch, and that was good enough for him. It was like she'd said to Marcos; Logan was never one to ponder motives or imagine conspiracies. He was so adorable in his funny, quirky way, so smart and factual and dry. Surely Marcos's family would appreciate that. Surely they'd understand what a terrific kid he was.

She headed down the hall, calling out, "Okay, Logan, let's get—"

She stopped in the open doorway of the bathroom and let out a bloodcurdling scream. "Logan! What have you done to your hair?"

Logan looked from his mother to his reflection in the mirror and back again. "I cut it off."

Nina dropped to her knees, wanting to weep at the little piles of red hair on the vanity and floor. She grabbed Logan by the shoulders, turned him to face her.

He appeared to have cut his hair in great chunks. The edges were jagged, and some patches on the sides were nearly bald. He looked like he had mange.

"Why…" she began, then stopped herself. There was no point asking why. The damage was done. Knowing why wouldn't change that.

She looked him sternly in the eye. "Never do this again," she said.

"'Kay," he said.

She knew he'd obey her. Once a procedure was established, he followed it. The problem was, she had no way of knowing what he'd do next in time to say, *Logan, never use a meat thermometer or anything else to disassemble a brand-new magenta ink cartridge for the ink jet printer* or *Logan, never pry open any smartphone or other electronic device and remove the battery and SIM card.* He followed his own unpredictable logic.

But that was a problem for another day. What was she going to do now?

If I leave right this minute, and stop at a Supercuts on the way—

But what if there was a wait? What about her potato salad? Potato salad did not improve by being unrefrigerated. Should she call Marcos and say she'd be late? Or maybe call Eliana, or their mother? Pick up a cooler somewhere to put the potato salad in?

She let out a sigh that turned into a groan. They were off to a fantastic start.

THE SISAL WELCOME MAT lay upside down on the flagstone walkway off the main house at La Escarpa. Marcos had set it there to dry yesterday, after he'd hosed down the outside of the house and cleaned all the exterior windows.

He picked up the mat and walked it to the front door, just as Tony came outside with an armload of cushions. While Marcos squared up the mat on the still slightly damp decking boards, Tony set the cushions in the porch swing. Then they both walked over to the rail and looked out at the big fenced yard.

The buffalo-grass lawn stretched out smooth and bright with its parallel lawn-mower tracks like comb marks, and the smell of cut grass lingered in the air. All the shrubs and flower beds had fresh blankets of cypress mulch. Near the front porch steps, the *esperanza* bush was loaded with bright yellow blossoms like little trumpets.

"Place looks pretty spiffy, huh?" asked Tony.

"Yeah," said Marcos.

They'd been mowing and edging, weeding and planting, for the better part of a week. Marcos had borrowed Tony's mower and tidied the grass around the bunkhouse, as well. Likely, no one would end up at the bunkhouse today, but it was Marcos's home, and Nina would pass it on her way down the driveway. He wanted it to look like the home of someone who had his act together.

"Steaks are marinating, and I've got plenty

of brats and hot dogs to throw on the grill," Tony said. "Lauren put together some kid-friendly hobo packets with potato chunks and cheese and zucchini and such, and we've got your mom's *charro* beans, and Dalia's flan. Alex brought over about a gallon of *pico de gallo*, and Eliana made a fruit salad with ingredients no one ever heard of that cost fifty-seven dollars to make. You think that's enough?"

"Yeah," Marcos said. He didn't cook, but he'd bought the chips, buns, paper plates, ice and drinks—so many drinks. Beer, craft and otherwise. Bottled water. Four different kinds of soda, and a variety of juice boxes, because maybe Logan wasn't allowed to drink soda.

"I'm excited!" Tony said. "Are you excited?"

Marcos gave his brother-in-law a sidelong look. Tony was bouncing on his feet, about to burst out of his skin. And Marcos? His mouth was dry, his knees felt like they might give way any second, and he had this gone sensation deep inside him that he hadn't experienced since Syria.

"Yeah," he said.

"I can tell! You look exactly like Dalia when she's excited. Your eyes are a tiny bit wider than usual and your nostrils are kinda flared." He clapped Marcos on the shoulder. "I'm so happy for you, man! You're gonna love being a dad."

Marcos swallowed. "What if I'm…not good at it?"

"You will be! I know you will. And me and Alex are here for you. I know our kids are younger than yours, but we'll help any way we can. We're your brothers now."

Marcos's chest tightened, like his heart had suddenly grown too big. He knew Tony wasn't just saying that; he meant it. He was grateful for the effort everyone was making.

But words never came easily to him, especially at times like this, and all he could say was, "Thanks."

And here came Nina's RAV-4 rounding the bend in the gravel drive.

Marcos's stomach seemed to drop away from his body, as if a shell he'd loaded had failed to fire. He stood rooted to his spot, hands gripping the porch rail, while Tony opened the door and called, "They're here!"

Everyone came pouring out of the house. Marcos got caught up in the movement of the crowd, and by the time Nina had parked, they'd all gathered just off the porch steps—

Marcos, his mother and sisters, Tony, Alex, Lauren, Peri, Ignacio, Durango the border collie and five barn cats—like one of those British period dramas that Eliana liked to watch, where the entire family and all the servants lined up in front of the manor house to greet visitors, only the Texas version.

Nina parked in front of the cedar trees and got out of the car. Marcos's heart pounded in his chest. Should he go out to her? Offer to carry something? This was the mother of his child. He should be helping, not standing here like a clueless chauvinist, but he didn't know how. If Nina and Logan had been a broken gate or something that he could fix with tools, or even some wayward livestock, he'd know exactly what to do, he wouldn't even have to think about it. But here he'd just get in the way.

One time when he'd lived in California, he'd witnessed a blowout on the Pacific Highway and pulled over to help. The man and woman were dressed nice, like they were out on a date. Marcos had jacked up the vehicle, taken off the busted tire and put on the spare all by himself, right in front of the guy and his girl, while the guy hovered uselessly behind him. As he'd spun the tire iron, Marcos had wondered, *How do you get to be a grown man and not know the first thing about such a basic skill?* He'd pretty much despised that guy.

Now he *was* that guy.

By now, his mother and sisters had reached Nina's car. Dalia took the covered dish out of Nina's hands. Eliana hugged her, and Renée clasped her hands and said, "Hello, dear, and welcome."

Logan clambered out of the backseat. He was on the far side of the car, so Marcos couldn't see him well, but he saw Renée look at him funny for a second before greeting him too.

Then they all headed to the yard gate, and Marcos saw the reason for the hesitation.

"What's the matter with his head?" he asked Tony in a low voice.

"Hey, Logan!" Tony called. "What happened to your hair, bro?"

"I cut it off," Logan said, sounding unconcerned.

"What'd you do that for?" Tony asked.

Logan shrugged. "I didn't have anything else to do."

Renée gave Marcos a sly smile. Marcos had cut off his own hair when he was about the same age. When asked why *he'd* done it, he'd said, "Why not?"

"He's a sight, I know," Nina said. "He did it just as we were about to leave the house. I wanted to stop for a haircut along the way to get things evened up, but the places I passed weren't open yet, and I didn't want to be late."

Her voice sounded strained, and she was smiling a little too hard. Probably this whole thing wasn't easy for her either.

And here at last was a problem Marcos could solve.

"I've got some clippers in the bunkhouse," he said. "I've been cutting my own hair and other guys' hair for ten years."

Logan had almost reached the porch steps by now. Marcos crouched down by him. "What say I go get 'em and we tidy up what's left of your hair?"

Logan gave him a cool, appraising look. "'Kay. Make it look like yours."

Marcos hurried out the gate and down the drive to the bunkhouse. It felt good to have something to do. A mission.

By the time he got back with the clippers, Logan was swathed in a makeshift plastic cape fashioned from a kitchen trash bag and some binder clips, and perched on a bar stool that someone had brought to the front porch.

The whole extended family was standing around, ready to watch Marcos cut his son's hair. *Yeah, that's not weird at all*, Marcos thought. He'd been glad enough when they were planning this deal, to know there'd be people around as a sort of buffer zone, but he hadn't expected all the people around for the entire time.

The back of his son's head looked a lot smaller and more vulnerable than the heads of fellow Marines, but the principles were the same. Marcos plugged his clippers into the nearest outlet and went to work. A few passes and a couple of changes of clipper guards later, Logan had a regulation haircut.

By now, two more barn cats had shown up. They all bapped at the clipper cord and chased tufts of hair. Ignacio laughed at them with that all-out belly laugh that always made Marcos smile. Had Logan laughed like that when he was a toddler?

"There you go," Marcos said, brushing tiny hairs from Logan's neck. "High and tight."

Nina pulled a compact mirror out of her purse and held it open for Logan. "Looks good, huh?"

"Yeah," he said. He ran his hand over his head from front to back, just like Marcos always did after a haircut, though he'd never really thought about it before.

Marcos took the plastic cape off Logan and shook the hair out over the porch rail. Dalia already had a broom ready. She swept the tufts of red hair off the edge of the porch. "There. Now some bird can use it for a nest."

Logan clambered down from the barstool. Marcos steeled himself and said, "Logan, you want to see the horses? Maybe go for a ride?"

That ought to thin the crowd. Surely they wouldn't all go to the horse paddock.

Then he looked at Nina. "I mean—if that's okay with you."

"The horses are very safe," Dalia told Nina. "I put Ignacio on Buck all the time. Buck's been at La Escarpa since we were little kids, and Painted Pete is an old roping horse, very steady."

"All right," Nina said. "Sounds like fun."

Good! A new mission. Marcos could do this.

CHAPTER EIGHTEEN

MARCOS DIDN'T SPEAK on the walk to the horse paddock, to Nina or anyone else. It was as if he'd used up his word quota for the day. Nina was glad Dalia and Lauren were there to help her keep up some small talk. Lauren took pictures along the way with her big, fancy camera. Ignacio went too. Dressed in his little cowboy boots and cowboy hat, he jabbered happily, walking and running and plopping down, chasing grasshoppers, lifting his arms for Dalia to pick him up. Logan simply walked, as silent as his father.

They went past the house and out through a gate at the back corner of the big fenced yard. Behind the back fence stood a red barn— a storybook barn, Nina thought, picture-perfect. To the side of the yard, and sharing its fence, was a big rectangular space. The horses, a spotted one and a golden brown one with a black mane and tail, were standing alongside each other at the far end, under the shade of a big oak tree.

Dalia crouched by Logan and pointed to the horses. "See how they're standing, nose to tail? That's so they can swish flies away from each other's face."

"Huh," he said. "That's smart."

"They sure are far away," Nina said.

"They'll come," Dalia said. She looked at Marcos. "You want to do the honors?"

He put his fingers to his lips and let out a loud, piercing whistle. The horses turned their heads, then came running. It didn't take them long to cover the distance with those powerful legs and pounding hooves.

"Wow, they're big," Nina said. She'd always liked horses in the abstract, but up close and in the flesh, they were pretty intimidating. Marcos and Dalia put lead ropes on them, led through the gate and secured them to the fence like it was no big deal.

Dalia introduced the horses to Logan. "The brown one is Buck, and this guy—" she patted the spotted horse's shoulder "—is Painted Pete. Now, before we saddle them, we have to give them a good brushing to make sure there aren't any grass burrs or bits of dirt or anything that might hurt them if it got pressed into their skin. So we're going to get their tack and grooming kits from the tack room and get started on that."

Logan and Nina followed Marcos and Dalia into the red barn. The tack room smelled of leather, grain and hay. While Dalia fitted Logan with a helmet, Marcos loaded up two squarish buckets with brushes and bridles and things. He mutely handed one to Nina and the other to Logan, then picked up a saddle and its accompanying tack off a holder that stuck out from the wall. Dalia picked up another, and she and Marcos carried them outside and set them along the top of the fence. The squarish buckets had big hook pieces that fit over the middle fence rail.

"All right," Dalia said. "Ignacio and I are going to work on Buck. Marcos, how about if you and Logan take care of Pete?"

Marcos took a deep breath and looked at Logan as if Logan was the newest member of his artillery crew.

"Right. The first thing we're going to use is the curry comb."

He held up a black oval-shaped rubbery thing with lots of rows of blunt teeth and an adjustable handle on the back.

"Hold out your hand," Marcos said.

Logan did, and Marcos strapped the thing on. Then he took another, bigger curry comb from the bucket and put it on his own hand.

"Now the way we do this is, we swirl it around and around on his coat. Just his body, not his legs or face, and not his tail. Round and round. That's it! We want to make the hair fly. Don't get too close to his back legs. They're too sensitive for the curry comb. Stay right by me."

Six feet away, Dalia was doing the same thing with Buck, hand over hand with Ignacio. Lauren was getting shots of the horses being groomed.

The curry combing went on a long time. Ignacio lost interest after a while, so Lauren took care of him while Dalia finished up on Buck.

For the time being, Nina was at loose ends. It felt all wrong for her to stand here, not doing or saying anything, with Logan so close to the huge powerful animal. She should be right there with him, telling him what to do, keeping him safe. But she didn't know the right procedure here, and Marcos did.

He managed artillery crews in combat. Surely he can watch out for one small boy.

Marcos seemed more comfortable now

that he had something to do again. Nina was proud to see how well Logan paid attention to him and did exactly what he said. He looked older with his new haircut. Taller, even.

After the curry comb came a stiff bristle brush, then a soft brush for the face and legs, then a mane and tail brush. Marcos showed Logan how to grab a fistful of tail and brush just that part so he didn't pull the horse's hair.

At this point, Nina couldn't hold back anymore.

"Should he be standing so close to the horse's back legs?" she asked. "Don't horses kick?"

Marcos didn't even turn around. "Pete won't kick unless he's surprised or scared by something behind him. He knows we're back here, so we're all right. Plus, standing this close to his back legs, we're actually safer than if we were a little farther off. The horse can't get up any momentum this close."

"Feel his tail hair, Mom," Logan said. "It's rough."

Marcos kept his head bent over the horse's tail, as if the fate of the world rested on getting it properly brushed. Nina quailed at the thought of coming that close to him.

Don't be a coward, she told herself. *There's*

nothing to be shy about. You already made a baby with the man.

She stepped on over and felt the long wiry hairs. "Oh, it *is* rough. And it's two different colors."

"Pete's a tobiano," Marcos said. "That's a type of Paint horse. A lot of times they have two colors in their tails."

She dared a glance at him. Like the horses, he seemed uncomfortably big and powerful up close.

"I thought this kind of horse was called a pinto," she said.

"He is. A pinto is a horse with this type of coat pattern. Pintos can belong to a lot of different breeds. Paint is a breed based on specific bloodlines."

"I see," Nina said. "So…a pinto isn't always a Paint, but a Paint is always a pinto?"

"Actually, no. It's possible for a registered Paint horse to not be a pinto. If the genetics are right, a pinto dam and sire can produce solid-colored offspring."

"What's dam and sire?" Logan asked.

A deep flush rose from the collar of Marcos's shirt and spread to his face. "Dam and sire are horse words for mother and father."

Standing near Marcos, with their own offspring in between them, suddenly made the mild spring sunshine feel uncomfortably warm. Nina backed up again and watched as Marcos and Logan finished the tail and mane.

Marcos took a metal hook from the bucket. "Now I need to check his feet and scrape out any dirt or rocks stuck in his hooves. So I just run my hand down the back of his leg like this and…see? He lifted it right up. He knows what I want him to do."

Marcos showed Logan the underside of the hoof with its sensitive inner part and the hollow areas with their packed grass and dirt. Once all four hooves were picked clean, it was time for saddling and bridling, both multistep processes. How did anyone ever ride a horse if it took this long just to get ready? Probably it went a lot quicker if you didn't have children around to explain things to.

Finally they got the kids actually up in the saddles. Marcos had to shorten the stirrups a lot to fit Logan. And Pete was so tall! Quite a height to fall from, if Logan took a spill.

But Marcos still had Pete on a lead rope, and he and Dalia clearly knew what they were doing. Nina ought to sit back and relax and let them do it, and enjoy not being the one in charge for a change. This was what she wanted, right? Of course it was.

And yet…something about Marcos made it hard to relax. Those long lean legs, those wide shoulders, kept drawing her eyes. He had such a graceful ease about him—no fuss, just quiet competence and strength.

All this time, Lauren was taking lots of candid shots of the kids in her unobtrusive way.

"When we're done here, give me your email address," she said to Nina. "I'll send you some photos once I've edited them."

"Thank you, that's so thoughtful," Nina said. "It must be nice for the family, having you around as their official photographer."

Lauren smiled. "They're a fun group to photograph. Always doing interesting things, and all so good-looking and photogenic, and not the least bit self-conscious."

"Eliana said you were the photographer at Tony and Dalia's wedding?"

"That's right. That's where Alex and I first met. I realized later that I'd gotten a whooooole lot more candid pics of him than of any of the other groomsmen. That should have told me something right there…but one week later I was driving my van to Mexico, and Alex was still here. I didn't even come back to Texas until a year and a half later."

In the horse paddock, Marcos was saying something to Logan and pointing at Nina. Logan looked at her and waved. Nina waved back, her heart in her throat, as Lauren aimed her camera at Logan and snapped another picture.

"He's doing well," Lauren said. "Very relaxed, with a good natural seat and a good grasp of the reining. Not that I'm an expert. I did learn to ride in Mexico, on the ranch where I worked for a while, but I've only just started getting back in the saddle. I was already pregnant when Alex and I got together."

"Eliana told me," Nina said.

"I thought she might have. It's not a secret."

"Is your ex involved with Peri at all?"

"Nope. Totally out of the picture. He knows about her, but he'd already left me for someone else by the time I found out I was pregnant."

"I'm sorry."

Lauren shrugged. "The whole thing happened fast. We met on a beach, got married two weeks later and separated two weeks after that. By the time our divorce was final, we hadn't even known each other six months."

"Well, I think I've got you beat with short engagements and short-lived marriages. Marcos and I hadn't even known each other a full day when we got married, and I got served with annulment papers within a week."

"It's weird, isn't it? The whole thing is so *embarrassing*. You feel like you don't have a right to be upset, because it was your own fault for being so impulsive, and anyway you weren't even together that long. But none of that makes it hurt less. A lot can happen in a short period of time, and you can never go back to how things were."

Nina's eyes stung. "Yeah."

It was comforting, talking to someone who really understood, someone who'd been there.

"So what did Alex say when he found out about the baby?"

"Oh, he was just relieved to know there was a reason I was so commitment shy with him, as opposed to me not being that into him. Honestly, I think he would have married me on the spot. But the thought of getting involved with another man at that point—even a good, kind, hardworking, steady guy like Alex—was terrifying. I was planning to do what you actually did, raise the baby myself—in my van, no less. I thought I couldn't trust myself to get involved with Alex, not after picking a guy like Evan less than a year earlier. But Alex was patient, and eventually I came around. I finally realized that I may have been a fool to fall for Evan, but I'd be a bigger fool to walk away from Alex."

"I'm happy for you," Nina said. "He seems like a great guy."

"He is! He's so traditional that he's actually kind of unconventional. The whole family is wonderful. Renée is super sweet—she mothers everyone. Dalia seems stiff until you get to know her, but she's really lots of fun, and incredibly loyal. We've been best friends for twelve years now. And Tony's a big sweetheart. They're all willing to take you in, just like they did me."

"Thanks. That's good to know."

Marcos led Pete through the gate with Logan still in the saddle. Logan's face was flushed and his eyes were bright.

"Mom! Did you see me?" he asked.

"Yes, I did, sweetheart. You looked awesome! And Lauren got lots of pictures of you."

"Marcos says we can come back another day and ride some more. We'll come, won't we?"

"Yes, of course we will!"

Marcos secured the lead rope and helped Logan down from the saddle. "This guy here," he told Nina, "is a natural horseman. Calm and relaxed, light hand on the bit. Held his reins like an experienced rider. Pete was very comfortable under him. Responded well to his cues."

Logan glowed from the praise. It was rare to see him so openly excited.

Now that the riding was done, the saddles and tack had to be put away and the horses had to be groomed all over again. By the time they all headed back to the house, Nina was ravenous. She could smell something rich and meaty coming from the grill behind the house. Tony was manning it, wearing a Texas flag apron, and the rest of the family was getting things ready for an outdoor meal in the space between the house's two back wings. Alex already had Peri in her bouncy seat and was spooning what looked like pureed squash into her mouth. A vine-covered trellis spanning the two wings provided shade.

"Is it ready?" Dalia called out as they drew near.

"Just waiting on you, baby," Tony replied.

"Go inside and wash your hands, kids," Renée told them.

Dalia and Marcos answered, "Yes, Mom," in identical drawn-out, long-suffering tones that made everyone laugh.

"Seriously, Mom," Marcos said as he reached the edge of the pavers. "I'm thirty-two years old. I know to wash my hands after grooming a horse and before eating lunch."

"Well, I'm still your mother, and a little reminder can't hurt."

They went in through the French doors at the back of the house. Dalia and Lauren took Ignacio to his room for a diaper change, leaving Nina and Marcos alone with Logan.

Marcos led the way to the kitchen, a gorgeous room, with a strong rustic farmhouse vibe, but also clean and spacious with wonderfully clear counters.

He hooked his ankle around a step stool, drew it over to the kitchen sink and patted the top step.

"Here you go, bud," he said to Logan.

Logan climbed up, with Marcos and Nina on either side of him, and Marcos turned on the water. He and Nina bumped hands when they reached for the soap at the same time.

After that she kept her head down and concentrated on her hand washing. For a while they all lathered and rinsed in silence. Marcos's hands looked so big next to Logan's, but they had the same strong, lean, squared-off shape.

"This is a big sink," Logan said.

"It's old," said Marcos.

The enameled farmhouse sink was set under a window. It was worn and chipped, with double basins and double drainboards. Nina could picture mounds of garden-fresh vegetables on the drainboards, ready to be chopped or made into preserves.

"Is it original to the house?" Nina asked.

"Oh, no. This place was built before indoor plumbing was a thing. The original kitchen wasn't even attached to the rest of the house."

"Why not?" Logan asked.

"Two reasons," Marcos said. "People didn't have air conditioning back then, and they cooked over open flames. So kitchens got hot, and they caught fire a lot. If the kitchen was in a separate building, the rest of your house stayed cooler in the summer, and if the kitchen burned down, the whole house didn't have to burn down with it."

Nina liked hearing Marcos talk. It was hard to get him to say much, but when he did speak, he was logical, clear and concise.

"Eliana told me about that bad storm that destroyed the kitchen a few years back," Nina said.

"I missed all that. Happened when I was in Syria. Came home and found this whole end of the house rebuilt from the ground up."

He didn't sound sad about it, exactly, but Nina could read between the lines. She'd heard similar stories from a lot of veterans over the years. They came home changed, and home itself wasn't the same. It was disorienting.

"Well, they saved the sink, anyway," she said.

"Yeah. It got a few more battle scars—" he touched a chip in one corner "—but it's still in one piece."

"They're part of the charm," Nina said. "A beautiful old piece like this, solid and well made—a few chips in the finish just prove its quality and give it a character. It's strong enough to take some abuse without breaking."

Now that the words were out, she could hear a lot of unintended subtext. Marcos was strong and solid and well made, and he had a few dings of his own.

Marcos shut off the water and reached for a towel without looking at her.

"I guess," he said. Then he stalked back outside without another word.

It was a clear rebuff, and it stung. Nina took her time drying her hands and Logan's, then stood still a moment. She could hear Dalia's and Lauren's voices coming from Ignacio's room down the hall, and the more distant voices of the rest of the family outside. For a moment it felt as if she and Logan were the ones on the outside, cut off from everyone else.

Marcos's family was trying so hard to make them feel welcome, but maybe trying was all it would ever be. Maybe coming here was a mistake.

"I'm hungry," Logan said.

Nina put on a smile. "Well, then. Let's go get some lunch."

They walked outside. Marcos was sitting on a wooden porch chair, holding a water bottle. He didn't turn around at the sound of the door, but Renée did. She gave them a smile so warm that it made Nina truly love her.

"La Escarpa is a beautiful place," Nina said.

"Thank you!" said Renée. "I'm pretty partial to it myself."

"Have you seen the rose arbor yet?" Eliana asked. "It makes a great photo backdrop."

"No one's ever been able to tell me what kind of rose it is," Renée said. "And it's been here longer than anyone can remember."

"I didn't see it," said Nina. "I think we passed a rock garden on the way back from the barn, though."

Renée laughed. "The rock garden is a lot more recent. Up until a few years ago it was just an unsightly rock pile next to a big hole, and before that it was nothing but a low spot in the ground. Marcos went after it with an old Smith & Hawken garden spade one day when he was ten years old. Said he wanted to see if he could hook up to some underground cavern system or springs of water or something. Before I knew what was going on, he'd excavated a hole the size of a Volkswagen."

"I remember that," said Eliana. "I was four, and the hole looked like a portal to a magic kingdom."

Dalia made a scoffing sound. "Who even thinks about portals to magic kingdoms at age four?"

"I did!" Eliana said indignantly.

"Did you find the caves?" Logan asked Marcos.

"No, but I found other things," Marcos said.

"Like what?"

"Old iron stuff, mostly."

Alex perked up. "I haven't heard this story. What kind of old iron stuff?"

Marcos shrugged. "A plowshare, a pruning hook, an old musket. Some pretty cool fossils in the limestone."

"Dino fossils?" Logan asked.

"No, some sort of fish. Might have been a couple of stone arrowheads, too."

"Where is all this stuff now?" Alex asked.

"Probably in a shed somewhere," Marcos said.

Alex looked like he was in physical pain. "Prerevolutionary artifacts, possibly some pre-Columbian, and you chucked 'em in a shed?"

"Don't worry, Alex," said Renée. "They're safe and sound in a plastic tote in my garage. They turned up in the Great Decluttering when I moved to town. I've been thinking about displaying them in a shadow box."

"How come you get to decide what happens to them?" said Marcos. "I'm the one who unearthed them."

"Yes, in my yard, leaving a hole you never filled in." Renée turned to Nina. "I remember his dad worked him so hard that day, worming cattle, and after he finally turned him loose, what does the boy do but go right back to it, tearing up my yard! Martin always said he'd make him fill in the hole, but he never did. I think he was proud of him for showing such industry. Eventually I rearranged the chunks of limestone he'd dug out, planted some alyssum and stonecrop, and had me a rock garden. You can see the hole's still there, but over the years it's gotten a lot shallower."

"What if you made it into a pond?" said Logan.

"It's not quite big enough for that," said Dalia. "If you try to fill it in with water, it just turns into a mud hole."

Marcos rubbed his chin. "Maybe not. We could put a liner in there, get a pump, make a little fountain."

"Oo, a water element!" said Tony. "That'd be a nice addition to the outdoor grilling and entertaining area I want to put together."

"You could use a floating crystal ball for an accent," Eliana said.

"Hold on," said Dalia. "Would this fountain be toddler-proof?"

"I don't see why not," said Marcos. "We're not talking about a pool here, just a place for water to flow over some stones and things. There wouldn't be any place for water to collect in any quantity. The stones would displace it."

Marcos turned to Logan with a determined air. "What do you think? What if we did that, you and me? You want to make a fountain?"

"'Kay," said Logan. It was his go-to affirmative response, but pitched a little higher than usual, and Nina could see how excited he was.

"Good! They ought to have everything we'd need at Dancy's Hardware. We can go right now." Then he turned to Nina. "I mean—if that's okay. Is it okay?"

It was funny and sweet, how he kept running things by her. But before she could answer, Dalia said, "Whoa, hold on. We haven't even had lunch yet. And before you make any changes to my yard, you're going to have to show me a detailed plan, make a full list of supplies and get my approval on the design."

"Oh, come on," Marcos said. "We don't have to mess around with all that. I know what we'll need. We can eat a quick bite now, run to town to get the stuff and have the whole thing finished in a few hours."

"A few hours! This is a weekend project, not a single-afternoon project."

"The hole's already dug! That's the most time-consuming part."

Dalia shrugged. "My house, my rules."

Marcos sighed heavily, sounding a lot like Logan had the day Nina had told him that, no, he could not have a flamethrower for his birthday.

"All right, buddy, you heard her," Marcos said to Logan. "We can't do it today."

"That's okay," Logan said. "I'm coming back, remember?"

"Yeah," Marcos said. "I remember."

IT WAS A WONDERFUL, wacky, sprawling, action-packed, chaotic family meal, with a hundred things going on at the same time. Durango sitting with perfect border collie manners as Dalia balanced treats on his nose, then snapping them up when she gave him the go-ahead. Ignacio laughing his bubbly toddler belly laugh whenever Durango did this. Peri in her bouncy seat, making raspberry noises. Good-natured ribbing among all the siblings. Parents handing each other plates of food, and handing off children to one another as needed. Tony at the grill, expertly cooking. Logan looking up at him while clutching his empty plate, saying, "Ignacio's dad, please may I have another hot dog?" Tony smiling down at him, saying, "You sure can! And you can call me Uncle Tony if you want."

Nina watched it all, fascinated by the give-and-take, the sly teasing and affection. The Reyes boys had gone to school with the Ramirez kids, and they had a lot of memories in common.

"I'm all done," Logan told Nina. "Can I go swing now?"

"May I please," Nina said.

"May I please go swing now?"

"Yes, you may."

Logan took off at a run.

"That's an impressive swing set," Nina said.

It was built on gigantic proportions, out of oversize lumber that still looked bright and new.

"It's overbuilt," Alex said.

"No, it's not," Tony said. "I wanted to be able to swing on it myself."

When Ignacio saw where Logan was going, he wanted to go too. Dalia went with him.

"Aw, look at that," Tony said. "He wants to play with the big kid."

"You used to follow Marcos around the same way," Renée said.

"Yeah, I remember," Tony said. "I used to think he was so cool."

"Used to?" said Marcos.

"You know what I mean. I had a real hero-worship thing going on back then. I remember how pumped I was the first time I got invited to one of your pasture parties."

"Did I invite you?"

"Okay, maybe I just showed up. But you didn't throw me out! I was so happy to be there."

"Because you were in love with my sister. You were hoping *she* would be there."

"Well, yeah, that was part of it. But she didn't ever go to your pasture parties, except for that one time our senior year."

"Which is the only reason I didn't throw you out."

Tony slapped Marcos's shoulder. "Haha! Isn't he great? Y'all should've seen him at our little heart-to-heart right before the wedding. He gave me that death glare of his, and he said, *Just remember two things, Tony. I know how to kill a man, and I have access to over a thousand acres of family land.* Then he laughed and laughed, and said, *Haha!*

I'm just messing with you, man. And then he stopped laughing and his face went dead serious again, and he said, *Except I'm not, and don't you forget it. And don't you ever, ever hurt my sister."*

"Still true," Marcos said through a mouthful of food.

The camaraderie made Nina envious. She wished she'd had a brother who'd threatened her boyfriends, or a sister she could laugh with about it.

After lunch there was a whirlwind of cleanup and whisking away of children as Ignacio and Peri were put down for naps. Logan looked around in the sudden quiet and said, "I'm the only kid here now."

"Yes, you are!" said Renée. "Is there anything you'd like to do?"

Logan considered for a while before saying, "I'd like to see the chickens, please."

"What an excellent choice! Marcos, why don't you take Logan to the orchard to see the chickens? You can give them some scratch if you want."

Marcos looked at Nina. "Is that okay?"

He and Logan watched her with the same eager expression, like they were both kids and Nina was the grown-up.

"Sure," she said.

Marcos downed the last of his water and got to his feet. "Come on, Logan."

As they walked off with their identical strides, Nina watched with a prickle of disquiet. Everything had been *easy* for Marcos so far. Maybe it was because he and Logan were so much alike. She was glad, sort of. But something about it seemed unfair. She'd been the only parent in Logan's life for seven years. She'd toughed out those days of constant feedings and no sleep and struggling just to put food on the table and keep a roof over their heads, while still managing to find time and energy to make sure Logan felt valued and safe. And now here was Marcos, connecting with him effortlessly, just because they shared an inordinate amount of DNA. You didn't have to work for DNA. It was just *there*. And there was Logan, walking away from her without a backward glance.

She gave herself a little shake. *Don't be like that. This is what you said you wanted, for Logan to have his father in his life. Well, this is what that looks like. Don't make everything about you.*

CHAPTER NINETEEN

THEY WALKED ALONG the back of the house, to the corner of the porch, where Marcos took the wire egg basket from the hook on the post where it had been kept all his life. Then he and Logan went on through the old wrought iron gate in the side fence into the orchard. The hens made a suspicious *brra-a-a-a-a-ak* sound as they entered, but when Marcos headed toward the bin where their scratch was kept, they decided he was an okay guy after all.

He let Logan take a small scoop of scratch and spread it out. The chickens went right to work on it.

"What is this stuff?" Logan asked.

"A mix of grains and seeds. It's not their main food—it's like a dessert for them. It's called scratch because they like it so much they'll scratch around in the dirt for it. Scratching is good for them. It keeps them from getting bored, and it helps them eat some grit. Chickens don't have teeth, and the grit stays in their stomachs and helps break their food into smaller pieces."

Logan pointed. "That one looks different."

"Yeah, he's the rooster. The rest are hens. The hens are all his girls, and he takes care of them. If a predator gets in the orchard, like a hawk or a skunk or even a coyote, the rooster will fight it off, or die trying."

Maybe he should have left off the *die trying* part. Logan was a stranger to the grim realities of rural life. Over the years Marcos had seen some remarkable heroics from many roosters, and they'd often surprised him by defeating opponents a lot bigger than themselves. At the very least, they put up enough of a fight and made enough noise to allow time for someone to get a shotgun, if anyone was home. But against a mature coyote or a determined hawk, even the most valiant rooster was likely to end up as dinner himself, or die later from his wounds.

Logan gave the rooster a respectful nod and said, "Oorah!"

It was strange hearing the Marine battle cry coming from a little kid, but Marcos had to agree that it was appropriate. "Oorah," he said.

"I like their house," Logan said.

"Cool, isn't it? I helped my father make it when I was a boy. It's up high like that so predators can't get in. That little ramp is for the baby chicks to run up, because the steps are too high for them. The chickens stay out during the day, except when they're laying their eggs, and at night they all go inside and we shut the door."

The two of them went inside the coop, and Marcos showed Logan the double-decker nesting boxes. The bottom one nearest the door had a dozen or so eggs piled in it.

"How come they all use the same box when there's so many?" Logan asked.

"I don't know. They're not the smartest. But it does make it easier for us to gather the eggs. You want to put them in the basket? That's it, nice and easy."

When they stepped out onto the chicken coop porch, Logan suddenly perked up. "Hey! These trees are all lined up in parallel rows!"

"That's right," Marcos said, proud that his son knew what parallel meant. "They're planted in orchard rows. An orchard is a group of fruit trees. We plant them in rows so they can get the right amount of sunlight and have enough space to not crowd each other and still be close enough for pollination."

"Bees," Logan said.

"That's right. Moths and butterflies, too. Even flies and gnats are pollinators."

Wow. Our second-ever conversation alone, and I'm telling him about the birds and the bees.

"Is the fruit for the chickens?"

"No, it's for people. But an orchard is a good place for chickens. The trees give them shade and a place to hide from hawks. And the chickens eat the bugs that might hurt the trees. So it's healthy for both the chickens and the trees."

"Huh. Where's the fruit?"

"It's still too early in the year for it to be ripe. See those flowers? They'll turn into fruit later on. We have all different kinds planted out here. See this one, this plum tree? This is my tree. My father planted it for me when I was a baby. He planted trees for all his kids. This pomegranate tree is for my sister Dalia, and this pineapple guava is for my sister Eliana. And over here, this little Mexican lime—this is Ignacio's tree. His father planted it for him."

"I have one of those," Logan said.

"A Mexican lime tree?" said Marcos.

"A father."

He sounded perfectly matter-of-fact about it, like they were talking about Toyotas or something, but Marcos's stomach flipped over inside him.

"Oh," said Marcos. He didn't know what else to say.

"He doesn't live with us," Logan went on.

"Oh, yeah?"

Marcos felt ridiculous, making empty small-talk responses. Logan didn't seem upset about the subject, probably because Nina had been so careful to handle it right. Or maybe he just didn't miss what he'd never had.

"Yeah, 'cause when I was born, he wasn't ready to be a father yet."

Marcos nodded. "Yeah. Yeah, that happens sometimes."

"But when I grow up, I'm going to find him. That's what my mom did with her father. He wasn't ready either, when she was a kid. Then she grew up and found him, but he *still* wasn't ready, so she had to wait some more and find him again, and that time he was ready."

Logan gave Marcos a wise look. "Sometimes you have to wait a long time."

The words stabbed Marcos right through the heart. He understood perfectly now. It wasn't that Logan was disinterested in his father. From his point of view, there just wasn't anything he could do about it until he grew up, so why waste emotional energy? He'd clearly thought things through; he had a plan.

"What if—what if your father was ready before then? What if he was ready when you were still a kid?"

Logan's brow furrowed. "How would I know?"

"Maybe you wouldn't have to know. Maybe he'd find you."

"Huh," Logan said. "I never heard of it being that way."

"But what if it happened anyway? What if your father found you? How would you feel about that?"

Logan shrugged. "Fine, I guess."

For a moment, time seemed to stand still. Marcos could *feel* that Logan was his son. The sensation overpowered him. It was too much to keep to himself.

"Well then, I have something to tell you."

His heart pounded. Was he really doing this?

Then he took the plunge. "It's me. I'm your father, Logan."

Logan blinked. "You are?"

"Yeah."

Logan stood there, quiet and still. Marcos could almost see him mentally rearranging things to make room for this new piece of knowledge.

"And…you're ready now?"

The words stung. The idea of Logan having to wait for him to be ready was all wrong—like Logan was the grown-up here, and Marcos was a backward kid who took longer than expected to mature.

"Yes," he said. "I'm ready."

Logan thought some more, then said, "Does my mom know about this?"

Marcos suppressed a smile. "Yeah, she knows. We, uh, we knew each other a long time ago, she and I, but then…we lost touch."

What a cop-out. "Lost touch" was when you misplaced someone's phone number, not when you walked out on her. But Nina had said they shouldn't burden Logan with knowledge he wasn't ready for yet.

"Huh," Logan said again. He thought a while longer, then said, "Did she give you the box?"

"She did. I love it. And I showed it to my mom—you know, Mrs. Ramirez? She's your grandmother. Dalia and Eliana are your aunts, and Ignacio's your cousin. We're your family."

"Did you plant a tree for me?"

"No, I didn't. I couldn't, because—"

He'd almost said *because I didn't know about you*, but that sounded like blaming Nina, which was the last thing he wanted to do.

"I was away," he finished.

Logan nodded. "Fighting. Because you're a Marine."

"That's right. But I'm back now, for good. So how 'bout if we plant your tree together? We can go to the tree farm, and I'll show you the different kinds and you can pick."

"'Kay."

They walked out of the orchard in silence. Marcos set the egg basket on the fence post as he closed the gate behind them.

"Look, Logan—I'm sorry I wasn't there for you before. I wish I had been. I missed out, not knowing you. But I'm here now, and I want to be a father to you."

"'Kay."

Logan's go-to monosyllable sounded cold, but Marcos knew better. He saw the rapid rising and falling of the boy's chest, the trembling of his lower lip.

"I want to go play on Ignacio's fort now," Logan said.

"Okay," Marcos said. His son needed some space; he could respect that. He'd give it to him. He'd been given space enough himself for seven years and more.

Logan started to run off, but only made it a few yards before doing a full-speed U-turn, running full tilt into Marcos and hugging him tight.

Marcos's heart swelled. He swallowed hard over the soreness in his throat and held on.

CHAPTER TWENTY

AFTER MARCOS AND LOGAN had gone to see the chickens, Renée turned to Nina with an eager smile. "I brought over some photo albums from when the kids were young. Would you like to see? I thought it might be fun to look for family resemblances."

"Oh, thank you! I'd love that. I wish I'd thought to bring mine."

"That's all right. We've got plenty of time. Anyway, I've already had a preview. Marcos showed me the box. He usually plays it pretty close to the vest, but I think seeing all that stuff in the box made him so proud that he had to share it with someone." Her eyes moistened. "It was good of you to keep those things for him."

A few minutes later they were side-by-side at the dining table and having a fine cozy time of it, flipping through pages, filling in histories. It was strange and wonderful to see Marcos as a child, unscarred by life, smiling wholeheartedly at the camera. Eighteen months old, wearing nothing but a diaper, cowboy boots and a cowboy hat. Lying on the floor next to a newborn Dalia, with his legs curled up, holding a toy for her. Using a real hammer to drive real nails into a piece of wood at age four. Holding a swaddled newborn Eliana, looking gravely at the camera with eyebrows raised. On the back of a reddish horse, next to Martin, who was riding the buckskin horse that Ignacio had ridden today.

"Your husband was a very good-looking man," Nina said.

"Yes, he was. He was a real prize. And I won him!"

Nina smiled at the evident pride in Renée's voice.

Renée lightly touched Martin's face in the photo. "Family resemblance is a funny thing, isn't it? You'd think it would be cut-and-dried—this child looks like this parent, or has this one's eyes and that one's mouth—but really it's a lot more complex. Marcos and Dalia both take after Martin's side of the family, and Eliana looks like me. But sometimes Marcos reminds me so much of my brother, it's almost eerie. And even though Dalia and Eliana don't look much alike when you go feature by feature, they still look like sisters, especially when they're laughing, or sleeping. Mannerisms, posture, voices, they all have their effect. There's a lot of nuance. It's fascinating."

They came to some pictures of Marcos digging his hole in the yard. It really was an enormous hole. Then a birthday party of Dalia's. Tony was there, instantly recognizable by his infectious grin and outrageously thick head of hair. Dalia had her hair in a long braid. Marcos was a lanky preteen by then, geared up and armed to the teeth with two machetes, a pocket knife, a flashlight, a water bottle, a bandana headband—"Plus goodness knows what else inside those cargo pockets," Renée said. "He was always a big believer in cargo pants, let me tell you—plenty of places to stow all his stuff."

"Logan loves cargo pants too! I just wish I could find some that are long enough and still fit him in the waist."

"I know exactly what you mean. It's right in the transition between a little boy's size 7X and a big boy's size 8. They stop elasticizing the waist right when they make the waist size three inches bigger!"

"*Yes!* And the only way to keep his pants

from falling down is to fold the waist into a big old tuck and cinch it with a belt! It's like the manufacturers have never even *seen* a tall skinny boy with no hips!"

"Oh, yes, I remember those days well. Why don't you just bring all Logan's pants to me? I'll sew some one-inch elastic into the back of the waistband with a zigzag stitch. That's what I did for Marcos before he filled out."

Nina thanked her, but she tried to keep herself from getting too excited about the offer. It was the sort of thing people said without intending to follow through.

"I mean it," Renée said. "I'm sure you must be a very busy person, and I'd like to be able to help."

Renée was so warm and sympathetic that Nina found herself confiding.

"Sometimes I feel like I'm always telling Logan *no*. I don't want to stifle his curiosity, but I can't let him do whatever comes into his head, or he'd have the house down to bare studding within a week. I try to provide constructive outlets for him so he won't tear things up, but his mind moves so fast, it's hard to keep up with him. He doesn't like reading, and I can't just park him in front of the TV for hours—couldn't even if I wanted to, because he gets bored with it."

"Some children are naturally curious about how things work. It goes along with a strong mechanical aptitude."

"When do they outgrow the part where everything they do turns into a huge mess?"

Renée tilted her head. "Hmm. I'll let you know. But they do get to a point where they have something positive to show for it at the end, like a rebuilt engine for the lawn mower, or a new weighted gate for the cattle chute. What was Logan like as a baby? Was he an escape artist, like Marcos?"

"Oh, yes. He managed to climb out of his crib at eight months. He crawled early, walked early and could figure out how to open practically anything. He talked late, though. And his first word was *gear*."

"Marcos's was *wheel*! He crawled and walked early too. I lived in constant fear that he'd hurt himself, but oddly enough, he was the only one of my kids never to break a bone."

"What about…academically? Even though Logan hit every physical milestone early, he isn't reading well at all. I've done everything his teachers have told me to do. I read to him every night, but I get the feeling he's just enduring it. He's not even close to where he's supposed to be readingwise."

"Neither was Marcos at that age, or for many years to come. Dalia was two grades behind him, but once she started school, she passed him in no time. I was worried, but he didn't even seem to care."

"What did you do?"

"I mostly just waited. Gave him time and space to do the stuff he was good at, like playing with Legos and building things and digging giant holes in the yard. Some of his teachers put a lot of pressure on me. They basically said he'd be academically stunted for life if he didn't get radical intervention right away, but I just smiled and said I'd wait and see for another year."

Nina was impressed that sweet Renée would actually stand up to a teacher that way. Logan's teachers terrified her.

"Then when he was around ten," Renée went on, "something changed. He was less restless, more patient, better able to sit still and concentrate on things besides carpentry projects and small engines. He'd always been interested in military history and how things worked, so I got him some good kid-level books about Iwo Jima and the Mississippi River, and a biography of the Wright brothers and I don't know what all, and left them in his room without saying anything. For weeks they sat there untouched. Then one day I looked outside and saw him sitting in that hole he'd dug, grimly reading away. There was no looking back. He worked his way through piles of books about nature, technology and history. By the end of that school year he was completely caught up in his reading level."

Renée took a sip of iced tea. "Now, I'm no expert, and I'm not saying that approach would work with every kid, or that some kids don't need more intensive help. But I do think people are a little too quick these days to put a label on anything that deviates from a very narrow set of standards. Time is a great equalizer. Children develop at different rates, and I wonder if sometimes going all remedial on a kid will make him dig in his heels and resist, or lose confidence, when he would have been fine with the right environment and a little patience."

Nina sighed. "I'm not as strong-minded as you. I think I *have* put pressure on Logan, and

I haven't done a good enough job of shielding him from other people's remarks."

"Don't beat yourself up. It was easier for me. I wasn't alone. Martin was there for me to bounce ideas off and provide another perspective, and he always backed me up. That makes a huge difference. For whatever it's worth, I'll be there for you and help as much as I can. I'm not very wise, but I do have a lot of experience. And from what I can see, you've done a lot of things right. Logan is a smart, calm, confident boy."

"Thank you. It's worth a lot."

Just then, Marcos came in from outside through the kitchen door.

"Hi, honey," said Renée. "Where's Logan?"

"Hey, Mom. He's fine. Playing in the yard. Nina, can I talk to you outside for a minute? Alone?"

Nina's heart rate picked up. She wanted very much for Marcos to talk to her, alone. That instant, electric attraction that she'd felt eight years ago was still there, as strong as ever. Stronger, even. Seeing him today with his family—seeing him patient and humble with Logan—had made him even more attractive than usual. She wondered if he felt it too. With such a crowd around them both all day, it was hard to tell. But here he was now, bold and direct, without using any ruse or excuse to get her by herself, just saying what he wanted.

He gestured to the door he'd just come through, opened it for her and followed her out.

He led her to a corner of the porch. A porch swing hung there, made from reclaimed wood; it was a beautiful piece. But Marcos didn't sit down. He looked solemn and strong and a tiny bit anxious. He faced Nina, took a deep breath—

"I did something," he said. "I hope it's okay."

For heaven's sake. Was that all this was? More second-guessing himself? What did he do, let Logan pet a chicken?

Oh, well. It was progress, anyway, asking forgiveness instead of permission.

"What did you do?" she asked.

"I told him. I told Logan I'm his father."

For a moment Nina couldn't speak. "You what?"

"I know I didn't run it by you first. I know we said we'd wait. But the subject came up, and it felt like the right time."

"How on earth did the subject come up? What did he say? What did you say?"

After he told her, she stood there a while, processing the news. She had to admit, it did sound like he'd chosen the perfect moment—or, rather, the perfect moment had been handed to him. But he'd taken a lot on himself, and taken a lot away from her. She felt as if he'd pulled the rug out from under her.

"I have to go talk to him," she said.

She found Logan swinging on one of the enormous swings hanging from the outsized frame, going back and forth in great sweeping arcs. It really did look like fun, and any other time Nina would have hopped into the next swing and given him a run for his money.

Instead, she said, "Logan, I need to talk to you."

"'Kay," he said. His voice sounded normal, and he didn't look upset.

"Stop swinging," she said.

He gave her a pained look.

"Logan," she said in a warning tone.

He stopped pumping his legs and slowly came to a stop.

"Did Marcos tell you something when you were with the chickens?" she asked.

"He said roosters will fight to the death

if something tries to hurt their hens," said Logan.

"Oh? That's interesting. Did he say anything about...about being your father?"

"Yeah, but that was *after* we left the chickens."

Nina wanted to laugh, or scream. This kid was so *precise*.

"I see. So...what did you think of that?"

"It's fine. Now we don't have to wait 'til I grow up to find him."

"Yes, that's true."

She waited, but Logan didn't volunteer anything more.

"Do you...do you like Marcos?" she asked finally.

"Yeah," he said.

Maybe it was time to give up. An articulate discussion about emotions might be a lot to expect from any seven-year-old, let alone this one.

"All right, then," she said. "If you ever want to talk about this, I'm here."

"'Kay."

Marcos was waiting exactly where she'd left him. The sight of him standing there, this big, tough man, waiting to be chastised, melted away most of her annoyance.

"Is everything okay?" he asked.

"I suppose. I'd have preferred if the two of us talked it over beforehand, but in all fairness, he is your son too."

Marcos smiled. "Yeah," he said.

"So…how did he take it?" Nina asked.

"Pretty calmly. He's a cool customer. He did give me a hug, though."

"He *hugged* you?"

"Yeah. Is that okay?"

"Yes, it's okay. It's just surprising. Logan's never been much of a hugger. He was even an unsnuggly baby. I'd have found it a lot easier to believe if you said he'd given you a good strong handshake."

"Maybe he just likes me."

He sounded uncertain. Nina smiled. "Maybe he does. I'm glad. Honestly, it always concerned me a little that he wasn't more curious about his father. But maybe he was just compartmentalizing."

"Makes perfect sense to me," Marcos said. "He couldn't do anything about it at the time, so he set it aside against the day when he could."

"Something tells me I'm going to get a lot of insight into Logan's character, now that I have you," she said.

The moment the words were out, she wanted to take them back. "I mean, now that I have you around," she backpedaled.

He smiled. "Speaking of that...there's something else I want to talk to you about."

Her heart sped up again.

"Remember when we first met, I told you about the bridge on South Congress Avenue in Austin where the huge bat colony lives? And how they all fly out at dusk to go hunting?"

"I remember."

It had been after they'd left the bar and gone to the park. They'd already talked over all the places in Texas that they'd both visited, and now he was suggesting places for her to visit next. The bat bridge had been high on the list.

"I said I'd take you to see them one day," he went on.

Yes, he had said that. She hadn't forgotten. Her heart beat faster still.

"Well," he said, "I think Logan would really like to see them. So how 'bout we all go?"

Her heart dropped like a stone. What was wrong with her? Why were her emotions on such a free-for-all today?

"All of us?" she said.

He laughed. "Not the entire family, not this time. *All* as in the three of us. You, me and Logan."

"Oh. Yeah, that sounds like a more manageable crowd. Okay, sure. Let's go. You're right, Logan would love it."

"Good! Is tomorrow okay? Or maybe we should wait 'til next Saturday. It might be a late night by the time we drive back home. You have to time it right to see them fly out. I looked it up, and sunset this time of year in Austin is about eight thirty. Is that too late for a Sunday night?"

"Tomorrow's fine. He'll probably fall asleep in the car."

"You want to go early, walk around? South Congress is a pretty happening place. We can do some shopping, get something to eat. We don't have to schedule everything, just allow plenty of time and see what we feel like doing once we get there."

What Nina felt like doing now was laying her hands against Marcos's chest, backing him against the porch post and kissing him.

Don't be ridiculous. He's taking an interest in his son, trying to be a responsible, involved father. A month ago you would have been thrilled with that much. It's stupid to want more.

But she did.

Suddenly Nina was exhausted. It felt like an age ago that she'd found Logan cutting his hair at home. So much had happened, and she'd been flooded with one emotion after another. She hadn't had a day this eventful since…well, since she met Marcos for the first time.

He'd made her do things totally out of character for her. No, not *made*. Nobody had forced her to do any of it. Yes, part of it was her fragile emotional state brought on by her father's rejection. But only part. She'd chosen with her eyes wide open. She'd *wanted* to marry Marcos, less than half a day after meeting him.

She couldn't afford to lose control that way again. She had Logan now. She had to keep a handle on her emotions for both their sakes.

CHAPTER TWENTY-ONE

"I'M TIRED," Logan said.

The thin note of whining in his voice set Marcos's teeth on edge, but Nina just said with strained cheerfulness, "We know. We heard you the first ten times."

"Well, I am. How much farther is it?"

It was more than a thin note now. Marcos and his sisters never would have been allowed to use that tone with their mother. In their family, whining simply wasn't done. Surely Nina would have to correct him now.

But all she did was look at the map on her phone.

"What are you doing?" he asked.

"I'm seeing how much farther it is to the bridge."

"You mean you're actually going to answer the question?"

Nina didn't look up. "Why wouldn't I?"

Marcos lowered his voice. "Because he's whining."

She shrugged. "Sometimes he whines. He's seven."

"Well, when *I* was seven, I ran all over La Escarpa from dawn 'til dusk helping with ranch work."

Nina looked at him, stunned. Marcos was stunned too. He'd channeled his dad with that last remark.

"Well, he's not you, okay?" Nina said.

How had things come to this?

The first part of the afternoon had been one success after another. The hole-in-the-wall taco place Marcos remembered from way back. The eye-catching storefronts, a bright jumble of old Western-looking facades, painted murals and patterned tiles. The quirky gift shop that stocked vintage and off-the-wall toys, where Marcos had bought Logan a Transformer toy, a bat figurine and some blind-box action figures, the kind where you didn't know which character was inside until you opened the box. The vintage boutique where Nina had oohed and aahed over fancy old jewelry while Marcos ran herd on Logan and kept him from careening into fragile displays.

Buying that stuff for Logan had made Marcos feel like a rock star. He'd come close to buying Nina something from the boutique but thought it might be weird. She'd seemed to enjoy herself anyway. Told Marcos how nice shopping with another adult was, since she could really look at things and not be constantly on alert.

All in all, Marcos had thought he was doing great.

After the boutique they were all hungry again, so he took them to Amy's Ice Creams for some specialty flavors—Honey Bear Bomb, Lemon Cheesecake, and Texas Dirt Cake.

It was after the ice cream that things had started to go south.

"All right," Marcos had said. "Time to pound the pavement."

Nina had looked at her phone and frowned. "Aren't we going back to the truck first?"

"Nah. We're hoofing it. That's why I've been carrying this bag all this time, for when we reach the hill where we'll watch the bats."

He held up the military-surplus sling pack where he'd stowed a blanket and some binoculars.

"We're still pretty far from the bridge," Nina said.

"We're a whole lot closer than we were.

That was the whole point of parking where we did and moving in this direction. If we go back to the truck now, we'll be moving *away* from the bats. At this point, we're almost halfway there."

"But if we walk to the bridge, we'll still need to walk all the way back to the truck afterward. There's parking near the bridge, isn't there?"

"Sure. But we're so close already. The bridge is only…" He looked at his phone. "Zero-point-eight miles away. Logan can walk that, can't you, buddy?"

"Yeah," Logan said.

The way he said yeah irritated Marcos a little. His own dad *never* would have let any of his kids get away with a simple *yeah* or *no* to an adult. But Marcos was going to let it slide, because he was cool like that.

Now here they were, ten minutes and half a mile later, with Nina giving off an I-told-you-so vibe.

As for Logan…

What had happened to the little buddy he'd gotten along with so well at La Escarpa? Marcos had thought they really got each other. Now Logan was giving him a look that bordered on mutinous.

Logan wiped sweat from his forehead. "I'm hot."

Hot? You call this hot? Try the banks of the Euphrates in August.

The words were right there on the tip of Marcos's tongue. He bit them back.

"What's wrong?" Nina asked him.

"Nothing."

"Well, something must be wrong, or you wouldn't look like that."

He didn't answer.

"Marcos," she said.

"It's just—it's that whiny tone of voice," he said quietly. "It grates on me to hear him talk that way to you. It's disrespectful. My father never would have let me get away with talking like that to my mother, or to him."

"Well, Logan hasn't had a father, okay? He's just had me. And yes, maybe I've let him get away with some things. But I do my best. I don't want to be coming down on him all the time. And sometimes I just get tired."

A phrase drifted unpleasantly to Marcos's mind: *direct reflection of leadership.* As in, *Hey, Sergeant, I hear a guy in your squad drank a fifth of Jack and snuck a motorcycle into his room. Direct reflection of leadership, right?*

It was Marcos's fault things were all jammed up. Nina had warned him that the walk was too far for Logan, and he hadn't listened. This was all on him.

And it was up to him to get things turned back around.

He clapped his hands together and looked at Logan. "All right, change of plans. We're still zero-point-three miles from the bridge. We're still not going back to the truck. But you're not walking anymore. I'm carrying you the rest of the way."

"He's going to get heavy," Nina said.

"Heavy? Look at him, he can't weigh more than sixty pounds. Infantry rucksacks with full gear and ammo are more than that."

"I'm not a baby," Logan said.

"I know you're not," said Marcos. "I'm not going to carry you like a baby. I'm going to put you in a fireman's carry."

"What's that?" Logan asked.

Marcos crouched down, and within moments had Logan slung over his shoulders.

"This is how you get a wounded comrade away from danger," he said. "It's an important manly skill that I'll teach you how to do. Someday, you might need to carry me this way."

As Marcos started walking again, Logan giggled. There was no other word for it.

Nina fell into step beside him. Marcos's peripheral vision was obstructed by Logan's backside; he had to turn at the waist to see her face.

"We good?" he asked her.

She smiled. "Oh, yes. We're very good."

"WHOA, WATCH OUT, BUDDY," Marcos said to Logan. "Your Transformer about knocked over your mom's drink. Here, let's move you over to the edge of the blanket so your action figures can tromp around on the grass."

Nina lay back on her elbows, stretched out her legs and watched as Marcos helped Logan relocate his toys.

They were sitting on the hill beside the Congress Avenue Bridge, with a rugged plaid blanket spread out beneath them—the same plaid blanket that had been in the bed of Marcos's truck on their wedding night. She'd recognized it the second he opened his sling pack, and when she saw Marcos's self-conscious glance, she knew he remembered too.

Marcos came back and stretched out his own legs alongside of hers. She'd taken her shoes off, and her bare toes barely reached past his calves.

They weren't quite touching, but there was something intimate about how close they were, hip to hip, thigh to thigh. When Marcos's arm brushed hers, she actually shivered.

"Are you cold?" he asked.

He sounded surprised, and no wonder. It had to be eighty degrees in the shade right now.

Nina pretended she hadn't heard the question.

"There sure are a lot of people out here," she said.

The hillside was crowded with people waiting to see the bats come out. More people stood along the bridge, silhouetted by the setting sun. At the bottom of the hill, canoes, kayaks and riverboats floated in Lady Bird Lake, paddles and oars and engines at rest.

"Yeah," Marcos said. "Another time we should rent a canoe and watch the bats from the water. There are some good canoeing spots on the Colorado River. We could start early, make a day of it."

The words gave her a quick lift of pleasure. *Another time.* Their first outing as a family had had its rough moments, but Marcos wasn't done with her and Logan.

"I've never been canoeing," Nina said.

"Seriously? Never?"

"Never."

"How about kayaking?"

"Kayaking I've done, in the Pacific."

"Good for you," he said, as if he was truly proud of her. "Did you know kayaking is supposed to come easier to women? It's because of all the hip-swiveling."

She smiled. "Is that so? I don't think we go around swiveling our hips all that much."

"No, no, I mean because of the shape," he said. "Women just have—their hips are—the shape is different."

Was his face actually reddening?

"Anyway," he said. "Where in the Pacific did you go kayaking?"

"La Jolla."

"La Jolla is fantastic for kayaking! Kelp forests, dolphins, sea caves."

"Flying fish too. And seals. They pop up out of the water sometimes. They're cute, but they stink."

"Have you been to the Channel Islands? Huge sea caves there. You paddle on in, and everything goes dark and the sea lions start barking at you."

"I've heard it's beautiful, but I've never been. And La Jolla was a long time ago. I haven't done anything like that since Logan was born."

"Oh. Right. I guess it would be—yeah."

Logan trudged over and plopped down on Marcos's other side. "When will they come out?" he asked.

He was whining again. Nina's chest tightened, anticipating more tension.

But Marcos said calmly, "I can't understand you when you talk that way."

Logan took a breath, then asked his question again in a normal voice.

"Soon," Marcos said. "Around sunset."

"And they're all crammed in under that bridge right now?"

"Yep, all snug in their little crevices."

"The concrete holds on to heat," Nina said. "I was reading about it on the website. So the babies that aren't old enough to fly yet stay nice and warm while their mothers are out hunting bugs."

"The babies stay alone at night?" Logan asked.

"Yes, but they've got lots of good hiding places to keep them safe," said Nina.

"What about the fathers?"

"This colony is mostly mothers and babies. Each mother has one baby a year. It takes them about five weeks to get big enough to fly and hunt. By the end of the summer, when the bats go back to Mexico, the babies will all be big and strong enough for the trip."

"But where do the fathers live?"

"I...don't know, actually," Nina said.

"They live by themselves," Marcos said. "In hollow trees and things."

"Why don't they live under the bridge too?"

"Because you can't have that many male animals together all in one place, or they'll fight and cause trouble. It's better for everyone if they live alone."

Put that way, it sounded pretty bleak. Nina stole a sidewise glance at Marcos and saw him scowling slightly.

"Hey, Logan," he said, "show me again how your Transformer turns into a car."

It was getting darker by the minute. By the time the Transformer had been put through its paces, the first few bats were starting to trickle out from under the bridge. A few more, and a few more, streaming out like smoke, and then the smoke swelled into a huge dark cloud.

"See how they're flying?" Marcos said. "How they swarm? Not like birds. Even far away you can tell a bat from a bird, if you know what to look for. Bat wings are more maneuverable than bird wings."

"They're fast," Nina murmured.

Marcos showed Logan how to use the binoculars. Logan didn't say much, but Nina could see how intent and absorbed he was.

The dark cloud rose into the sky and snaked out, following the river east, the vanguard of the group dwindling to a point far away. The bats kept coming and coming.

WHEN IT WAS all over, and the blanket and binoculars were packed and everyone's shoes were on, Marcos announced that they were taking an Uber back to the truck. He'd used the app to book one while Nina wasn't looking, and the car was waiting for them when they reached the street. She'd been trying to figure out how to tactfully suggest doing that very thing, but he'd thought of it all on his own.

They didn't talk much on the drive home. Logan fell asleep within minutes of being belted in. The silence was pleasant and restful, like the silence on the drive to San Elijo after their wedding. Nina even had a mellow alt-country playlist going, only slightly updated from eight years ago. It felt good to listen to the music coming softly through the truck's stereo, and remember their day together, and glance at Marcos's strong profile once in a while.

Once they left the city, Marcos put the windows down and rested his arm in the open frame. Some sweet scent blew in from the countryside. Nina wished she knew the name of the bloom. She'd like to bottle it.

Marcos pulled into Nina's driveway and killed the ignition. Then he and Nina both turned around at the exact same moment to look at their son in the backseat. Logan was out cold, with a dinosaur loosely gripped in one hand and his new bat figurine in the other.

"He looks so much younger this way," Marcos whispered.

"I know," Nina said softly. "He always does."

There was a delicious sense of normalcy and security in the moment: a mother and a father watching their sleeping child.

"I'll help you get him inside," Marcos said.

They went around to the backseat. Marcos opened the door and crouched down. "Show me how to work this vest thing he wears," he said.

While Marcos watched, Nina unfastened the various buckles, clips and hooks. Together, she and Marcos gently slipped off the vest.

And suddenly Marcos was holding Logan, not in a fireman's carry this time, but in his arms, looking so natural and fatherly that Nina's throat ached. The bat fell from Logan's loose fingers. Nina caught it before it hit the ground, and took the dinosaur from his other hand.

Nina hurried ahead to unlock and open the front door, then led the way to Logan's room. Marcos stood silently while she pulled back the covers, then he carefully laid Logan down. Nina took off one shoe, and Marcos got the other. Without opening his eyes, Logan held out his hands, and Nina gave him the bat and the dinosaur. He clutched them to his chest and rolled onto his side with a small sigh, and she pulled the covers up to his chin.

They tiptoed out and she shut the door.

Her bedroom was across the hall. The bed

wasn't properly made; the fluffy duvet was bunched up, and strewn with what looked like every casual outfit she owned, which it might have been. She'd tried on a lot of different things this morning before making her final choice. The bench at the foot of the bed held a pair of thin plaid pajama pants and a pink T-shirt with a picture of a bespectacled koala bear and the words *Well Koalafied*.

And Marcos was standing at the open doorway, peering through, looking a lot like Logan had that afternoon, staring into the window of the shop with the action figures.

He turned with a quick, self-conscious smile, like he'd been caught doing something he shouldn't, and hurried back to the front room. Nina followed him.

"Can I get you something to drink?" she asked. "I have some of that turmeric-ginger tea you like."

She felt silly admitting this. She'd felt even sillier buying the tea, like she hoped and expected to have Marcos sitting in her kitchen one day, drinking it. Yet here he was.

"Yeah, thanks," he said.

She gestured awkwardly to the table, and he sat down.

"Nice place," he said.

"Thanks," she said as she filled the kettle. "It's small, but big enough for us, and close to work. I was glad to find something so nice that fit my budget. Your housing dollar goes a lot farther in Texas than in California."

"Sure does."

Nina opened the brand-new box of turmeric-ginger tea and took out a bag. She got a bag of yaupon tea for herself.

As she was pouring the hot water, Marcos said suddenly, "Nina, how'd you ever manage all this time on your own? I'm worn out after just one day. You've been doing it for *years*."

She set the kitchen timer and took the seat across from him.

"I don't know," she said truthfully. "I guess I just had to, so I did."

"Well, you're doing a great job."

She couldn't resist a little dig. "There were times today when you didn't seem to care much for my methods."

"I don't know what you're talking about," he deadpanned.

She gave him a shove on the shoulder, and he grinned.

"Okay," he said. "It's possible that…mistakes were made today. I may have overstepped my bounds a time or two."

"That's very big of you to say. To be fair, you may have had a point about the whining. Oh, and that whole I-can't-hear-you-when-you-talk-like-that thing? Genius."

"That was my mom's line. Couldn't believe it when I heard the words coming out of my mouth."

"Your mom's pretty smart."

His face turned serious. "So are you. You're a good mother. You set clear boundaries, and you enforce them, but you don't micromanage. And it's obvious that you enjoy being around him."

"Thanks. You're shaping up to be a pretty good father."

He shrugged. "Well, given my track record so far, almost anything is an improvement."

Nina remembered how he'd looked with Logan slung over his shoulders, smiling and strong and sure of himself.

"I mean it," she said.

Her gaze dropped from his heavy-lidded eyes to his mouth, lingering a moment on the devastating curve of his bottom lip, then to his leanly muscled forearms resting on her dining table. His hands were folded together, just inches from hers. His fingers slowly un-furled. Nina's heart skipped a beat.

Then he spread out his hands across the dining table and said, "This is a handsome piece."

You're a handsome piece.

Nina took a steadying breath. "I got it at a flea market in San Jose, from a place that makes reproductions of Spanish colonial furniture. It was a splurge. Logan was four, he'd long since outgrown his high chair, and I wanted a real table we could eat at together instead of the tiny IKEA thing I had. When I saw this, I had to have it. We lived on eggs and tuna for months afterward, but I never regretted the purchase."

"Three years ago," Marcos said. "I was living in a tent in Deir ez-Zor."

And all that time, I had a son.

He didn't say it, but Nina could feel him thinking it.

He could have FaceTimed with Logan from Syria. Nina could have mailed him Logan's drawings and photos instead of putting them into the box.

When the timer went off, Nina brought the mugs to the table. She'd made Marcos's in an *Apatosaurus* mug with a handle that was formed by the dinosaur's looping neck.

"My last year's Mother's Day gift," she said

as she set it in front of him. "Doesn't your son have excellent taste?"

Marcos chuckled. "He does. But maybe next year I'll steer him toward some fancy old-fashioned jewelry."

He wrapped his tea bag around his spoon, using the string to squeeze out the last few drops.

"Look at you," Nina said. "You've turned into an expert tea drinker."

"I ought to. I've drunk enough of the stuff."

"How's your stomach? Any more flare-ups?"

"Nope. Maybe it's all healed."

They drank their tea, and talked and were silent together. The silences got longer and longer; they were full of the palpable attraction between them that she'd been feeling all day. It was as real as the scent of ginger in the air, so real that surely any minute now, Marcos would act on it.

But he didn't.

Maybe she'd imagined the thing in the hallway. Maybe he'd just been appalled by her poor housekeeping. Maybe all this was, was a mother and father connected by their child, with a good working relationship. What was that word that she hated so much? Co-parenting. Maybe this wasn't anything more than effective co-parenting.

"Can I ask you something?" he said.

Her heart gave a quick painful throb. "Sure."

"When you decided to make up a fake husband, why did you buy a new ring off Amazon? Why not use the one I gave you?"

She stared at him. "Well, I… I couldn't. Not after our marriage ended."

"Why did that matter? You were pretending either way."

"Well, yes, but—the new ring didn't remind me of you."

She was too flustered to look him in the eye. She swirled her tea around in her mug and said, "I mean, I guess I still felt pretty sore and…raw about the whole thing. I couldn't wear the ring you gave me like it didn't mean anything. I couldn't be that pragmatic."

"I see. So the fake husband thing started pretty soon after the…the annulment, then?"

"Um…no. It was just a couple of years ago."

"Ah." He nodded, no doubt processing the knowledge that she was still feeling raw and sore about the dissolution of their marriage years after the fact.

"Why did you want to know?" she asked.

He shrugged. "I thought maybe you didn't like the other ring," he said. "Or maybe you threw it away."

She made a scoffing sound. "There might be some women out there who are dramatic enough or rich enough to throw away a gold ring as some sort of gesture, but I'm not one of them."

"Did you sell it back to the pawn shop, then? Or to one of those cash-for-gold places?"

She squirmed under his gaze. Why did he keep pushing about this? Hadn't she provided enough evidence of just how hopelessly hung up she'd been on him for the past eight years? For a second, she wished she could look him coolly in the eye and say she'd sold the ring and used the money to pay her utility bill.

"I still have it," she said. "In the back corner of my jewelry box."

There. Now he knew.

"I still have mine too," he said. "It went with me to Raqqa and Deir ez-Zor and back again. I keep it in an old Altoids tin with my grandfather's tie pin."

A warm burst of hope washed through her.

"I'm sorry I was so nasty at first, about the fake husband thing," he said at last. "Once I calmed down, I could see the need for it. I'm sure you had guys coming on to you all the time at the VA."

Flattering as this was, she was too honest to let him believe it.

"Well, I wasn't exactly beating them off with a stick, especially before Logan started school. Most men don't want to get involved with a woman who has a small child. But then I had a bad experience with this one guy, a Navy veteran. He got obsessed, found out where I lived—he basically stalked me for four months. I had to take out a restraining order."

Marcos sat up straight. "Did he hurt you?"

"No. Just creeped me out. It was a scary time, but it passed."

"Where is he now?" Marcos asked. His eyebrows drew down, and his chin jutted out, like he was ready to go hunt the guy down.

"Still in California, I guess—and doing much better, last I heard. It's okay—he gave up eventually."

"If he hadn't—if he'd hurt you or Logan—"

"He didn't. It's okay."

"It's not okay!"

The words rang through the quiet room. He got up, stalked around and said in a lower voice, "I left you alone and unprotected, with a child—my child. It was cowardly and dishonorable. I took a vow, and I broke it."

He turned to face her again. "I'm glad you found a way to shield yourself, even a little."

She started to speak, stopped, then tried again.

"The fake husband thing…it wasn't just about safety. It was a barrier to keep men from getting too close—all men, even emotionally stable ones."

An expression she couldn't identify passed over his face. "So… I take it you haven't dated a lot over the past seven-plus years?"

"Not at all. There's been no one since you, Marcos."

"There's been no one for me, either."

"Seriously?"

It was one thing for her to keep clear of romantic entanglements. She had a small child. But for Marcos—a handsome, dynamic man, out in the world—

"I had a lot going on," he said defensively.

He took his seat again, picked up his mug and set it down again.

"Back when I lived at Camp Pendleton, I

used to go exploring, up and down the west coast. Kept my camping gear in the truck, and whenever I had a chance I'd take off, find a new place, sleep under the stars. Then I met you. That morning in San Elijo—you were the first woman I ever took with me. The only one. You didn't turn up your nose at sleeping in the bed of a truck. You were as stoked as I was. I watched you fall asleep, and I thought to myself… I thought, *Don't mess this up.* But I did. If I hadn't…we could have been together all this time. I could have taken you and Logan to the Channel Islands, and the redwoods, and Big Sur."

Her heart pounded. *Careful*, she thought.

Then Marcos downed the last of his tea and stood to go.

Nina's emotions plummeted. So much for caution.

She walked him to the door. He reached for the latch, then turned and said quickly, "Will you have dinner with me? Just the two of us?"

And Nina was soaring again. "Yes," she said.

"Friday?"

"Yes."

"Pick you up at six?"

"Yes."

She dimly felt that she should have varied her answers a bit, but Marcos didn't look like he cared.

"Okay," he said. "Good."

And then Nina thought of something else to say. "Thank you for today. I had a nice time."

In spite of the moments of tension, it had been a good day.

"I did too," Marcos said. "We'll figure stuff out—where I fit in, how to share responsibility and discipline and all that. We're smart people—we can do it. Then we can present a united front. We have to, otherwise Logan will play us against each other."

"I agree."

His gaze softened and strayed down to her lips. He drew infinitesimally closer—

And turned back to the door.

"Right. See you Friday."

And he was gone.

ELIANA'S SCARED FACE peered at Marcos through his phone screen.

"What's wrong?" she asked. "Is Mom okay? Is the ranch on fire again?"

He frowned. "No. Nothing's wrong. Why would you think that?"

"Because you're FaceTiming me. You've never FaceTimed me in your life."

Marcos shrugged. "That doesn't mean something has to be wrong. I just need you to do something for me."

"And you have to FaceTime me to ask? The last time you asked me to do you a favor, it was to shut up and drive."

"Yeah. And you did great at that! But this time it's something different." He took a deep breath. "I need you to take me shopping. I have a date."

For several seconds she didn't speak or move.

"Hello?" Marcos said. "Are you there? Is my screen frozen?"

Then Eliana's mouth fell open in an O and her eyes filled with tears.

"Are you *crying*? Ana, what the heck?"

The image in his screen fluttered and bounced in time with some thunking sounds. Eliana had dropped her phone, and she was squealing. Marcos sighed, then smiled.

Eliana's face appeared in the screen again, shining with joy.

"Oh, Marcos! I'm so glad. You and Nina are *perfect* for each other!"

"I didn't say it was Nina."

"Don't be silly. Of course it's Nina."

Yes. Of course it was Nina.

"So when's the big day? We have to plan. Do you want me to come over?"

"Come over? Now? It's ten o'clock at night."

"I don't mind. There's not a moment to lose. We've got a lot of planning to do. Successful dates don't just happen, Marcos."

He started to reply that his first date with Nina just happened, without any real planning, but Eliana would just point out that it hadn't exactly ended on a high note, with him curtly dropping her off afterward, and Dalia would say it hadn't technically been a "date" at all.

"We have until Friday," he said. "I just wanted to get ahold of you tonight before you went to bed so you could pencil me in."

She smiled. "No, you didn't. You called because you wanted to celebrate, but you didn't know how, and you knew I'd do it for you."

She wasn't wrong. He liked seeing her excited. It gave him the feeling that maybe he could do this. He'd messed up plenty in the past, but he was on the right track now, and it felt good. Maybe it wasn't too late.

CHAPTER TWENTY-TWO

MARCOS SHOWED UP at six o'clock on the dot, looking jaw-droppingly gorgeous in a beautifully cut indigo-colored shirt, dark jeans that hugged him just right and black boots—and carrying a dinosaur gift bag. He always looked good, but usually in an accidental sort of way. It gave Nina a sweet pang to see him so polished and spiffy and a bit nervous, like he was on a job interview.

His gaze traveled down her dress, a little spaghetti-strap number with a ruffled skirt that ended just above the knee, and back up again. Nina loved that dress. She'd done a lot of twirling in front of the mirror while getting ready. Judging from Marcos's smile, he liked it too.

Behind her, the oven chimed, and she realized she was keeping Marcos waiting at the doorway.

"Come in," she said. "I'm almost ready."

His boots thumped on the hardwood floor as he followed her.

The babysitter was sitting at the sofa, her books and notes spread over the coffee table. Marcos walked over to her, his best-foot-forward look still very much in evidence.

"I'm Marcos," he said. "Logan's father."

Nina's eyes prickled at the sight of a man, ordinarily reserved to the point of sullenness, now determined to make a good impression on the babysitter. That, and the pride in the words *Logan's father*.

As he got a good look at her, recognition dawned in his face. "Wait. Do I know you?"

She gave him an apologetic smile. "I'm Tabitha. I think you met my sister Chloe. She used to babysit Logan."

"The makeup vlogger?" Marcos sounded truly startled.

"The same," Tabitha said.

"Tabitha is studying to be an engineer," Nina said from the kitchen. "She and Logan really hit it off."

She slid a foil-covered casserole dish into the oven and set the timer.

"Dinner will be ready in twenty minutes," she told the babysitter. "Make sure Logan puts up his Legos before bed. In-process creations don't have to be taken apart, but no loose bricks left on the floor."

Marcos nodded in approval. "Good policy. No one wants to step on a stray Lego."

Logan came out of his room, clutching a Lego creation in one hand and a *Parasaurolophus* in the other. He eyeballed Marcos and said, "Hey."

"Hey," Marcos said. "I have something for you."

Logan took the bag and plopped right down on the floor with it.

"That's a great gift bag," Nina said.

"It's seen a lot of use," said Marcos. "Just about every birthday of my childhood, I got one of my presents in this bag."

Logan pulled out the tissue paper, reached inside the bag, and drew out—

"Books," Nina said brightly. Logan didn't say anything at all, just pulled them out one by one and set them on the floor in a pile, not even looking at the covers, like he was getting them out of the way to find the erector set that must be hiding in the bottom of the bag. Then he turned the empty bag upside down and shook it. Nothing more came out.

Marcos crouched down beside him. "I

know you're not crazy about books," he said. "But these are special."

He picked up one of them. "See this? It's called *The Way Things Work*."

Logan gave him a suspicious look. "What things?"

"Lots of things. Can openers, zippers, pianos. Windmills. Batteries. The internet. See this woolly mammoth? He's part of everything that happens in the book. The people want to find a way to wash the mammoth, or pick him up or make him fly. And the book shows how you could do all that with real machines."

"David Macaulay rocks," said Tabitha from the sofa, fist lifted high.

"I know, right?" said Marcos. "This next book is by the same guy. It's called *Underground*. It tells about all the tunnels and pipes and columns and things that go underneath a city."

"For real?" Logan asked.

"For real. And this…" He opened the third book. "This one is about a great big American river called the Mississippi. It's over two thousand miles long, and it runs through ten different states, through mountains and forests and cities and swamps. See this turtle?

She hatches out of her egg at the headwaters—that's the river's starting place—and travels all the way down to where it empties into the Gulf of Mexico. She sees a lot of other animals and people, and lives on a steamboat for a while, and even finds some pirate treasure."

Logan flipped through and pointed at a picture. "What's this?"

"Those are locks and dams. Machines that keep the river from flooding."

Nina came closer to take a look. The book had the big, flat dimensions of a children's picture story book, but with smaller type and more text. The wide margins were filled with unbelievably detailed illustrations of animals, maps and machinery, intricately labeled in neat, hand-printed all caps.

"This book is beautiful," she said.

Marcos smiled. Then he looked at Logan, and his expression turned serious.

"My mother, your grandmother, gave me these books," he said. "She kept them safe for me after I grew up and went away. Now they're yours."

Logan didn't even look up from the page. He sat there, cross-legged on the floor, drinking in the pictures, with the same absorbed fascination he typically gave to machinery.

"Logan," Nina prompted him.

"Thanks," he said.

"Logan."

"Thank you," he amended, still not raising his head.

Before Nina could correct him further, Marcos held up a hand to her and shook his head.

"This reaction is thanks enough," he said. To Logan he said, "You're welcome. I'll see you later, bud."

"Yeah, g'bye," said Logan.

Outside, Marcos's truck gleamed in freshly washed splendor, dwarfing Nina's RAV-4. He went around to the passenger side and opened Nina's door for her, getting there fast without appearing to hurry. It was a small gesture, but it made her feel precious and cherished.

"So what's the plan for tonight?" she asked after he got in and shut the door. "Or is there a plan?"

He turned and faced her, suddenly all business. "Oh, there's a plan, all right. We will proceed to the Huisache Grill, where a reservation has been made for eighteen thirty. During the interim between our arrival and the designated time, we will remain in the outdoor seating area, or alternatively visit any or all of the boutiques within easy walking distance. Following dinner, we will stroll to downtown New Braunfels for possible shopping in various antique and gift shops."

"Great!" said Nina. "Is there a DOD seal on that memorandum? Can I get a hard copy? Did you follow the six-step Marine Corps Planning Process?"

Marcos smiled as he started the ignition. "The itinerary was framed based on input from a consultant."

"Let me guess. Eliana?"

"Yeah. She's surprisingly astute for someone who used to sneak behind the sofa to nibble on cupcake-scented Play-Doh."

"Did she tell you about the man she's started seeing?"

"Yeah. *Rinaldo.*" Marcos rolled his eyes. "Where does she even *find* these guys?"

Nina knew where Eliana had found this one—on Tinder. But she kept that to herself. "He sounds nice. Eliana said maybe the four of us could go out together some night."

"Ha! Never. It won't last long enough for that. I mean Eliana's thing won't last, not—" He pointed vaguely back and forth between Nina and himself. "She's had more boyfriends than I can count, and you know how many I've had a chance to meet and intimidate? Zero. They're all gone before she gets to the point of wanting to bring them home. I'd like to meet and intimidate them too. I'd be good at it."

"You'd be brilliant at it. Well, I'm sure you'll get your chance. Eliana's only twenty-six. She's bound to settle down at some point."

He gave her a doubtful look. "We'll see."

He turned in to a lot off San Antonio Street, parked alongside a wooden fence, checked his watch and nodded in satisfaction. The restaurant was tucked away behind some shops. Asian jasmine covered much of the building's front, giving it a cozy, grotto-like appearance.

Marcos led Nina around the side to the back entrance. A big, gracious patio with a fire pit and a winged-pig statue blended into outdoor seating and a small village of tiny boutiques.

"Shop, or sit?" Marcos asked.

"Shop," Nina said.

She loved cozy little boutiques filled with lovely items from designers she'd never heard of, though most of her clothes and Logan's came from big box stores.

The very first place they visited had an adorable pair of cowboy boots—soft, supple brown leather, embellished with embroidered leaves and vines in ivory thread with pops of turquoise.

Marcos saw her staring. "You like those?"

"They're adorable."

"Then you should have them."

She shook her head. She'd taken a peek at the price and there was no way she was spending that much for footwear. "I already have a pair of cowboy boots."

"Those are work boots. These are for dancing. If you're going to live in Texas you need boots for all occasions. Dress boots, work boots, riding boots, dancing boots. My dad had one pair just for weddings and funerals. You could wear these with that dress you have on right now."

"I don't know. I'm not sure I could pull off that look."

"Sure you could. Try them on."

She sat down and kicked off her mules. She'd never been one for fancy shoes, especially high heels. She couldn't think straight with cramped toes, and Logan kept her way too busy to sacrifice practicality for style. Eliana always wore elegant shoes that looked like they would pinch but that she claimed were perfectly comfortable. Quality like that cost more than Nina was willing to pay. She usually settled for cheap flats that wore out quickly and got replaced with more cheap flats. Now that she took a good look at them, her mules were getting pretty worn.

A salesgirl handed her a pair of socks. Nina pulled them on and slid her feet into the boots. They felt solid, sturdy, durable. She could see the craftsmanship in the stitching, the molding of the upper, the shape of the sole. And that leather scent! No wonder people got so attached to their boots.

Marcos was watching her. "How do they feel?"

She stood and walked around, then looked at herself in the full-length mirror. Wow. The boots gave the dress a punch that she never would have predicted.

"They feel perfect," she said honestly.

He had his wallet out before she could say another word.

"You don't have to—" she began.

"I'm getting them," he said.

"But I really don't need—"

He held up an imperious palm. "Nina, let me take care of you."

The salesgirl gave Nina a quick, secret smile.

"Would you like to wear them out of the

store?" she asked. "I can cut the tag off for you."

By the time Marcos returned from taking the box holding Nina's flats out to the truck, it was time for them to be seated.

There was something luxurious in being taken care of. In the gentle pressure of Marcos's hand at the small of her back as they were being shown to their table. In the way he pulled the chair out for her. In his gentle urging for her to have a glass of wine, though he himself had given up alcohol.

The Huisache was as beautiful inside as outside—cottage-like, rustic and elegant, with rooms opening unexpectedly out of other rooms, and lots of odd spaces gracefully fitted up with weathered siding and bits of architectural salvage. Their table was in the main room, which was furnished with old draw-leaf tables, similar but not matching; a crystal chandelier hung from one of the exposed beams in the cathedral ceiling.

Every sight her eyes rested on was a fresh source of delight—including the man across the table from her.

She thought she might be too excited to eat, but the aromas from the kitchen quickly changed her mind. It felt strange and wonderful to drink wine and order from a menu that featured words such as *brie*, *portobello*, *tenderloin* and *charcuterie*.

"I'd forgotten how much I like grown-up food," she said over grilled duck breast and herbed baby potatoes.

Marcos took a bite of beef medallion and shut his eyes. "Man. I'm glad beef isn't one of the things that set my ulcer off."

After dinner, they strolled through a downtown filled with neat businesses in old buildings—a hardware store, some more fancy-looking boutiques, a performing arts theater, and an old-fashioned barber shop with gold paint on the windows and an actual spinning barber pole. The shops were closed, but it was fun to look in the windows. Then Marcos took her to the Faust Street Bridge, a historic truss bridge that spanned the Guadalupe River.

"Didn't I see a Faust Hotel in New Braunfels?" Nina asked.

"Yeah, there's a heavy German influence in this area."

"My grandparents on my father's side were German—the ones who lived in this area. I called them Oma and Opa. I loved their little white farmhouse with its ramshackle barn and split-rail fences. I called it a farm. Really it was just ten acres or so. I was ten before I even knew I had any living grandparents on that side. They knew about me, though, and they were desperate to meet me. I was their only grandchild. But my mom kept me away from them."

"Why'd she do that?"

"I honestly don't know. I don't know what they ever did to her. But she held a grudge for some reason. Once I found out they existed, she made them out to be ignorant rednecks. I didn't know what to expect when I finally went to see them for the first time, but they turned out to be these good, wise, sturdy country folks. They had a horse named Starlet, a strawberry roan with a white marking on her forehead in the shape of a heart. She had the sweetest face, and the sweetest disposition. Opa put me on her back and led me around, that first year. He said he'd teach me to ride the next year, but he had his stroke and Starlet got sold." She sighed. "I wish I'd had more time with them."

"That's awful that your mom kept you away from them. My grandparents lived right in town—well, my dad's parents lived on the ranch until I was five. Then they turned the ranch over to my parents, retired and moved to town. We used to have holidays with both sides of the family, all of us together. I never thought about it at the time, but I see now how special it was. Not only parents with an intact marriage, but both sets of grandparents too."

He talked about camping trips he'd gone on with his mother's father and his cousins, places he wanted to take Nina. Enchanted Rock. The Davis Mountains. The Llano Estacado. Caddo Lake. He wanted to take her hiking, diving, caving, parasailing.

"I used to want to see the world," he said. "Now I just want to go travel around my home state, with you."

The bright green water sparkled in the setting sun and rushed over a shallow waterfall that gave it furrows like comb marks. The trees seemed to glow with a golden light, casting long shadows over the river.

"Want to go down to the shore?" Marcos asked.

"All right."

He'd hardly touched her all evening. Now he took her arm to help her down the slope to the water's edge. They both took off their boots and socks. Marcos folded up the legs of his jeans, gave the cuffs of his sleeves another couple of turns and undid the third button of his shirt, revealing a broad triangle of lean, muscular chest.

They waded into the cool, smooth water for a while, and then Marcos went back to the shore and skipped stones. Nina watched from behind. He was deadly serious about the whole thing, choosing his stones with care, planting his feet apart in a broad stance with his left side toward the water and his knees bent and staring out over the water for a long still moment. Then all at once his wrist cocked and his arm whipped around as his body spun into a deep lunge, the fabric of his shirt caught in a sudden tight twist from shoulders to waist. She didn't keep track of the number of skips; she was too preoccupied by the crisp outline of his form against the twilit sky and the knotting of his calf muscles. Even his Achilles tendons were a thing to be gazed at and treasured.

"Your hair is in those spirals again," he said, making a spinning motion near his face with one hand. "I like it. I like it straight too. But the way it is now—that's how you had it at the Gristmill."

"Yes. I'm surprised you noticed. You barely looked at me that entire evening."

"I might not have made much eye contact, but believe me, I looked. Under the circumstances, I wasn't in a good position to flirt."

"I've got news for you, Marcos. You're not much of a flirt under any circumstances."

He smiled. "That's true. I'm too direct. I either keep it all inside or just say what I want."

She stepped closer to him. "And what do you want now?"

He stood a long moment facing her, with that sober mouth and those intent green-flecked eyes.

"I want to kiss you," he said.

"Well, what's stopping you?"

He cupped her face in his hands and lowered his mouth to hers.

And suddenly the restraint that had kept him on a tight rein all evening was—not gone, but drawn back. He was kissing her like there was no tomorrow, his mouth eager and searching, his arms fully enveloping her, pressing her to him. The past and its pain, the memory of his rejection and all those lonely years without him, vanished like smoke. There was only now, and that was all she needed.

She held tight to the warm, solid mass of him, ran her hands along the rippling muscles of his back, the velvet of his close-cut hair. He smelled of pine, woodsy and sharp and clean.

He pulled back and looked down at her, his lips parted, his eyes full of a yearning that was half pain. She could feel his breathing, shallow and rapid in his chest, and hear her own pounding pulse.

Then he kissed her again, more deeply than before.

"I missed you, Nina," he said. "I missed you so much. Don't ever go away."

The little niggling voice that had been telling her all evening that she'd better keep her head on straight because Marcos had done her wrong before reminded her now that she hadn't been the one to leave in the first place.

But she only said, "Never," before circling the back of his neck with her hand and pulling his face back down to hers.

What stopped them was an alarm going off on his watch. They ignored it at first, but it kept going, sharp and insistent. Finally he took her arms in his hands—gently, his thumbs rubbing her skin—and rested his forehead against hers.

He let out a sigh. "Well, that's it," he said. "It's time."

"Time? Time for what?"

"For me to take you home."

Silence. Then, "You set an alarm to take me home? What, do I have a curfew?"

He pushed her gently away from him and let go. It felt like part of her had been ripped away.

"I told you. I want to do things right this time."

She ought to be pleased, she supposed. He was being responsible, showing self-control. She watched him walk away.

Then he whirled back around, took her by the shoulders and kissed her again.

And tore himself away a second time.

"I STILL CAN'T BELIEVE you actually set your alarm," Nina said on the way home.

Marcos stole a glance at her profile—rounded forehead, short straight nose, firm chin—silhouetted against the passenger-side window. Those spiral curls were rumpled now from his hands, and she was smiling.

"I couldn't leave it to chance," he said. "Couldn't trust myself enough for that."

He walked her inside the house and stood there holding his truck keys while Tabitha gave her report. He had a dim sense that he ought to be paying more attention to what the babysitter was saying—he was Logan's father, after all—but all he could think of was Nina in his arms, her lips against his.

"Would you like a cup of tea?" Nina asked after Tabitha left.

He shook his head. He'd planned this part in advance. He'd resolved that he wouldn't even sit down.

"Will you come to Sunday dinner at La Escarpa?" he asked.

"I'd love to. That's a lot of days away, though. Will I see you before then?"

A wave of pleasure stirred in him.

"I'm free in the evenings. Can Tabitha watch Logan again?"

"Probably. I only wish she had better daytime availability. I still haven't found a permanent babysitter for when I'm at work. I have someone for tomorrow, but that's it."

He thought a moment. "How about me?"

She looked at him. "Seriously?"

"Sure, why not? He can come out to La Escarpa when I'm working there. I have a section of fence I have to put up. It's something he can help with, and he'd like it. He'd like seeing the come-along and how it works. My dad and I strung many a mile of fence together when I wasn't any older than he is."

"You're sure he won't be in the way?"

"I'm sure."

Another kiss on the front porch of her house, and he was off like a shot. He was fighting every instinct he had, but he was winning the fight. He'd dropped his girl off in good time, kept his impulses in check.

He could do this. He had to. Had to prove himself to her, win her back. He couldn't mess up again.

CHAPTER TWENTY-THREE

EVERYTHING IN MARCOS'S life that summer was good, and getting better. Five months after the perforated ulcer incident, he was finally back in top physical form. He had a nice place to live, private and quiet. He was on good terms with his family and enjoying ranch work more than he would have thought possible twelve years ago. His financial situation, while not all it should be, was okay, and improving.

Best of all, he had an amazing woman in his life, who happened to be the mother of his child; he was crazy about her, and for some reason she seemed to be crazy about him too.

He was consumed by her. She was his first thought on waking and his last at night, and wove her way through all the thoughts in between. He called just to hear her voice and sent her texts throughout the day. Every time he saw her or talked to her he kept thinking the whole thing was too good to be true—

she was going to get tired of him, but she always seemed happy and excited to see him or hear from him. It seemed unbelievable that she could feel about him the way he felt about her, but it appeared to be true.

He loved her sleek hair, her stubborn chin, her fearless blue eyes; loved how strong, capable and downright forcible she was, and at the same time so feminine, so nurturing to him and Logan. He loved the way her curves fit against him, soft but firm, here in the oversize wooden chair on the front porch of the bunkhouse.

Nina had cooked dinner at his place that evening, and now he felt sleepy and content and full of good food. There seemed no limit to the number of wonderful things Germans could do with potatoes. The July day had been a scorcher, but now a cool breeze was taking the edge off. It stirred the grasses that shone with sunlight out in the northwest pasture.

"Logan, what are you doing over there?" Nina asked.

Logan looked from his mother to the hole he'd excavated with the old Smith & Hawken garden spade, and back again. "Digging," he said.

"Ask a silly question," Marcos murmured into her hair as he kissed the top of her head.

Nina chuckled. "I see that you're digging. Why are you doing it?"

"I want to find a spur."

"Oh? What makes you think you're going to find a spur buried over there in the dirt?"

"Because I already found another spur before dinner."

"Oh yeah?" Marcos held out his hand. "Let's see it."

Logan handed him a rusted U-shaped object with a shank sticking out of the curve and a roughly star-shaped object attached to the shank.

"Yep," he said. "That's a spur, all right."

"How about that?" said Nina. "I wonder how old it is."

"Alex might be able to figure it out."

"We can fix it up again, right, Dad?" Logan asked.

Being called Dad still gave Marcos a rush. No one had told Logan to do it. He'd just started one day all on his own.

Marcos handed the spur back to him.

"I don't know, bud," he said. "We can get some of the rust off for sure with a mild acid.

But I don't know how good of shape it'll turn out to be in underneath. We'll do what we can."

"Bull riders wear spurs, right?"

"They sure do."

Logan was on a cowboy kick. The day before, Tony and Marcos had taken him out to Mr. Mendoza's place for some time on Brush Hog. After the men had their turn, Mr. Mendoza put the bull on an easy setting and let Logan give it a try. Marcos loved riding the mechanical bull, but he loved to watch his son even more.

"Whoa," Mr. Mendoza had said to Logan. "Have you done this before?"

"No," Logan had said.

"Are you sure? You're not a secret bull-riding champion?"

"No."

"Well then, I guess you're just a natural. You've got rhythm and nerve, and you're strong."

Mr. Mendoza had gone on in that vein for a while, bragging on Logan, before turning to Marcos and saying, "You got yourself a fine ranch hand here."

And something inside Marcos had gone cold and tense.

He knew now, in a way that hadn't been possible before, just how proud of him his own father had been. When he imagined Logan turning into a surly teenager, talking to Marcos the way Marcos had talked to Martin—

Well, he wouldn't think about that. For now, Logan loved the ranch and all things cowboy. After the trip to Mr. Mendoza's to ride Brush Hog, Marcos's mother had found his old chaps for Logan to wear. They were a little big, but he'd worn them the next day when Marcos took him for a ride all the way around the boundary line of La Escarpa. Marcos had liked watching the solemn respect in his son's face grow as the ranch went on and on and on, and Logan slowly began to comprehend just how big it was.

There was no reason for that respect to ever turn sour. Logan would have no cause to feel trapped here the way Marcos had. This was just a temporary stop, until Marcos figured out something else to do for a living. Just what that might turn out to be, he didn't know. But he had an idea or two.

He hadn't talked to Nina about any of this. He was still thinking it through. He wasn't going to come to her with some half-baked scheme.

Nina laid her head on Marcos's chest, her

glossy hair fanning over his shirt, and started running her fingertips lazily up and down his forearm, sending tingles throughout his body. "Eliana's been telling me about the Persimmon Fest. She's going to ride on the float with this year's Persimmon Queen and court. She said she still has her dress and tiara and sash from when she was queen."

Marcos chuckled. "Of course she does."

"She said there'll be live music at the Persimmon Pavilion. Lots of local bands."

"Mmm-hmm."

"And carnival rides and festival food and craft booths and…"

He took hold of her chin and raised her head. "Baby, do you want me to take you to the Persimmon Fest?"

"Yes," she said shyly.

"Then I will."

She snuggled against him excitedly. "Oh, thank you! Thank you!"

He chuckled. "You might want to save your thanks until you get there. It's not that big a deal—just a small-town agricultural festival like a million others across the south. This one happens to have a guy dressed up as a persimmon frolicking around, instead of a watermelon or a pecan or a cotton boll."

"But this one *is* special, because it's ours."

"If you say so," Marcos said.

He'd loved the Persimmon Fest when he was little, scoffed at it when he got a little older and stopped thinking about it at all after he went away. But if Nina wanted to go, they'd go. It might actually be fun to see the thing through her and Logan's eyes.

Nina took a deep breath, held it a second and let it out slowly. Marcos recognized that move. It was her about-to-go-home sigh. He tightened his arm around her shoulders, wishing he could keep her here, but she sat up anyway.

"All right, Logan," she said. "Time to put the shovel away and wash up. We've got to head home."

Logan kept digging.

"Logan," Nina said.

"I don't want to."

"You heard your mother," said Marcos.

With a quick "Yes, Dad," Logan set the shovel against the porch and skedaddled inside the bunkhouse.

"Wow," said Nina after the front door shut behind him. "Did you see what just happened here? Do you have any idea how incredibly attractive you are to me at this moment?"

"Mmm, what?" said Marcos. He was thinking about the curve of Nina's calves and pretty little ankles drawn up over his thighs.

"The way you did that just now. And you weren't even *trying*. That male voice just gets a different reaction somehow. I mean, I'm not exactly a pushover myself. But things he balks at coming from me, when *you* tell him to do them, he snaps to attention and gets them done without question or comment."

"Does he? Well, you're a strong disciplinarian yourself, and great at things that I don't have a clue about. So I guess we balance each other out."

"I guess we do. It's so restful, having you around."

"It's pretty nice having you around too. Both of you."

She uncurled her legs and started to get up. Marcos gently pulled her back down, and she gladly gave in.

"Kiss me," he said.

She smiled at him and laid a hand against his cheek. Her touch was so soft and light that it made a shiver pass through him. Then she slid her hand around the back of his neck and lowered her face to his. Her hair came down like a curtain and tickled his neck. He reached up to meet her lips. Her mouth tasted sweet, like apples.

"I don't want you to go," he murmured.

"I have to."

"I know. But I don't like it. I don't like saying goodbye to you all the time. I want to say good-night instead. I want you to be there when I wake up. I'm not going to pressure you to stay—I don't mean that. I just... I'm looking forward to things being different."

It was the most commitment-like thing he had said since they got back together. It didn't express half of what he felt, or meant. But judging from the look in her eyes, a sort of soft delight, she understood.

Then, to prove to her that he wouldn't pressure her to stay, he gathered her up in his arms, got to his feet, stood there long enough to show her how light her weight was to him and set her down.

Back in the house, as he helped her collect Logan's things, he said, "I want to take you to Tito's some night this week."

"That bar?"

"Yeah, but it's not a *bar* bar. It has a restaurant right next door with just a pass-through in between, and board games that kids can play. It's a very family-friendly place."

"You want Logan to come too?"

"Oh, yeah. I want to show both of you off to people I went to school with."

"I'd love that," Nina said. "It would be a good chance for me to catch up to Logan. Between bull-riding at the Mendozas' place and the days he's spent in the quilt shop, he's already met half the town."

Marcos had kept Logan almost every day this week while Nina was at work. On days when he'd worked for Mr. Mendoza, he'd dropped Logan off at the quilting and knitting shop with his mother. Renée had proudly introduced him to every customer who'd come through the door.

"Have you seen his scarf?" Marcos asked. His mother had started Logan on a knitting project.

"No, but I heard about it. I wondered how you felt about your son knitting."

"I feel fine about it. Sailors and Marines used to knit. They sewed too. They were so isolated on their ships for months at a time that it made sense for them to make and take care of their own clothing. My mom taught me to knit when I was younger than Logan. I was good too."

Nina smiled and kissed him. "You are full of surprises."

The bunkhouse seemed dark and empty after Nina and Logan drove away. Marcos had to find a way for them to be together. Enough income, a bigger house—he'd make it happen. He had to.

NINA SIPPED HER craft beer and checked out Marcos from a distance, admiring the fit of his jeans and his strong, straight posture. He was standing at the bar while Mr. Mendoza told a story to another man, nodding whenever Mr. Mendoza looked at him for confirmation. Three of the Mendoza brothers listened, grinning, and putting in their two cents' worth once in a while.

Marcos's lips were slightly turned up at the corners, which for him was a big emotional display, at least in public. No one watching him now could possibly imagine the other side of him, the one that sent Nina goofy, affectionate texts all day. It was a privilege that she alone enjoyed.

Marcos was right—this *was* a nice place. The atmosphere was jovial but not rowdy, probably because people willing to pay eight dollars for a locally-brewed beer weren't generally looking to get drunk. They wanted to relax, socialize, savor the beer and the company. So many friendly people, interested in her and Logan—there was no way she would be able to remember all their names, but at least she'd made a start. Apparently everyone in town wanted to meet the mother of Marcos Ramirez's secret child.

"Nina?"

A woman stood across the table, holding a glass of something purplish. She had a sheaf of dark hair over one shoulder, a sweet smile and big, soulful eyes.

"Annalisa! Have a seat. What are you drinking?"

Annalisa sat down and took a sip. "Blackberry mead. It's delicious—you should try it. Is your little boy here?"

"Yes. Right over there, playing Jenga."

"Aw! He and Marcos have father-son haircuts."

She gave Nina a sly glance. Nina felt herself blushing.

"I'm happy for you, Nina," Annalisa said. "It's sweet that you're back together after all these years."

"I think so too."

"I heard Marcos is living in the bunkhouse now?"

"That's right. Oh, and I read your book! I loved it. There's a copy of it at the bunkhouse. Only fitting, after how it got Alex and Lauren together."

"Good! I heard Alex and Lauren did a fantastic job fixing the place up."

"They did."

It was the sort of house that seemed to belong exactly to its location, like an organic part of the environment. All the stuff along the hallway wall that had been found in the building before the restoration, or excavated from outside—the big metal *R* that no one could explain the origin of, the rusted gear thing—looked exactly right and at home, along with the ornate wall sconce Lauren had found at an architectural salvage place in town. The crude, sixties-era fireplace had been antiqued with a German smear and topped with a mantel made out of a mesquite tree that used to grow in the goat pen on La Escarpa. If the rusted old spurs that Logan had unearthed couldn't be restored enough to be functional again, they'd look great on that hallway wall. Then Logan would be part of the history of the place, just as Alex and Lauren were.

Yesterday, Marcos had moved his own old Legos to the bunkhouse—for Logan to play with, he'd said, though he seemed to be getting a lot of use out of them himself. He and Logan had plans for making a Lego castle together—not a castle from a kit, but a model of an actual Welsh castle. When Nina asked how they would handle the curves for the towers, Marcos gave a complicated answer that she didn't quite follow but that convinced her that they could pull it off. She loved hearing him and Logan talk about it, this big, engrossing project that she was absolutely not responsible for. Marcos had set aside the second bedroom for Lego storage; he called it Logan's room. Whenever Nina heard those words, she thought of how it really would be Logan's room after she and Marcos got married. The lease on her rental house was only for six months. It made sense for her and Logan to move to the bunkhouse. Nina's work commute would be longer, but not by much, and Marcos's work and family were right there.

Whenever she thought of these things, that voice in her head told her to slow down and not get her hopes up. It was too early to be thinking of marriage, especially given their track record. She wanted to believe that this time, the voice was wrong. True, she and Marcos weren't actually engaged; he hadn't even told her he loved her yet. But what he'd said that evening about wanting her to be there when he woke up—what else could it mean? He wanted the three of them there, in that house, as a family.

The house was small, but big enough for a man, a woman and a child. Alex and Lauren had made it work. So could Marcos and Nina. Her reproduction Spanish colonial dining table would look perfect in the eat-in kitchen, and Logan's beanbag chair would fit nicely in that corner of his room by the window.

The crowd at the bar gave a roar of laughter as Mr. Mendoza clapped Marcos on the shoulder. From behind the bar, Tito, the baby of the Mendoza family, said, "You'd better hope the Department of Labor doesn't get wind of your occupational procedures, there, Dad."

Annalisa glanced over. "Mr. Mendoza must be telling the story about how he sent Marcos up in the scoop of the dozer to saw the top branches off that hackberry tree."

"Yes, with the chainsaw-on-a-pole tool.

Marcos said he got 'voluntold' for that job because he's the tallest."

Mr. Mendoza had called Marcos over a few minutes ago to tell the story but had ended up doing most of the talking himself. Nina suspected that Marcos was just there to verify that Mr. Mendoza wasn't exaggerating. Apparently the story had already gotten around.

"I guess you went to school with Tito?" Nina asked Annalisa.

"Yes, and his brother Javi."

"Javi's the one who went west to work in the oil fields, right?"

"That's right." Annalisa's smile turned wistful. "He's making good money, but I wish he'd come home. It's rough, dangerous work, and those oil towns are full of rough, dangerous men. It's not a good scene."

"I can imagine. Like Gold Rush towns in California. Places that don't have any women or children living in them tend to be places where men don't show much restraint."

"Yes, and some men like it that way. But Javi…" She sighed. "Well, I just wish he'd come home."

"Maybe he will," Nina said.

"Maybe. Marcos did, and he swore he'd

never be back. And I guess you did, too, in a way."

"It was my grandparents who lived here, not me. And I only ever visited them a few times as a kid. But I did love it—partly because I was never strongly tied to a place myself. I moved around a lot growing up."

"Have you been to your grandparents' place since you moved?"

"What's left of it. It was sold years ago, and the new owners knocked down the house and built a new one in a different spot. I couldn't even tell where the windmill and the garden and everything used to be. It's like it's all been erased."

"That makes me sad."

"Me too. There's something profound about a place like La Escarpa, where the same family has lived for almost two centuries. Plus, practically speaking, it's great to have all that *space*. The other day Logan asked Marcos to tell him about what he did in the Marine Corps. Marcos started explaining artillery to him, one thing led to another and now they're planning to make trebuchets in the northwest pasture. You can't do *that* on a town lot."

Annalisa laughed. "No, you sure can't."

From the next room, someone called Annalisa's name. She turned and waved.

"I've got to go. I'll see you at our next salon appointment."

She'd barely vacated her seat when Eliana showed up, immaculately pretty in a turquoise sheath dress. She gave Nina a light, floral-scented hug and sat on the bench beside her.

"I like your boots," Eliana said. "Are they new?"

"Yes. Marcos bought them for me."

"Good for him. Now he needs to take you dancing in them. There are so many nice old dance halls around here. We should all go."

"That would be fun! We could finally meet Rinaldo."

Eliana waved a hand dismissively. "Oh, that's over. Turned out he didn't like cats—as in, he actively disliked them. Can you imagine? I don't need that kind of negativity in my life, so I ended it."

"Oh," Nina said. She didn't know what else to say.

Eliana was watching her. "You don't think I'm flaky, do you, Nina?"

"No," Nina said truthfully. "I don't know that disliking cats would be a deal breaker for me personally, but who am I to talk? I went nearly eight years without a date, only to get back together with my ex."

"That's because you two were clearly made for each other. It was meant to be. I love stories like that. But what's *my* story going to be? I see the way Dalia looks at me. She's afraid there's something wrong with me that I can't choose a man and settle down, and maybe she's right. Maybe I'm just terminally flaky."

"You're not flaky," Nina said. "You're attractive enough to get asked out a lot, pragmatic enough to end a relationship that you know is doomed and optimistic enough to keep trying."

Eliana brightened. "That's a lovely thing to say. Well, I know one thing I've done right, anyway—getting you and Marcos back together. It was a genius move—and I wasn't even trying to matchmake! Maybe I have an instinct for getting the right people together. I just haven't learned to do it for myself."

She leaned over to look across the passthrough. "Speaking of which. A friend of mine had a date last night, and I need to find out how it went. You and Logan are coming to Sunday dinner at La Escarpa, right?"

"Right."

Marcos came back to the table, slid his arm around Nina and dropped a kiss on her cheek. "Hey, baby. You miss me? Hi, Ana."

Eliana tilted her head and smiled at the two of them as if they were a work of art. "You two are so beautiful together. You ought to make more babies. Okay, bye now!"

Nina felt her face flush. She'd been thinking more or less the same thing for a while now, though she hadn't put it into words. But Marcos looked startled.

"Where did *that* come from?" he asked.

"Oh, just Eliana being Eliana. Who's that guy she's talking to?"

"Behind the counter? That's the Mahan kid. He works here."

Was he the friend whose date Eliana wanted to check on? Interesting.

"He's cute," Nina said.

Marcos gave her a look. "What do you mean, *cute*?"

"Handsome and appealing in an innocent sort of way. Looks about eighteen, though."

"He's a good bit older than that. Just a couple of years behind Eliana in school."

"Is he? Well, now."

"Well now, what?"

"Oh, nothing. Just wondering if maybe there's a little something there."

"Between Luke Mahan and Eliana? Nah. Luke is like the whole town's kid brother. He lost his father in an industrial accident when he was young. Terrible thing. Everyone sort of got in the habit of looking out for him. He's a likable kid, and Eliana likes taking care of people. And bossing them around. That's all that is."

Nina wasn't so sure. Luke certainly didn't look like Eliana's type—he was the ultimate boy next door, not the least bit sophisticated—but there did seem to be a spark between them.

"Marcos?" said a voice behind them.

They turned and saw Keith Randall standing there with a beer stein in his hand.

"And *Nina*?" he added. "Well, now. Suddenly a whole lot of things are starting to make sense."

Marcos stood and shook Keith's hand. "Hey, Keith. It's been a while."

"Yeah, a few weeks now. Guess you've been busy."

He and Nina smiled at each other.

"Yeah, I've been meaning to call," Marcos said, "but I've had a lot going on. There is something I've been wanting to talk to you about, though, if you can spare a minute."

"Sure," Keith said.

He started to set his beer down on the table, but Marcos was already headed for the front door.

"Good to see you, Nina," Keith said as he followed Marcos outside.

Well, that was…odd. Why did Marcos want to talk to Keith alone? What could he have to say to him that couldn't be said in front of Nina? Keith was his mentor…but Nina was his girlfriend.

Don't be like that. Of course there are things he's more comfortable talking over with another veteran. That's why we got him a mentor in the first place.

Still, it bothered her. What was Marcos telling Keith? And why couldn't he tell her?

"So, YOU AND NINA," Keith said. "When did that start up?"

"It's a long story," Marcos said.

"Give me the abridged version."

"Okay. Nina and I were briefly married years ago. I'm her child's father but I didn't know it until earlier this month. Now we're back together and I want to marry her."

"Oh, I *see*," Keith said. "Wow. You really *have* been busy."

"Yeah. I'm seeing Nina and Logan every chance I get, and working my two jobs. The land-clearing work is about finished. I can probably stay on at the ranch a while, but I need to find something I can do long term. What about what you do, surveying? It seems like interesting work—technical, physical, outdoors. Is it something I could learn to do?"

"I'm sure you could. You would need a degree, though. Two-year, preferably four."

Marcos lowered his head and rubbed the back of his neck. "Ah. I see."

"You could handle the coursework," Keith said.

"Maybe. But the idea of being back in a classroom—" He shuddered. "Not to mention navigating the GI Bill."

"If you were seriously interested, though—"

"I don't know what I'm seriously interested in. I just need to find a good way to make a living and support a family."

"Is there a future for you on the ranch? Opportunities for expansion? Sounds like you've got plenty of land. And you and your sister and brother-and-law are young, energetic, enterprising people with decades of ranching experience between you."

Marcos's stomach tightened.

"I don't think so."

"Why not?"

"I just don't. It's okay—I'll figure something out." He shook Keith's hand again. "Good seeing you."

"Good seeing you too. When can we get together?"

But Marcos was already halfway through the door, which made it easy to pretend not to hear.

SOMETHING WAS WRONG.

Nina could see it the second Marcos walked back through the door. He looked almost angry. When he met Nina's eyes he smiled, but not very convincingly.

"Everything okay?" she asked as he joined her at the table.

"Yeah."

She waited for more, but it didn't come. Should she press? Did she dare? Clearly something was up—and clearly he didn't want to tell her about it. She couldn't ferret it out of him without coming off like a nagging girlfriend.

She'd have to let it go, and trust him.

"I'm having a good time," she said.

"Good."

"I've met so many people. They all look shocked when I tell them I'm from California, but most of them seem to be getting over it. I finally asked Tito about it, and he said it's a whole thing, Californians coming to Texas, and then trying to make Texas like California. I knew a lot of Californians were moving here, but I've never considered it from the Texan point of view. Tito said I should make it clear that I like Texas just the way it is, and I should be fine."

Marcos didn't answer. His eyes were shuttered, and he seemed to be someplace deep inside himself.

"Marcos?"

He snapped to attention. "Yeah. That's true."

Had he even heard her?

Her expression must have communicated something to him, because he pulled her to him for a quick kiss.

But the mood had been spoiled.

It was as if Eliana's baby-making remark had unleashed something. For the rest of the evening, someone or other kept asking Marcos and Nina when they were going to get remarried. Marcos's face grew more and more closed off; he barely spoke and didn't seem to be taking an interest in anything anymore.

Nina went on talking and laughing with the people she met, but she was growing more uneasy with each passing minute.

What if he'd never truly cared for her at all? What if his pursuit of her was nothing more than an outworking of guilt, or chivalry, or obligation to his son?

If he was faking, then he was a good actor. The way he'd kissed her beneath the Faust Street Bridge, the things he'd said to her there... He'd meant them, hadn't he? He loved her.

Though it couldn't be denied that he'd never come out and said the words. She was pretty sure he'd come close a few times.

But what was that thing Marcos had said just the other day? *Close only counts in cornhole and howitzers.* It had cracked her up then. Now it seemed chillingly prescient.

No, Marcos couldn't have faked his feelings for her. But maybe he'd run out of steam. Maybe he didn't have the staying power to see things through.

Logan's Jenga partner had gone home. He wandered over to Nina and Marcos's table.

"Dad, will you play checkers with me?" he asked.

"Not now, bud," Marcos said. There was something strained in his voice that Nina had never heard there before. His face looked drawn and hard.

I'm losing him. He isn't interested anymore. He doesn't want to be tied down to Logan and me. He's going to go away and break both our hearts, and it's my fault for letting him get close.

She knew she was being ridiculous, but something like panic was rising inside her, and she couldn't stop it.

A smiling woman holding a cocktail came to their table. "Marcos Ramirez! It *is* you! I'd heard you were back in town. Do you remember me? Mrs. Cooley! I taught you in third grade. Aren't you going to introduce me to your wife and child?"

Marcos abruptly got to his feet and walked out of the building without saying a word.

Nina was stunned. For a moment she and Mrs. Cooley stared at each other. Then Nina said, "Excuse me," scooped up Logan in her arms as if he were a toddler and followed Marcos outside.

"Marcos? What's wrong?"

He didn't even turn around. "Sorry, I—I just needed some air."

Some *air*? Had he really just said that?

"That was really rude," she said.

"I know."

The words were tight and clipped. What was his problem?

It wasn't his father's death that made him leave before, said the dry, hard little voice in Nina's head. That was just who he was.

Or who *she* was.

Part of her had expected it all along.

But no part of her expected what happened next.

"Mom, you're squeezing me," Logan said.

She took another step toward Marcos—

And he physically bolted, actually ran away from her, and stumbled to his knees. Next thing she knew, he was hunched over a gutter, vomiting blood.

MARCOS LAY ON his back in an urgent care facility with an IV in his arm, a tiny pillow under his head and a thin blanket over his body because Nina thought the air conditioning was too cold.

She smiled down at him, the glaring fluorescent ceiling light making her hair glow like a halo.

"Idiot," she said tenderly. "Why didn't you tell me?"

"I didn't want to believe it was happening again," he said. "I kept telling myself it would go away. And the pain didn't get *really* bad until today."

"Your stomach was hurting for *days*? Marcos!"

"Yeah, it started yesterday. Looking back, I was in deep denial. And by the time it got bad, we were at Tito's, and I didn't want to ruin your evening. I thought I could power through."

Was that really his voice? It sounded thin and weak, like a sick old man's.

She combed her fingers through his hair. "That's ridiculous. You and I, we're…well, we're together, aren't we?"

She actually sounded unsure.

"Yes," he said. "Of course."

"Then we're a team. And you should trust me with things like this. It wasn't like I couldn't tell *something* was wrong, you know. I'm not dumb."

Her eyes filled with tears.

"Babe, don't cry. I'm going to be okay."

She nodded, but the tears spilled over.

"Nina? What's wrong?"

"I just thought… The way you were acting tonight, I thought you were bored with me."

"Bored with you?" He reached up and ran the backs of his fingers over her cheekbone. "If you thought that, then maybe you *are* a little dumb."

She leaned down and kissed him softly on the forehead.

"Are you feeling better yet? Those drugs should be kicking in by now."

He was being given intravenous meds to stop the bleeding and nausea. Nothing for pain—NSAIDs were bad for ulcers—but with the bleeding stopped, the pain ought to go away on its own, or so the doctor said.

"Lots better. Kinda floaty. Like I been tranked."

She scanned his IV medication labels. "Hmm. Looks like you have. Your nausea inhibitor is also a tranquilizer."

"Huh." He had a vague sense that that ought to bother him, but he couldn't work up the energy to care. He just wanted to lie here, and enjoy his stomach not hurting and look at Nina.

She frowned. "Why are you sticking your tongue out at me?"

"I'm not."

"Yes, you are. You're doing it right now."

The doctor walked in. "Increased tongue movement is a side effect of Phenergan. Nothing to be concerned about."

She turned to face them, chart in hand. "All right, Marcos, here's what's happening. The bleeding has slowed, but your hemoglobin and hematocrit are seriously low. So we'll admit you to the hospital tonight and—"

"No," Marcos said.

He said it in a matter-of-fact tone of voice, like someone had asked if he wanted fries with that.

Nina looked at the doctor, then said, "Marcos, do you understand what she said? You've lost a lot of blood. You need to go to the hospital so they can monitor you."

"Nope nope nope," he said.

His arm jerked up randomly, and he hit himself in the face.

"Another side effect?" Nina asked the doctor.

"Yes," the doctor said shortly. "Mr. Ramirez, I don't think you understand."

"I do, though. You want me to go to the hospital. I don't want to go. And you can't make me. That's about the size of it, isn't it?"

"I can't force you to be admitted, no. And your levels are not dangerously low. But they're close. I strongly advise you to check in to the hospital, or at the very least, to follow up with a gastroenterologist as soon as possible. You need to find out what's causing these ulcer flare-ups."

"All right, I hear you. No hard feelings, yeah? Thanks for the meds that slowed the bleeding, and for the trippy meds that made me stick my tongue out. Seriously, thanks. I'll be paying my bill and going home as soon as my IV bag empties out."

The doctor gave Marcos the patiently annoyed look that he was so used to seeing from doctors.

"Thank you, Doctor," Nina said. "Can I have a minute alone with him, please?"

The doctor nodded and walked out.

"Marcos," Nina started, "why—"

"Hey!" he said, sitting up with a start and slapping himself in the face again. "Where's Logan? Did we leave him at Tito's?"

She took him by the shoulders and guided him gently back to the exam table. "Lie down! No, we did not leave Logan at Tito's. Your sister took him to your mom's house. Then I drove you here in your truck because you refused to go to the ER."

"Oh. Okay. Good."

"Marcos, why don't you—"

"Wait. You drove my truck?"

"Yes. You don't remember?"

He started to slap himself again but she grabbed his hand and held on.

"I love you," he said.

He hadn't meant to say it, but the words were out and there was no taking them back. He didn't *want* to take them back.

Her face softened into a smile. "I love you too, Marcos. Now, why don't you want to go to the hospital?"

"Because I don't like hospitals. They take over. You have to sign over half your soul just to get a bed. Anyway, you heard what she said. I'm only borderline low with my hemo-whatsits. And she admitted herself that she can't make me go."

"She also said that if you don't go, you should at least follow up with a gastroenterologist."

He didn't answer right away. Finally he said, "I have the name of one. Keith gave it to me."

"Well, then. We'll make you an appointment tomorrow, and we'll find out what's making you sick."

He wiggled his fingers in front of his face. "Look at my amazing hand. I never really noticed it before."

"Marcos," Nina said sternly.

He gazed at her. "What if we *don't* find out? What if I go through the whole stupid exhausting doctor process for the umpteenth time, and at the end of it I still don't know what's wrong with me?"

"This time isn't going to be like the other times, Marcos."

"Why's that?"

She looked him full in the face with those steely blue eyes. "Because this time, I'll be there, advocating for you. I won't let them give you the runaround. I'll *make* them find out what's wrong."

A flood of warm comfort spread through his body. It might have been the Phenergan again, but he didn't think so.

CHAPTER TWENTY-FOUR

TONY STOOD ON the doorstep of the bunkhouse, holding a covered pot of something that smelled of beef and vegetables and a hint of lime.

"Is that *caldo*?" Marcos asked, waving him inside.

"Sure is! Dalia made it. Best thing in the world when you're sick. You want me to dish you up some right now?"

"Please." Marcos hadn't been aware of his hunger, but now that he smelled the good broth, he was ravenous. He sat down at the kitchen table.

Tony took a bowl down from one of the open shelves. "So how you doing?"

"Still a little shaky on my pins, but better."

"Good! How'd it go at your doctor's appointment? Any clue as to what's causing this?"

"Yes! Turns out I have a whole syndrome. There are tumors on my pancreas that make my stomach produce way too much acid. The acid eats through my stomach lining, and that's why I have an ulcer that won't go away."

Tony set the steaming soup in front of Marcos and joined him at the table. "No kidding? You seem awfully cheerful about something that sounds so horrible."

"I am. Because after all these months of pain, all these doctors talking down to me and giving me the runaround, I finally have an answer. I can't tell you how good that feels, Tony."

"Then I'm glad. So is there anything that can be done?"

"Yes. Now that we know what's wrong, the condition can be controlled. There are meds to cut down on the acid, and treatments to shrink the tumors. I should be able to live a normal life."

"That's great news, brother."

Marcos took a spoonful of clear amber broth with bright vegetables and chunks of beef, blew on it and put it in his mouth. He shut his eyes and let out a moan.

"That's the stuff," he said.

When he'd chewed and swallowed, he said, "Nina went with me to my appointment. She'd made a timeline of all my flare-ups going back to February, all the tests I'd had, my hospitalization, everything. She really fought for me. And the gastroenterologist listened to her, and did tests that the others didn't do. She was…she was great."

Tony nodded. "It's nice, having a strong smart woman in your corner, isn't it?"

"Yeah."

"Hey, what is that on your fridge?"

"A get-well card. Logan made it. That's him and me riding the fence at La Escarpa. I'm on Buck and he's on Pete."

Tony tilted his head. "Oh yeah, I see it now. Is that your first dad card?"

Marcos felt a smile breaking through. "Yeah."

"Nice. So, I wanted to talk to you about work."

"Yeah, I'm sorry to be leaving you in the lurch this way. I should be good to go soon, and I'll get caught up."

"Oh, no, take your time. I mean, yeah, we need you, but don't get back in the saddle before you're ready. We don't want you coming off a horse or keeling over on the tractor or getting trampled by a bull or—"

"I get it," said Marcos. "Anyway, when I do come back, I'll be just here. My job with the Mendozas is over, at least for now. All the major work at Masterson Acres is done, and the pad sites will have to wait on the builders."

"Yeah, I know. That's what I wanted to talk to you about." Tony braced his arms on the table. "I've been approached about doing the construction work at Masterson Acres. You know I haven't done any big jobs since before Dalia and I got married, and I've never done anything as big as this. But I haven't been out long. Still have my contacts and equipment. Still know what I'm doing."

"You want to take the job?"

"I do. It would mean a lot of money. It could bankroll some things we want to do at La Escarpa. But it would also mean me not being around so much in the short term. Which brings me to what I wanted to talk to you about."

Something inside Marcos went cold, in spite of the hot soup. He knew where this was heading.

"In a way, the timing might be exactly right," Tony went on. "You and Nina are clearly getting closer. Maybe you're thinking you might be supporting a family before long. This could help with that. I'm not talking about a temporary thing, you filling in for me while I'm away. With a fresh infusion of cash, we could expand our operation. Buy more land, increase our herd. More cattle, more goats. You could be a part of that. You could be a partner."

"I don't have the cash for a buy-in," Marcos said.

"I know—I'd be providing the cash. What you'd be providing is more manpower. Dalia's putting together a package for you as we speak. Your share would be a sweat equity kind of thing. You'd get fully vested over time. Dalia can tell you the details. What do you think?"

What Marcos thought was that he'd just been offered a partnership—no, a chance to work his way *into* a partnership—on his own family's ranch, by a kid who used to follow him around and crashed his pasture parties in high school.

Tony leaned back in his chair, looking pleased. Marcos took a big spoonful of soup and slowly chewed.

Pay attention, bud, Marcos's father used to say when showing him how to do something on the ranch. *You'll be my partner someday, and you need to know this.*

"I'll get back to you," he said at last.

Tony looked a little put off at first, but quickly recovered. "Sure, I get it. I know you need to run it by Nina. I'll leave you to it, then. Glad you're feeling better, brother."

"Thanks. And thanks for the *caldo*."

After Tony had gone, Marcos sat alone in the kitchen, feeling as if the walls were closing in on him, trapping him on the place he'd wanted so badly to escape.

He could almost hear Keith's voice in his head. *Why do you think you feel that way?*

But Marcos didn't want to analyze his emotions. He just wanted to get away from them.

The dish drainer by the sink was covered with clean dishes, neatly arranged. Nina had left them there to dry last night. She'd been spending a lot of time at his place. Taking care of him.

Well, Tony was right about one thing. If Marcos was ever going to have a future with Nina and Logan, he had to raise some cash, and make provisions for a good, steady income. But there had to be another way.

And maybe…maybe he'd just thought of one.

He took out his phone and made a call.

CHAPTER TWENTY-FIVE

Coming over. Big news.

EVERY TIME NINA peeked at Marcos's text, those four words gave her the same sweet thrill. She was in full nervous housecleaning mode; even when the nerves were happy nerves, they still needed an outlet.

She hadn't been home much the past few days. Juggling Logan, her job and Marcos's care had kept her busy. There'd been plenty of catching up to do, housework-wise. By the time she heard him pull into her driveway, the second load of laundry was spinning in the dryer, the kitchen-cabinet and drawer fronts gleamed, and the whole house smelled like lemon oil.

"Is that Dad?" Logan called from his room. He could recognize the sound of Marcos's truck engine too.

"Yes," Nina said as she hurriedly stowed the furniture polish under the sink.

Was she being silly? Maybe a little. It wasn't like she expected an actual proposal at this point. But after the days she'd spent taking care of Marcos in his drugged and weakened state, she was confident that he wanted to marry her. He'd never said it in as many words, but the desire was clear. He'd just been waiting to be on solid financial footing. Starting tonight, they'd be planning for a future together.

After driving him back to the bunkhouse from urgent care, she'd made an executive decision to stay the night. She still thought he ought to be in the hospital, and though she couldn't make him go, she could at least watch over him to make sure he didn't hemorrhage and bleed out all alone. Logan had slept at his grandmother's, in Marcos's old room.

Recovery-mode Marcos was a revelation. Funny and sweet. Grateful and affectionate and helpless. It was like all his defenses were down. She'd wondered at first if Phenergan might be one of those truth-serum type drugs, but she'd looked it up, and apparently it wasn't, though "altered mental status" was listed as a potential side effect. She suspected he was just drowsy and relaxed and not holding back.

He went on sticking out his tongue and slapping himself in the face for the ride home, all while rambling about how much he loved her and Logan, and how he wanted them with him forever. Once she got him into his bed, he was sound asleep within minutes. She slept on the sofa, waking every hour or so to steal into his room and brood over him.

She took off work in the morning to take care of him, went to the center for the afternoon, stopped by her house to shower and get a change of clothes for Logan, picked up Logan at Renée's and went back to the bunkhouse. Except for a few hours of sleep each night, she'd been working nonstop in some capacity for days. It was exhausting and exhilarating at the same time, like when Logan got sick and she was on her own, having to do everything.

She looked out the living room window. Her heart skipped to see Marcos hurrying up the sidewalk with that long-legged, lowered-head stride. He had a bouquet of flowers in one hand and a plastic grocery bag in the other.

She met him at the door with a kiss. The cellophane wrap around the flowers crinkled against her back as he put his arms around her.

"Hey," said Logan's voice from the hallway.

They pulled apart. "Hey, bud," Marcos said. "I got you something."

He handed Logan the grocery bag. Logan reached inside and pulled out—

"Pistachios?" Nina said.

"Yep. A whole bag of them to himself, because he loves them so much."

"Wow!" Logan said, sounding several notches more excited than usual. "Can I really eat them all myself?"

"Sure!" Marcos said.

"Hang on," Nina said. She took a bowl out of a cabinet, opened the bag and put a small handful of pistachios into the bowl.

"That's enough for one night," she said. "Now, take them outside so you can spit the shells. You can have the rest later."

"Why can't I have them all at one time?" Logan asked.

"Trust me—that many pistachios at one time would be too much for your digestive system to handle. I'll put the rest in the pantry for you."

"But they're still mine, right?"

"Yes, all yours. Now what do you say to your father?"

"Thanks, Dad."

"You're welcome. Go on outside now while I talk to your mom."

After he'd gone, Marcos handed the flowers to Nina. "And these are for you."

"Thank you. Come to the kitchen with me while I put them in water."

He hopped onto the counter while she filled the vase, then pushed himself up, supporting his weight on his hands, and swung himself back and forth in an excess of energy, his triceps standing out in stark definition.

"What made you think of pistachios?" Nina asked.

"There was a display of them in the produce section. I was at H-E-B anyway, getting road-trip food."

"Road trip?" she asked.

"Yeah. That's what I have to tell you. Babe, I got a new job."

No surprise there, though judging from the look on his face, he *expected* her to be surprised. But why the road trip? Was he heading out of town to buy cattle?

He took her hand and pulled her to him, between his knees. He settled his hands around her hips.

"Out West," he went on. "In the oil fields. I'm leaving tomorrow."

She stared at him. "Wait. What? How?"

"Okay, I don't exactly have the job yet," he said. "But Javi says it's a sure thing. They're hiring—I'm qualified. I've just got to show up. They know he's a good worker, and he's vouching for me. I'll stay with him until I get situated. Then I'll get my own place."

So many things were wrong here that Nina hardly knew where to start.

"Javi Mendoza," she said.

"Yeah. He's been out there a while. Started out a floor hand and worked his way up to lead hand. Thinks I could do well there too."

"What…what brought all this on?" she asked.

"I need the money," he said, as if this were obvious. "It's time I made some serious income. This is my chance. And that means we can be together. You, me and Logan. I'll go out West, live cheap, earn big and sock away savings until we have enough cash to make a start somewhere."

Make a *start* somewhere? What did that even mean? He had a start here—more than a start. A past. A future. None of this made any sense.

He was watching her. "What's wrong?" he asked.

"How long are you planning to stay out West?"

"I don't know. Six months, a year. We'll see."

She wrenched away from him and braced her hands on the opposite counter.

"Are you upset?" he asked.

"Of course I'm upset. You've made a major decision without even consulting me."

"It's just a job."

"No. It's a job and a move across the state."

"To make more money, so we can be together. Did you miss that part?"

"Assuming you even want to be together anymore, once you get there."

"What are you talking about?"

She turned back around. "I've heard what those oil towns are like. All that wild, rough living. All those rowdy men together, partying hard to blow off steam in their downtime."

"Ah, it's not that bad."

"How do you know? Have you ever been there?"

"Have you? Where are you getting *your* information?"

"Annalisa Cavazos."

Marcos made a scoffing sound. "Annalisa

just wants Javi to come home because she's hung up on him."

"Yeah? Well, I'm hung up on *you*, Marcos. How do you think I feel? I don't like the idea of you going a thousand miles away from me for months at a time, and I don't understand why you would want to."

"It's not a thousand miles. It's not even four hundred. And I told you, this is for us, for our future. I can't stay in Limestone Springs forever, piddling around as Tony and Dalia's part-time hired man."

"But Tony and Dalia offered to bring you on full time. Offered you a *partnership*."

Silence. Then, "How did you know?"

"Dalia."

"She had no business telling you that."

"Why? Is it a secret?"

"It's irrelevant, because I'm not going to do it."

"Why not?"

"For one thing, it's not enough money."

"That's not what Dalia thinks. She and Tony want you to take a bigger role on the ranch. This could be a great opportunity long-term, to generate enough capital and man-power to make La Escarpa big. You could be part of that."

She hated how she sounded, like a nagging wife. But she wasn't Marcos's wife, and she was starting to get a terrible feeling that she wasn't going to be.

His voice hardened. "I can make more out West."

"In the short term. But you have a future on the ranch. And you've got a free place to stay, so your expenses would be lower."

He shook his head. "If I take that offer, I'm going to be trapped here forever."

The words were like a slap in the face.

"That's what this is about," she said, her voice shaking. "You're afraid of being trapped—with me and Logan."

"That's not what I said."

"But it's what you meant. You honestly think you can go away for six months, a year, or more, and you're going to be willing to come back and pick up where you left off? What about that Lego castle you said you'd make with Logan? What about his riding lessons? The trebuchets you were going to build together? What about the Persimmon Fest?"

He let out a harsh bark of a laugh. "You're seriously upset about missing out on the Persimmon Fest?"

"Don't make fun! It's not just that and you

know it. You're turning your back on all that? On us?"

"You're not listening to me. This is for you and Logan, for our future. This is how I make a way for us to be together."

"That isn't all on you. I have a job too, you know. Anyway, if you wanted to be with us, you would stay with us, instead of going away across the state to a place notorious for wild living."

"You don't trust me?" His voice was cold now.

"If you really loved me, you wouldn't ask me to. You wouldn't plan this move without me and then waltz in here and announce it like it's a done deal. You're walking away, just like you did before. Only this time you don't even have the guts to be honest about it. It's a soft breakup."

"A what? That's not—"

"Well, I'm not going to let myself be pushed out of your life little by little. I can't put Logan through that. So let's just cut to the chase. If we're done, we're done."

Her voice cracked. Marcos slid off the counter and reached for her, but she twisted away.

He lowered his arms. His eyes were wide with shock. "You're breaking up with me?"

"I'm calling a spade a spade. Goodbye, Marcos."

"Babe, I—"

"Just go."

"Nina!"

The tears were spilling down her cheeks now. "Go!"

His expression turned to stone. He walked out of the house without another word.

CHAPTER TWENTY-SIX

THE DRIVE HOME passed in a surreal blur. Marcos felt hollowed out inside, stunned. What had just happened? How had things turned so bad, so fast? Everything was knocking around inside him, with no way to make sense of any of it. All he wanted now was to get away. There was nothing left to do but pack his things and start driving.

The house was too quiet. He'd gotten used to having Nina and Logan around. It didn't seem possible that he was alone in there.

Only he wasn't alone in the house after all. A shadow moved in the hallway, followed by a muffled thump.

Then, "Marcos? Is that you?"

His heart hammered in his chest. "Mom! What are you doing here?"

His mother walked out into the living room. "Waiting for you."

"Haven't you ever heard you're not supposed to sneak up on combat veterans?"

"I thought you said you didn't have PTSD," she said innocently. "Besides, I didn't sneak. You walked in on me. And I texted you that I was coming."

He pulled out his phone, and there was his mother's message. Coming over. Got a surprise for you.

He silently laid his phone on the table.

"Well?" said his mother. "Don't you want to see the surprise?"

"All right."

She took his arm and led him to the long hallway of the bunkhouse. The broad space held a display of various pieces of artwork, architectural remnants and found objects. Alex and Lauren had started it when they renovated the place.

It had recently been added to. A shadow-box of flint arrowheads now hung near the rusted gear, along with the set of spurs Logan had unearthed.

High above it all was the old flintlock musket Marcos had dug out of the ground when he was ten years old.

Except it never looked that good when he excavated it. Someone had cleaned it up and refurbished it. The metal still had the patina of age, but most of the rust was gone, and the barrel and lock shone with a light coat of oil. The gunstock was new. There was even a tiny chip of flint in the jaws at the end of the hammer.

Marcos reached up and lifted it down from its pegs. "Who did this?"

"A gunsmith Alex knows. One of his reenactor friends specializes in antique weapons. He said it's an India Pattern musket. That's what the Mexican infantry carried at the time of the revolution. And somehow it ended up here. Doesn't it look wonderful?"

Marcos nodded. "When did he do the work?"

"He started weeks ago. I got the idea that first day Nina and Logan came out to the ranch. I thought it would be a nice homecoming gift for you. I'm so happy for you, honey, and so glad to have you back here. You've really come full circle."

Marcos stood there a long moment, swallowing over the lump in his throat, before finally returning the musket to its pegs.

"The gunsmith did a great job," he said. "If Tony and Dalia ever Airbnb the place out, they ought to take a picture of this wall and post it. Market the bunkhouse as a historical property. People would go nuts over that."

"Airbnb? What are you talking about? You live here."

"Not anymore. I'm leaving."

"Leaving? Where are you going?"

"West Texas. To work the oil fields."

"What? No! What happened? Did you and Nina break up?"

"No! I mean—yes. But that was after, not before."

"After what?"

"After I told her I was leaving. I tried to tell her—I did tell her—that I was doing it for her, for us. To build up my savings, so we can get married and I can provide for her and Logan. But she didn't believe me. Didn't trust me to live in an oil town without her."

"Well, can you blame her? After everything she's been through with her own father? That girl's up to her ears in abandonment issues. And let's face it, Marcos, you don't have the best track record with her."

"But this is different. I'm different. I'm doing this for her! Why doesn't anyone believe me?"

"Because if you really want to marry Nina, why not stay here and accept Tony and Dalia's job offer?"

He turned away and rubbed the back of his neck. "Does everyone know about that?"

"Is there a reason we shouldn't? More to the point, why didn't you take it? Nina and Logan already live here. You both have family in the area, a support network—that's important when you have kids, and even more so now that you know about your condition. And now you have the chance to be a partner on a ranch that's growing. Why would you go away when you have—"

"Fifteen hundred acres of good land with water and fencing, houses and barns, an established herd, a reputation, a good name, a heritage. Yeah, I know. I've heard it all before a million times from Dad. I know his whole speech by heart." He lowered his voice to his dad's gruff rumble. *"Do you have any idea how rare and precious that is, Marcos? How many men would give their right arm for what you were born to?* That's what he asked me, after I reenlisted the second time. And you know what I said to him? I said, *Then go find one of those guys and adopt him. Maybe he'll be grateful and obedient enough to satisfy you."*

Silence.

"I didn't know you told him you'd reenlisted again," his mother said. Her voice was shaking.

"Of course you didn't know. He didn't tell you. He just went out and worked himself to death. Whenever he was upset, he worked. When Tony and Dee went on their first date, he regraded the driveway. When Ana was in the hospital that time, he took down that big cedar tree—with an axe. And when I told him I'd re-upped and made up my mind to go career, he went out to the hay parcel all alone."

He sank to the floor and rested his elbows on his knees. They both knew the rest of the story. How his mother got worried because Martin had stayed out so long and wasn't answering her calls. How she finally drove out to the hay parcel only to find that he'd collapsed, with Merle the border collie doing frantic laps around him. How the firefighters and paramedics made record time, but it was too late. He was already gone. He'd died alone except for the dog.

But she didn't know about that last conversation. His father hadn't told her, and Marcos hadn't either when he came home for the funeral.

He couldn't regret reenlisting. He hadn't done it to spite his father, wasn't being stupid and rebellious. He'd loved being a Marine. But this was how it happened, and the long and short of it was that his father was dead now and it was Marcos's fault.

"So now you know," Marcos said. "He offered me what he valued most in the world, and I threw it in his face. It's my fault he went out and worked himself to death and left you alone."

His mother sighed. "Oh, Marcos. That's not true."

She sat down beside him on the floor and linked her arm through his.

"I know there was a lot of conflict between the two of you for a long time. But he was just as much to blame for that as you were. All his life he was haunted by this fear of what would happen to La Escarpa after he was gone, whether it would stay in the family or get carved up and sold. He didn't want to be the one responsible for losing it. And that made him put too much pressure on you. I saw it at the time, but I couldn't make him see it. The truth is, even if you'd stayed and taken over the way he wanted you to, that wouldn't have guaranteed anything. We can't control the future. The fact that it's still in the family now—that's a blessing, a gift. Something to be grateful for. Not something you can force."

"If it's not something you can force, then why is everyone trying to force me? I'm happy for Tony and Dalia. I really am. But why do I have to get rolled into their plans for La Escarpa? Why is everyone so determined to make a rancher of me?"

"Well, let me ask *you* something. If you're so dead set against ranching, why did you ever come back?"

"I got discharged, remember?"

"Yes. But that doesn't mean you had to come home. You could have stayed in California, or gone somewhere else. You were a single man with no children, or so you thought. You could have gone wherever you wanted. But you came here. Why?"

Marcos was quiet a long time before answering. Finally he said, "When I was in Syria for the Raqqa Campaign, I met an SDF guy, one of the Kurds. His name was Renas. When he found out I was from Texas, he wanted to hear all about my ranch. I think he assumed all Texans had ranches—and I guess I didn't do much to change his mind. I told him about La Escarpa, and he hung on every word. He said his family used to be nomadic herdsmen. They'd go back and forth between high pastures in summer and mountain valleys in winter. But when he was eight years old, the Iraqi government forced his family off their land. It was this whole thing designed to change the ethnic composition of northern Iraq. A quarter-million Kurds and other non-Arabs got displaced. The government invalidated their land titles, seized the land and then turned around and leased it to Arabs. Renas said to me that what I had was special, and I should treasure it."

He took a deep breath. "Not long after that, I came home for Tony and Dee's wedding. Everything seemed strange to me then, after two years in northern Syria. But the strangest thing was this place, La Escarpa. Fifteen hundred acres, continuously in the hands of one family for over a hundred years. I guess I saw the place with new eyes. I thought about how I would feel if we got run off our land the way Renas's family got run off theirs. Just imagining it made me furious. Then later, when I got discharged, I was so worn out from being sick, so tired of everything. And I just wanted to go home. I—I could *feel* that I belonged here."

His mother squeezed his arm.

"Can you imagine what Dad would have said to that?" Marcos asked. "How he would have looked at me when I told him? I would have given anything to be able to tell him that I finally got it. That he was right."

"He knows now. And, Marcos, that last argument was not the sum total of your relationship. The other parts happened too, the good parts. If your father had lived, the two of you would have made peace. You just ran out of time. And that's on him as much as it's on you."

She turned toward him and took his face in her hands. "And if he were here with us tonight, he'd tell you the same thing I'm telling you. You're a father now. You have a woman who loves you and a son who needs you, and you're about to throw all that away to prove something that doesn't need proving."

"What if I already did?"

She smiled. "Oh, I think you have more fight in you than that."

"WHERE'S DAD?"

Logan stood just inside the back door, holding his empty pistachio bowl.

Nina sniffed and swiped her eyes. "He had to go. Did you enjoy your pistachios?"

"Yeah."

It was a drawn-out, suspicious yeah. Logan wasn't the most intuitive or empathetic kid, but he looked uneasy. Clearly *something* was wrong.

What would he say, what would he feel when he found out? Nina was going to crush him the way her mother crushed her, with Ray and Jim and all the other men who cycled through their lives.

But not now.

"I'm not feeling so great," she told him. "I'm going to go lie down for a while. Don't take anything apart, okay?"

"'Kay."

It occurred to her as she crawled into bed that it had been a while since she'd had any deconstruction disasters to deal with. Between ranch work, big Lego projects and everything else Logan had been doing with his father, he'd shown a lot less interest in taking apart major appliances. Now whenever she heard a disconcerting silence and went to check on him, she was likely to find him poring over one of the books Marcos had given him. He still couldn't read more than a few words of them, but he could stare at the illustrations. And he did, a lot.

This was what Logan had needed all along—not some special activity or educational aid, but a person. His father. And now he'd lost him. What would fill that void in his life? Even if Marcos stayed involved with Logan now that he and Nina weren't together—even if he didn't ghost them like he had before—it wouldn't be the same.

Fresh tears stung her eyes. She wished she could undo Logan's whole experience of Marcos and go back to the time when Logan's father was still the unknown future recipient of the box on the top shelf of the closet.

CHAPTER TWENTY-SEVEN

MARCOS OPENED THE DOOR before his sister had a chance to knock.

"Thanks for coming, Ana."

"You're welcome. What's the occasion?"

"I need your help."

Eliana set her purse down on the kitchen table. "You're going to have to be more specific."

"Mom didn't tell you?"

"Tell me what?"

"Huh. I was starting to think you all know everything I've done and everything I'm going to do before I do it."

"Believe it or not, we do sometimes talk about things other than you, Marcos. So what's this about?"

"Nina."

Her smile faded. "Oh, no. What did you do?"

He was a little offended that she assumed he'd been the one to mess up, but there wasn't any time to waste, and anyway she wasn't wrong.

"It's a long story. The gist of it is I was stupid, but I'm over it now."

She made a circling "more" motion with her hand.

Marcos sighed. "Tony and Dalia offered me the chance at a partnership at La Escarpa, but I decided to go to West Texas to work in the oil fields instead. Nina thought I was just trying to get rid of her and Logan—which I wasn't, I swear. But we had a big fight and she broke it off with me. I know I was wrong. I want to stay, work at La Escarpa, win her back and marry her."

He expected a lot of time-wasting exclamations and questions, but Eliana just studied him a moment and said, "Okay, got it. So what you need is a grand gesture."

"Yes! Exactly."

He never would have put it in those words, but he did know he needed something out of the ordinary. Consulting Eliana had been the right move.

"First things first. Do you have a ring?"

He shrugged. "She still has the one I gave her eight years ago—assuming she hasn't thrown it away since last night."

"That's a wedding ring. I'm talking about an engagement ring. Do you have one of those?"

"No. Do we really need one? Can't we just agree to get married again and then do it?"

Eliana's gaze pierced him through. "No! You asked for my help for a reason, Marcos, and I am telling you right now, you've got to go big or go home. That woman has been raising your child alone for the past seven years. Do *not* be cheap now."

"I don't care about the expense. But there's no time. How would I know what size to get? I can't exactly take her ring shopping at this point."

"Way ahead of you. She wears a size six."

"What? How could you possibly know that?"

"I found it out weeks ago. I asked her if I could try on her fake wedding band to see what I thought of that style. Then when she wasn't looking, I checked it against the ring sizer I'd stowed in my purse."

He stared at her, speechless.

"What's the matter?" she said.

"Nothing. Just—thank you. And promise me you'll never use your powers for evil."

She smiled sweetly. "Aw. You're so cute. All right, let's go. Time to hit the shops."

"Hold on. I've got a better idea. Have you still got that ring sizer?"

"Yes. Why?"

He told her.

"Oh yeah," Eliana said, a hint of admiration in her voice. "That's good. Okay, now let's see what you're going to wear."

She stalked to his closet, threw the door open and started flipping through shirts. She froze on a black button-down with a sheen to it. She'd chosen it for him on their second shopping trip, when she'd helped him prepare for his first date with Nina.

"This one," she said, handing it to him.

He took it. "This is going to work, right, Ana?" he asked.

It was a stupid question. He knew she couldn't give him the assurance he craved.

"We'll soon know," Eliana said. Then her face softened. "Nina's loved you this long in spite of all the inane stuff you've done. I'd say you still have a fighting chance."

WHAT NINA HAD first noticed about Marcos, other than his drop-dead good looks, was his intensity. For him, anything worth doing was worth doing with all his might. Once decided, he was all in…until he wasn't. That was the problem with people who formed quick judgments and attachments. They could unform them just as quickly.

I thought Letters from Iwo Jima *was a stunning film*, she'd told him in The Bad Oyster the night they'd met. And he'd looked her right in the eye and said, *Will you marry me?* And she'd laughed, because of course it was a joke. But then he'd said, *I'm serious. What's to stop us? I* dare *you to marry me.* And he'd been so compelling and gorgeous that she'd said, *Fine, I will*, sure that that would put an end to the joke and make him back down, but also half serious, and wondering what it would be like if they did it. And it went on that way the rest of the night and into the wee hours of the morning—not a constant harangue, but something they both kept coming back to, flirting with the idea and each other. And when the sun was about to rise over Kate Sessions Park, and Marcos had looked up the opening time for the county clerk's office online, she'd said, *We can't do it* today. *There's a waiting period or something.* So he did another Google search and said, *Nope. No waiting period in the state of California.*

Every objection she raised, he had a comeback for. When she asked about rings, he found directions to the nearest 24-Hour Pawn. And so she went with him, and they actually looked at rings there in the glass case. And she found an antique filigree one that was just her size, and he found a plain platinum band, and she figured that was the end of it, the joke couldn't go any further.

But then he took out his wallet and paid for her ring. And she stood there a minute, breathless with do-I-dare excitement, and then paid for his.

And they went to the county clerk's office, and got married. And it was all very thrilling and exhilarating, until it was over.

And then it sucked.

THE PHONE WAS RINGING...*again*.

Nina hit Reject.

She felt sore inside, achy, like she was coming down with something, though she didn't seem to have a fever. Heartsick, that was what she was. That was a real thing. She'd experienced it before—not just over Marcos, but over her dad, and to a lesser degree, over Ray and Jim and the rest of her mom's disposable boyfriends.

But never as bad as this.

She'd managed to get up long enough to feed Logan and make herself cry looking at the pictures Lauren had taken at La Escarpa the first day she and Logan had gone there. Logan and Marcos, grooming Painted Pete. Logan on horseback, with Marcos leading him.

Her hand still rested on the phone. She picked it up, placed a call and pulled the covers over her head.

"Hey, there," Aunt Cessy said. "How are things at home? Got everything squared away?"

"Afraid not. I'm sorry, but it looks like I'm not going to make it to work today after all."

"Why? Nina, what's wrong?"

Nina let out a sigh that turned into a groan. "I broke up with Marcos…or he broke up with me. I broke up with him, but it was his fault."

"What? Tell me what happened."

She did.

A long silence followed. "Are you still there?" Nina asked.

"I'm here."

"Do you think I overreacted?"

Now that she'd had time to think things through, self-doubt had set in. Maybe she'd let her own insecurities and hang-ups sabotage her relationship with the only man she'd ever loved.

"Not exactly," Aunt Cessy said slowly. "You're right to be concerned that he made a major decision without you. But it sounds to me like there's something more going on here."

"That's what I told him. It's a soft breakup."

"Maybe. But from what you've described, he sounds pretty sincere about wanting to stay together. And he's not a devious man. If he wanted to break up, he'd just do it, like he did before."

"But why else would he go away?"

"I don't know. But doesn't it seem strange to you that his response to a partnership offer is to find another job across the state, the very same day? It's like he's trying to burn his bridges with the ranch. Maybe there's more to the story than meets the eye."

Nina thought. "He was pretty set against the ranch when I first met him. I was surprised he agreed to work there as a hired man at all. At first I thought he was just desperate for work, any work. But once he started, he did seem to enjoy it."

"And then he quit, and got another job far

away, and made a lot of noise about how he's doing it for your future. That sounds like a smokescreen."

"Well, maybe it was. Maybe he wasn't trying to weasel his way out of our relationship after all. Maybe something else *is* going on with him. But if so, why didn't he tell me about it? And why didn't he change his mind when he saw how much I didn't want him to go away? Bottom line is, if he loved me, he'd fight for me."

And he hadn't. He wasn't the one who'd been blowing up her phone with calls and unread texts. That was Eliana.

Aunt Cessy sighed. "I'm sorry, sweetheart. I know it's hard."

"And I'm sorry to be leaving you in the lurch this way. I just don't have the fortitude to face people right now. But I'll be back at work as soon as I can."

"I know you will."

As soon as they'd hung up, the phone rang with yet another call from Eliana. Nina hit Reject again.

By now Marcos must be well on his way northwest. He could be having an ulcer flare-up right now, on the road, without her to take care of him. How far apart were the towns in

West Texas? Was it all desert out there? Did they even have hospitals?

She wished she'd never gone to that first dinner with the Ramirez family, never met Eliana at all, never come to Texas to begin with. Just stayed in California without ever getting a glimpse of how outrageously glorious life could be with Marcos. She and Logan had done all right on their own. But going back to that life felt like poverty.

Someone was knocking at the door. She froze in bed, ready to wait them out.

"Moooom!" Logan called. "Someone's at the door!"

She groaned.

The worst part of all this was knowing she could have avoided the pain if she'd listened to that cautioning voice and kept her expectations low, instead of letting her hopes soar, again. Was this all life was, a series of disappointments? Was wisdom nothing more than practiced pessimism?

She buried her face in her pillow. She had to get a grip. She had Logan. *He* loved her, even if Marcos didn't, and he wasn't going anywhere. And she was the grown-up. She could make things safe for him, and she would, even when she felt like this.

She hadn't yet told him his father was gone—physically gone, hundreds of miles away without a proper goodbye, and gone from their lives. She didn't know how she would do it. It wasn't as if she and Marcos had been engaged; there was no reason for Logan to expect them to get married. But Logan and Marcos had grown close, in their terse, matter-of-fact way, faster than Nina would have believed possible. And now Marcos was gone again. How could that be anything other than a crushing rejection?

Nina shuffled to the door in her worn slippers, paisley pajama pants and oversize Tweety Bird T-shirt. Eliana stood on her doorstep, looking perfectly put-together as always. She breezed right into the house the second Nina opened the door.

"Get yourself cleaned up," she said. "We're going out."

Nina stared stupidly at her. "How are you here? You just called me like thirty seconds ago."

"That call was from your driveway. Come on! Hit the shower. Chop-chop. We're burning daylight."

Nina trudged back down the hall. "No. I'm going back to bed."

"Too bad, I'm not letting you. I'll go in the kitchen and bang on pots and pans until you get up again. You've spent enough time pining over my idiot brother."

"Enough time? We just—"

She was going to finish the sentence with *broke up yesterday*, but at that moment Logan appeared in the doorway of his room, no doubt attracted by the mention of banging pots and pans. Eliana pointed at him.

"You too, young man. Time to take a bath and put on your best clothes."

"I took a bath yesterday," Logan said.

"Well, you're getting another one today."

"Where are we going?"

"Someplace fun. You'll see. Now hit it!"

The force of Eliana's personality was enough to make him do it, and to get Nina through her shower. After that, Eliana took over—choosing her clothes, and doing her hair and makeup for her. She picked Logan's clothes too, including some nice new jeans that Renée had elasticized at the waist.

Less than an hour after Eliana had arrived at the house, she was driving the three of them to a location she refused to disclose.

Not that Nina was curious.

"I don't want to be cheered up," she said.

"Okay. But you're going anyway."

Nina stared out the passenger window as the miles passed, not paying attention until a familiar-looking water tower caught her eye.

"You're taking me to *Gruene*?" she asked, incredulous.

"What did you expect? Barhopping in Austin? That wouldn't be very practical at ten in the morning with your son along, would it?"

"I didn't expect you to take me back to where it all began! This is a fine way to cheer a person up!"

"Maybe I'm not trying to cheer you up."

Nina stared at Eliana's serene profile. "What is *wrong* with you?"

Eliana pulled into a parking lot. "Relax, we're not going back to the Gristmill. We're going to a completely different part of Gruene."

"Gruene is tiny! It technically isn't even a town, it's just part of New Braunfels. It isn't big enough to even *have* completely different parts."

"You'll be all right," Eliana said cheerfully. "We're going to walk down to the Guadalupe River. It's nice."

It did not sound nice at all. Most of Nina's significant encounters with Marcos had involved rivers, oceans or lakes. Most of his marriage proposals in San Diego had taken place in sight of the Pacific; they'd watched the bats fly out over Lady Bird Lake. The Guadalupe was connected both with the Gristmill, where they'd met again for the first time in eight years, and with the Faust Street Bridge, where they'd shared their first back-together kiss. Now here Nina was, back at the Guadalupe. There was even another bridge.

Eliana parked the car and turned off the ignition.

"Let's go," she said.

Nina didn't move. "Please will you just drive me back home again? I simply can't do this right now."

Eliana unfastened her seat belt. "Get out of the car. You'll thank me later."

Finally, Nina obeyed. Maybe if she went through the motions, Eliana would be satisfied and take her home.

They walked down a gentle slope to the cypress-lined riverbank. It was early yet, warm but not hot. A woman on the bridge was holding a big camera. Her dark hair was caught up in an attractively messy updo. She looked a lot like Lauren.

Nina stopped. *Was* it Lauren? Or was Nina

imagining things, populating the place with Marcos's relatives and near relatives?

Then a man stepped out from the shadow beneath the bridge, and Nina knew she must really be losing it now; she was having a full-on, straight-up hallucination.

He was standing in calf-deep water with his jeans turned up, just like at the Faust Street Bridge. It wasn't a hallucination. It was Marcos, in the flesh—the tall, broad, magnificent flesh—surrounded by… Were those floating candle blossoms?

He was gazing steadily at her, his jaw tense, his eyes bright and soft.

Eliana knelt beside her. "Let's get your boots off. You're going wading."

Nina accepted her help without question. The whole thing had an otherworldly, dream-like quality.

Marcos held his hand out to her—and not just his hand, but his whole arm, fully extended. It was a dramatic gesture, but there was nothing false about it.

She stepped into the shallow water and took his hand. He gripped it tight. From somewhere up above came the sound of a camera going off.

"I thought you'd gone west," she said.

"No. I'm staying. You were right, Nina. The ranch is my home now. And… I'd like it to be yours too. Yours and Logan's."

Floating right in between them was a perfect white lily. Marcos knelt right down in the water, cupped it in his hands and held it up to her. It was made of silk, and it was tethered to a little lead weight to keep it from drifting away.

From deep inside the petals, something flashed.

She put her hands over her mouth.

Marcos reached inside the lily and took out a diamond ring with an antique filigree setting—a lovely thing.

Nina heard her breath catch.

"I remembered you liked the old stuff best, that day on South Congress," Marcos said. "This is very old. My mom has a stash of all the old family rings and things, going back to before the revolution. She let me have my pick."

He held up the ring. "I asked you this once before—well, more like ten times before, all in the same night. I got a lot of stuff wrong back then, but I was right about you. You're the best woman I know, and I want to spend the rest of my life with you. Nina, will you marry me?"

By now she was crying too hard to say anything, so she just nodded again and again. Marcos slipped the ring on her finger. It fit perfectly.

He put his arms around her. She held tight to him.

She was dimly aware of voices around them, of the faces of his family, of Logan splashing in the water, of the cheers of strangers. But this, here, was the center of everything.

She held him like she would never let him go.

EPILOGUE

NINA WAS DREAMING about her grandparents' house. She hadn't spent all that much time there, but the details of the property were clearer in her memory than any of the places she and her mom lived when she was growing up. The split-rail fence. The rutted driveway, little more than a track, with grass growing thickly between the pebbly furrows. The shrinking white clapboards. The crumbling brick chimney. The framed picture of her father in his uniform.

And the smell of potato pancakes in the morning.

She opened her eyes.

Marcos was coming in sideways through the bedroom door, shirtless, wearing the soft gray pajama pants that Nina had given him for Christmas, and carrying a tray.

Logan squeezed through under the tray, nearly upsetting it, and bounced onto the bed. "Happy birthday, Mom! We made you breakfast."

She sat up. The plate on the tray was piled high with fluffy, golden-brown, crinkly-edged patties. "Mmm. Is this what I think it is?"

"It's potato pancakes! Aunt Cessy gave us the recipe. And Dad only burned two of them."

"Hey!" Marcos said. "They were just a little scorched on the edges."

He set the tray down on the duvet. "I got some of those brats that you like, and two figs off Logan's tree."

The figs were sliced in half, with their succulent golden centers exposed, and arranged in a dainty little dessert bowl.

"I thought that tree finished bearing back in June," Nina said.

"I did too, but looks like it's giving us a bonus fall crop."

"Mom, did you know figs aren't really fruits? *They're flowers.* Flowers that are— what's the word?—inverted. That means inside out. And they feed on wasps."

Nina gave him a skeptical look.

"It's true," Marcos said. "We were reading about it in that horticulture book my mom gave us for Christmas. There's this special

kind of wasp that can only reproduce sym-
biotically with figs. Their whole life cycle is
pretty metal."

"Metal means hardcore, Mom," Logan
said. "Don't be grossed out about the wasp.
It's not in there anymore. The fig digested it
with special enzymes."

"Oh, it takes a lot worse than that to gross me
out," Nina said. "I'm pretty hardcore myself."

She picked up one of the slices and popped
it in her mouth. "Mmmmm! Delicious."

"Told you," Marcos said to Logan. "Your
mom is tough."

She wasn't expecting much in the way of
gifts. She'd told Marcos earlier, *We've already
had our beautiful wedding, and we're still
trying to get established. So how about if we
forego expensive personal gifts this year, and
get each other things for the ranch instead?*

Like what?

*Oh, I don't know. Surely there are some
things you'd like that could help you do your
job better.*

He'd thought a while. *Maybe a headlamp?*

A what, now?

*A lamp for your head. You strap it on, and
that leaves your hands free, in case you're out
dealing with livestock or faulty fences at night.*

I want a headlamp, Logan had put in.

There, see? Practical and fun. So that takes care of your menfolk. Now I've just got to figure out what to get you.

Get Mom a headlamp too, Logan had said.

I think two headlamps is probably enough for one family, said Nina. *Especially when the ranch needs so many other things. Didn't you say the tractor tires should be replaced soon?*

Marcos had laughed. *You want me to get new tires for the tractor for your birthday? You don't even drive the tractor.*

No, but I should learn. There's a lot of stuff I should learn to do around here. I want to pull my weight.

Babe, you're already taking care of the garden, working part-time at the center and homeschooling our son. You've got enough on your plate.

I can do more. I want to be able to help you.

You help me so much already. Then he'd given her a thoughtful look. *That does give me an idea, though. Hmm...*

That was the last he'd said on the subject.

"How are the potato pancakes?" he asked now.

"Perfect. Crusty on the outside, tender on the inside. Just like you."

After breakfast, she opened Logan's gift—a pair of riding gloves. She'd had a few riding lessons from Marcos, but she wasn't yet riding as much or as well as she wanted. It was hard to get saddle time, since Logan rode every day. She was happy to let him monopolize the horses, though, proud of his progress. She knew Marcos was too. It had been over a year since his first lesson that day on La Escarpa, the first day he and Nina had come to the ranch.

"For my gift, you have to step outside," Marcos said.

"Aw, honey. Did you get me tractor tires after all?"

"You'll see. Get dressed."

The air felt deliciously cool when she stepped onto the front porch of the bunkhouse. A fine mist scarfed the northwest pasture.

"Did you rotate the horses' pasture?" she asked Marcos. "I can see one of…"

She trailed off. That wasn't Buck, and it sure wasn't Painted Pete. This was a strawberry roan with a flaxen mane and tail.

Then the horse lifted its face, and Nina saw the white heart marking on the forehead.

She clasped her hands together. "Is that…? It can't be."

But it was.

Marcos whistled, and Starlet came running.

She stopped near the fence and looked at Nina with soft brown eyes. The whole character of her face was sweet and mild and wonderfully familiar.

"How…how did you ever…? Marcos!"

"It took some doing. I've been at it for months. Cessy couldn't remember who Starlet got sold to, but she helped me track down one of your grandparents' old neighbors. He said a family in Bandera took her. So I tracked them down. They'd sold her to a friend, and that person sold her to someone else. Eventually she became a lesson pony at a barn that shut down a few years ago. After that the trail went cold for a while, but I found her at last, basically free-ranging it on some acreage where a retired couple live, not five miles from your grandparents' old place. I asked them if they were willing to sell, but when they heard my story they *gave* her to me. That freed up enough cash for some nice new tack, including a saddle you're going to love."

Nina rested her head against Starlet's neck.

She stayed that way a long moment, breathing in that clean horse scent.

Then she put her arms around Marcos and kissed him.

"Thank you," she said. "This is the most wonderful gift anyone has ever given anyone else in the history of ever."

Marcos glanced at Logan. "Oh, I can think of a better one. Now go get your boots on, woman. If we're going to become full partners at La Escarpa, you're going to have to learn to ride."

* * * * *

⬢ HARLEQUIN
HEARTWARMING

#383 BUILDING A SURPRISE FAMILY
Butterfly Harbor Stories • by Anna J. Stewart

Being nicknamed Butterfly Harbor's most eligible bachelor has taken Ozzy Lakeman by surprise! But he's more surprised by the town newcomer and single mom-to-be, Jo Bertoletti, a woman he can't get off his mind...or out of his heart.

#384 THE SECRET SANTA PROJECT
Seasons of Alaska • by Carol Ross

Travel blogger Hazel James has scheduled her holiday at an unexpected but much-needed locale—home. Major disruption to her peaceful Christmas: Cricket Blackburn, her brother's best friend and the love of her life she can't quite seem to get over.

#385 STEALING HER BEST FRIEND'S HEART
The Golden Matchmakers Club • by Tara Randel

Heidi Welch wants the house Reid Masterson intends to flip for a profit, which puts it out of her price range. Will they make a deal or take a chance on a friendship that has grown into love?

#386 A COWBOY'S HOMECOMING
Kansas Cowboys • by Leigh Riker

Rancher and widowed single mother Kate Lancaster needed help. But she'd never accept it from Noah Bodine—the man she was drawn to...and the man she blames for her husband's death.

HWCNM0721

Visit
ReaderService.com
Today!

As a valued member of the Harlequin Reader Service, you'll find these benefits and more at ReaderService.com:

- Try 2 free books from any series
- Access risk-free special offers
- View your account history & manage payments
- Browse the latest Bonus Bucks catalog

Don't miss out!

If you want to stay up-to-date on the latest at the Harlequin Reader Service and enjoy more content, make sure you've signed up for our monthly News & Notes email newsletter. Sign up online at ReaderService.com or by calling Customer Service at 1-800-873-8635.